W9-AOG-667

The Lost Band

Also by Don Coldsmith

Trail of the Spanish Bit
The Elk-Dog Heritage
Follow the Wind
Buffalo Medicine
Man of the Shadows
Daughter of the Eagle
Moon of Thunder
The Sacred Hills
Pale Star
River of Swans
Return to the River
The Medicine Knife
The Flower in the Mountains
Trail from Taos
Song of the Rock
Fort de Chastaigne
Quest for the White Bull
Return of the Spanish
Bride of the Morning Star
Walks in the Sun
Thunderstick
Track of the Bear
Child of the Dead
Bearer of the Pipe
Medicine Hat (Norman, 1997)
The Changing Wind
The Traveler
World of Silence

RIVERS WEST: *The Smoky Hill*

Runestone
Tallgrass
Southwind

The Lost Band

A Novel

Don Coldsmith

University of Oklahoma Press : Norman

A novel in the Spanish Bit Saga

Time Period: late 1700s, shortly after *Medicine Hat*

All of the characters in this book are fictitious, and any resemblance to actual persons, living or dead, is purely coincidental.

Library of Congress Cataloging-in-Publication Data

Coldsmith, Don, 1926–
    The lost band : a novel / Don Coldsmith.
      p. cm.
    "A novel in the Spanish bit saga; time period: late 1700s, shortly after Medicine hat"—T.P. verso.
    ISBN 0–8061–3226–4 (alk. paper)
    1. Indians of North America—History—18th century—Fiction.
2. Indians of North America—Great Plains—Fiction.   3. Great Plains—Fiction. I. Title.

PS3553.O445 L67 2000
813'.54—dc21

                                    99–056914
                                         CIP

The paper in this book meets the guidelines for permanence and durability of the Committee on Production Guidelines for Book Longevity of the Council on Library Resources, Inc. ∞

Published by arrangement with Bantam Books. Copyright © 2000 by Don Coldsmith. All rights reserved. Published by the University of Oklahoma Press, Norman, Publishing Division of the University. Manufactured in the U.S.A.

1 2 3 4 5 6 7 8 9 10

To those of any culture, present or past, who have struggled against all odds to preserve their heritage.

Introduction

When the *Trail of the Spanish Bit* was published in 1980, I had no idea that it was the first of a series. It was merely a book about a lost Spaniard in the Central Plains in 1542, injured and unable to get home.

I couldn't determine what tribes or nations he might have encountered, so I created a composite, a fictional nation of hunters based on the buffalo culture as the horse came into use. Most American Indians' names for their own groups translate as "the People." That part was easy. I then borrowed a creation story that was Kiowa, slightly modified, marriage customs from the Cheyenne, an educational system that is Arapaho-Cheyenne, and added some cultural traits from Comanche and some more from the Kiowas.

As the series expanded, so did the culture of the People. I added some customs, each true and valid for some of the nations of the Great Plains: a Sun Dance, an annual gathering, a tribal Council. And, in the Council circle, I left an empty seat. In the Kiowa Council circle is a traditional empty place in honor of one of their bands, killed in a genocidal raid more than two centuries ago in the Northern Plains.

In my story, however, it is the place of the Lost Band. At some time in the past, this band simply failed to arrive for the Council and Sun Dance. Their fate is unknown, an ongoing mystery through the centuries covered by the previous books of the Spanish Bit Saga. It has been a part of the history of the People.

A few months ago, a letter from a reader posed a question: *What happened to the Lost Band?* I had no idea. I had never really wondered about it very much. Yet, the more I thought about it, the more intriguing the mystery became. . . . What did happen? And what would happen if . . . ?

DON COLDSMITH

The Lost Band

Prologue ~•~→

It was the Moon of Roses . . . June by the white man's calendar, and the time for the gathering of the People for the all-important Sun Dance. It was a time for thanksgiving, an acknowledgment of their dependence on the return of the sun. Once more, Sun Boy's torch had triumphed. Renewed, it had brought about the retreat of Cold Maker to the icy mountains somewhere in the North. The warming rays of the new torch had restored the grass in April, the Moon of Greening. The ritual burning of last year's dead crop had awakened new growth. In logical sequence came the return of the buffalo, and it was right to offer prayers and sacrifices of thanksgiving.

It was also a time of fulfillment of vows and the making of others. . . . A time for renewal of patriotism, for ceremonies of healing, and attestations of faith. It was a time for politics, as the leaders met in the formal Big Council and recounted the activities of their respective bands. In the event of the death of the Real-chief, the principal leader of the nation, a new election would be held. But that would not be, this year. They had a strong leader, who was a member of the Northern Band.

Most exciting of all for the young, and for those not immediately concerned with politics or vows or thank offerings, was the gathering itself. Partly religious festival, partly country fair, partly a time for games and contests and gambling and trading horses. It was a time for the meeting of old friends, for the return to their parents of teenagers who had spent a season with relatives in another band to learn of other places and people and to return, more mature and capable. Is it not so, that for a time in one's youth, almost anyone is wiser than one's parents? But parents grow wiser in one's absence, too.

The first group to arrive was the Mountain Band, though they had farther to travel than any, with the possible exception of the Red Rocks. Sycamore River had been preselected for this season, a favorite site for the People. It was inconvenient for the two bands on the western edge of their territory. The Council would probably choose one better suited to their wishes for next year, though. It would even out. . . . There would be jokes, of course, that the Eastern Band might not be able to find a site so far away to the west. Their reputation for foolishness was well known.

Travel had been good, and the Mountain Band arrived even before the Northern Band, who had much of the responsibility for the location of the Medicine Lodge. The family of the Real-chief was also responsible for the selection of the medicine bull, the finest buffalo available. Its head would be positioned in a lifelike pose, facing to the east. Its skin would be stretched over an effigy, to form what might be the focus of an altar in other religions.

The Southern, or Elk-dog Band, was next to come. Their summer range was nearest the site on the Sycamore where the Sun Dance would be held. They were so named because, being nearest to the approach of the Spanish, the Metal People, they had been the first to acquire the horse. . . . A dog as big as an elk. That had been many lifetimes ago, more than two hundred winters. Now, it was as if the People had always possessed the horse.

The Southern Band began to erect their big lodges in their traditional sector. Each band camped in the same relative position as its seats in the Big Council. Starting with the east, the direction of Sun Boy's appearance and the position of all openings and doorways, the accustomed camping places progressed around the circle. First to the south was the empty place reserved to honor the Lost Band, which had disappeared even before the coming of the Spaniard, Heads Off, who had ridden the First Horse. He had become an adopted Person, and had risen to a position as a respected subchief. He might have risen higher as a leader, his descendants insisted, had he not been an outsider.

Between the empty place for the Lost Band and that of the Southern Band would camp a group of newcomers. They were the New Band, related but not identical to the People. They had been around for a generation or two, were well respected and had earned a seat in the Council. For a short while there had been a theory that this *was* the Lost Band, but the New ones said no, they could trace their lineage well back, and saw no connection. Thus they occupied only a small space between that seat and that of the Southern Band.

The Red Rocks lived, hunted, and wintered far to the southwest. They were usually accompanied by some of the Head Splitters, once an enemy of the People but now an ally. Head Splitters had no Sun Dance of their own, but enjoyed the excitement to be found in attending that of the People.

To the northwest quadrant camped the Mountain Band, wintering in the foothills and emerging onto the plain for the warmer months.

The big Northern Band lived and hunted mostly between the Platte River and the Kenza, or Kaw. Their place in the circle was a prestigious one. The last few Real-chiefs had usually been Northerners. Their reputation was that of a producer of leadership, just as that of the Southern Band was for things of the spirit. . . . Medicine. It was not a completely accurate tendency, any more than the Eastern Band's reputation for foolishness, but . . . Well, the moccasin seemed to fit.

The Eastern Band . . . *Aiee!* There were so many stories. . . . The man who bought a worthless horse, convinced by the previous owner that it could defecate gold nuggets instead of dung. In the other bands, a particularly foolish mistake might be met with a sidelong remark . . .

"Was his grandmother not from the Eastern Band?"

It must be admitted that the Eastern Band had produced great leaders, such as Red Feather. Still, it had produced even more clownish fellows who seemed to be pleased with the attention that their foolishness engendered. They always seemed rather disorganized, and were expected to be the last to arrive for the Sun Dance.

As the first of the People began to settle in, young men organized the traditional games and contests, and began to race their horses. A few rode out to watch for newcomers.

"Here come the Red Rocks!" a scout called.

There was a flurry of activity as the young men formed an impromptu mock war party to ride out and greet the new arrivals. A full, frontal charge met the Red Rocks well away from the camp, raising a cloud of dust and some serious scolding from the women of the travelers. The young men of the Red Rocks joined in the wild ride with enthusiasm, circling the column with the others and voicing the full-throated war cry of the People. After a couple of circuits they fell into a quieter pace, visiting with friends not seen since last season as they rode.

There were a few young women among the riders. It was not uncommon among the People for unmarried women to engage in such activities, or in the hunt with the men. What better way to attract attention or to observe the skills of potential husbands? Some even participated for the sheer joy and excitement of the occasion. A young married woman who as yet had no children might ride with her husband.

Through all of this the older men watched from their willow backrests, smoking and visiting, recalling the times when they, too, had ridden like the wind.

"Your nephew rides well, Little Badger."

"Yes . . . I taught him all he knows."

"Red Tree did not speak of knowledge, but of riding," observed another in a friendly jibe.

The whole group chuckled.

"They do ride well, though. We can take pride in our young men."

"And women . . ."

Another general chuckle.

"That goes without saying. . . . *Aiee,* look at that one! Is that not the daughter of Fox Woman?"

"I am made to think so. *Aiee,* she has grown up."

It was several days before the Eastern Band straggled in. The Medicine Lodge, an open-sided brush arbor, was nearly finished. There were a few remarks about how the Eastern Band might have been lost, or killed by their powerful neighbors beyond the range of the People.

"I think not," someone answered. "They camp next to the enemy, who pity their ignorance and spare them."

It was merely talk, for they had been at peace for some time.

When the Eastern Band was finally in place, the announcement was made that the Big Council would be held on the following evening.

By custom, the People began to gather as the shadows grew long. Purple twilight crept up out of the wooded canyons and gullies and spread across the rolling prairie.

The area selected for the Council fire was separate and apart from that of the Sun Dance lodge. Ceremonies there would not begin until after three days of announcement by the keeper of the sacred bundles and his assistants. For now, the Council would be a telling by the chief of each band of their activities since the last Sun Dance. Most of it was already known, of course. This would be only a formalizing of the happenings since the last gathering.

The pipe bearer filled and handed the instrument to the Real-chief, and then a burning twig. Spotted Hawk lighted the tobacco, blew the ritual puffs to the four directions, then to sky and earth, and handed the pipe to the band chieftain at his left.

The ceremony progressed quietly as each successive dignitary repeated the ritual and passed it on. Hawk received the pipe, knocked the dottle from it, and handed it to his pipe bearer, who quickly stepped aside to sheath the instrument.

"It is good!" announced Spotted Hawk. "Let us hear now of the doings of the People."

He turned to the leader at his left, Little Feather of the Eastern Band, who now rose to address the Council.

"I am Little Feather, chief of the Eastern Band of the People. We have had a good season."

There was a disturbance in the rear, and a few giggled.

"Any season when they survive is a good one," someone whispered.

An older woman looked at the youth who had spoken with a burning glance.

"Any season when any of us survive is a good one, stupid," she hissed.

Little Feather waited patiently for the disturbance to quiet and then continued, telling of a rather uneventful season. He finished, and Spotted Hawk nodded. The Real-chief turned to the next band chief in the circle. Blue Fox, of the New Band, who now rose for his narration.

Before he could speak, however, there came an interruption. There was a stirring in the rear, and Spotted Hawk looked around in irritation. He would not tolerate such lack of respect.

Hawk's eyes fell on a strange sight. A tall warrior was picking his way through the seated crowd. His garments were much like those of the People, but cut just a bit differently. His moccasins, too, were not quite like the familiar pattern. He was young, no more than twenty winters. He carried himself with a sense of confidence that spoke of experience. Although weary from long travel, he was still an imposing figure.

Yet, this was a very rude thing on the part of a stranger, to interrupt a ceremony of the host group. A couple of young men rose to intercept the newcomer, and he shook them off.

"I must speak to the Council," he protested.

The young men looked toward the Real-chief, who waved them aside.

"Let him speak," he snapped irritably. The solemn rhythm of the Council was already damaged. It would be best to handle this distraction at once and have it done. Still, he resented the intrusion.

The stranger moved on toward the five and began to speak. He used the tongue of the People, yet there was an accent that was unfamiliar. His voice was strong and carried a ring of confidence and pride.

"I am Story Keeper," he announced, "chief of the Forest Band of the People!"

There were gasps and hoots of derision, and the stranger held up a hand for silence.

"You have no Forest Band?" he asked majestically. "You once did!" He pointed to the empty spot in the circle, reserved to honor the memory of the Lost Band.

"That," he said in a ringing voice, "is my seat in the Council!"

It took some time for the crowd to quiet. That in itself was a thing of wonder. It was unheard of for any event to disrupt the formal solemnity of the Big Council. There might be moments of levity as each of the band chiefs gave his own report, but *aiee* . . .

Reactions ranged from outright disbelief to amazement to scorn to laughter to anger at the supposed impostor, who simply stood with dignity while the excitement swirled and eddied around him.

Spotted Hawk, with the aid of the subchiefs and a couple of the respected holy men, managed to regain control of the situation.

"Enough!" he bellowed. "Let us continue," he added in a calmer tone as the crowd began to quiet. "Our visitor, if he speaks truth, would be the next to give his report to the Council, no? We will hear him out, and then decide if he is what he pretends."

He waved a hand at the stranger to continue.

"Thank you, my chief," the tall man nodded. "I have waited long for this moment." He paused, and his face now showed the strain of pent-up emotion. "All my life . . . And there were those before, who waited many lifetimes. . . . I will tell you. . . ."

Now, for the first time, he paused and seemed to lose his composure.

"Would you wish to wait until later?" asked the Real-chief. "Do you need some food?"

"No, no," the stranger shook his head. "I have eaten as I traveled. I apologize, my chief. I will continue." He took a deep breath. "This is the way the old men told it to me."

He now fell into a rhythmic cadence, the singsong in the oral tradition of the storyteller. Every story must begin with Creation, must it not? The listeners waited patiently through the well-known part about the Old Man, astride the hollow cottonwood log, thumping with his stick, as another man or woman emerged with each thump. The People crawled out into the sunlight, one at a time. The stranger knew the story well, and his performance lent him credibility.

He hurried it a little, barely touching on the incident where Fat Woman became stuck in the log, preventing the coming of more People into the world. Even so, he *knew* about it.

Story Keeper also seemed to know many of the tales of the early history of the People. . . . How they were given the buffalo, taught to make lodges of their skins, and how to utilize their flesh, horns, and bones for many purposes. How the People had moved from the north to escape the pressures of their warlike neighbors and the threat of severe winters. The listeners had heard all of this before, many times, and waited impatiently.

It must be said, however, that the stranger did his job well. By the time he reached the point where the People selected their present area to settle, most of the listeners were convinced.

Then, when he began to speak of the activities of the Forest Band, now considered the Lost Band, people began to nudge each other to closer attention. This was an unheard-of situation, if true, to listen to stories of the People that they had never heard before.

Part One

White Moon ∿→

1

This was long ago, before the coming of the horse. The People hunted the buffalo, and deer and small game. They gathered nuts and berries and plums. The Forest Band had more of these than the bands farther west, who had more buffalo. . . . Each place to live has its problems and its good things, no? But they got along well, usually. Sometimes in the moons of late winter there was hunger, if they had not stored enough food, or if there was some unusual happening. Is the time just before Awakening not called the Moon of Hunger? Then, sometimes, it was the Moon of Starvation. But not usually. Times were good.

The Forest Band of the People had attended the Sun Dance, and all the bands had scattered again, each to its own area. . . . The Western Band, not so far west then, had not yet divided into Mountain and Red Rocks Bands. There were the Northern and Southern Bands, and the Eastern Band, living like our own Forest Band, in the forested area north of us. Not so successfully, of course. You know how they are, the Eastern Band.

One main problem of those of us who hunted the forests was always conflict with others. Our hunters would encounter hunters from other tribes, and there would be arguments, sometimes fighting.

In that terrible year long ago, when the Forest Band returned from the Sun Dance to one of their favorite camping places, there were strangers living there. They were cutting poles and building houses, and it was not good. There was much anger on the part of the young men of both sides. The strangers spoke a different tongue, but knew some hand signs, so the chiefs were able to smoke the pipe and hold a council. It was agreed that there was no need for bloodshed, that it would be better to live in peace. Besides, the newcomers were big and strong and there were many of them.

So, the People moved on, still in their usual area for hunting and camping, but a little farther to the south. The hunters sometimes encountered those of the invading new people, the "Shaved-heads," but by agreement, they respected each other's rights. The treaty seemed to be working.

It was a hot summer, it is said, and that led to some irritation and impatience, maybe. It was in the Moon of Ripening, when they were beginning to gather and prepare food for storage against the coming Moons of Long Nights and Snows, that the trouble began.

There was a young man, Big Dog, nephew of the band chief. He was a capable hunter, a good swimmer and wrestler, fast in a running race, and very handsome. Such a young man as we admire, who would someday be a leader, and whom all the young women saw as an ideal husband. But so far, he was more interested in hunting and sports and races and games. He was bright and cheerful and friendly to all of the young women, but had courted no one in particular yet. He did have a temper, which may have caused all of the trouble.

Dog had been hunting with two friends, Black Snake and Jumper. They had stalked a deer very skillfully, and Big Dog finally struck it with an arrow. The three hurried after the big buck as it made its last dying leaps through the trees and brush. They lost sight of it, and when they finally picked up the trail of blood and tracked it a little way, they found a hunter in the process of kneeling to cut the throat and bleed the deer. Other hunters stood behind him.

That is my kill! stated Big Dog, using hand signs.

The other hunter laughed. *I cut the throat!* he indicated. *The kill is mine!*

Dog rushed forward in anger and was met by the massed strength of the other party. His companions hurried to his aid. Jumper never even reached the fight, but was struck down by an arrow in mid-stride. Black Snake was struck a glancing blow with a war club and fell. When he tried to rise, half conscious and confused, he was overwhelmed by the enemy hunters. They tied his hands, and as his head cleared, Snake saw his friend Big Dog, also subdued and trussed. Snake realized that the side of his own head was covered with sticky blood. Dog had suffered a knife wound across his chest and another on his left forearm, but was awake and alert, and cursing quietly.

There was a time of considerable discussion, with gesturing and pointing, which Snake did not understand. Finally the hunting party, numbering about eight men and boys, seemed to come to a decision. They cut the thongs that bound his wrists and motioned for him to go away. *Tell your people,* their leader gestured.

What about him? Snake asked, pointing to Big Dog.

We keep him! the other signed.

It was not until then that Snake noticed a still form beside that of the deer. Dog had killed one of the other party before he had been dragged down.

Go! Go on!

My weapons? he signed in question.

No! Tell your people.

There was an urgent council, and much discussion. The leaders of the Forest Band were indignant at such treatment. Some wanted to attack immediately. Woodchuck, the band chieftain, was more calm and deliberate in his approach, even though his nephew was involved.

"That would spill more blood," he reminded. "As it is now, we have lost one life, that of Jumper. The others have lost one, but they spared Black Snake, here. Is that not a good sign? Let us approach them and ask for our young man back again."

It was agreed that such an approach was worth trying. A delegation was chosen, a dozen men including the best hunters of the People, but also several of their wisest elders. They assembled a few small gifts for the leaders of the other group and approached their town, half a day's travel away, on the next day.

They were met with an attitude of haughty superiority, but were led through the village, now appearing much more settled, as well as larger. There was a large meeting house near the center of the town, and they were taken there. The meeting house quickly filled with people, whose faces were stony and grim.

"This is not good," said Woodchuck.

In due time a few of the town's leaders arrived, obviously late as an intentional slight to the visitors. Their faces were hard, too, but they sat and smoked the pipe with the visitors, as was only proper. They accepted the small gifts from the visitors, and finally Woodchuck brought up the subject of their visit.

We have come about the incident between our young men, Woodchuck signed.

Never mind . . . A misunderstanding, answered the other leader with a smirk. *It is over.*

No, Woodchuck protested. *One man is dead on each side, but you hold one of ours prisoner.*

The other chief pretended to be surprised. *We released one,* he signed, pointing to Snake. *We kept only the killer, the crazy one.*

Woodchuck tried to ignore the insult. *Young men are sometimes foolish, no? He can learn better judgment, after we take him home.*

The other man smiled and spread his palms, helplessly as if perplexed. *We no longer have him,* he signed.

Woodchuck's heart sank. *Where is he?* he demanded.

The chief shrugged. *Who knows? We sold him to a party of traders. That might help improve his judgment.* He smirked again.

A slave? demanded Woodchuck.

Of course. We found him difficult to handle. . . . Crazy, you know.
But these traders knew how to cure that. He will be much calmer now.

Where did they go? demanded Woodchuck, barely controlling
himself.

They did not say. East, maybe. They left this morning.

They caught up with the traders in night camp that evening. They
were friendly, as traders should be. Woodchuck saw a number of
slaves, an ankle of each tied by a thong about a pace long to the
ankle of the next. These prisoners were of both sexes and various
ages, but Big Dog was not among them.

We are looking for a young man, he explained, after the usual
greeting.

Yes, we have several fine ones. The trader gestured toward the
prisoners. *Look them over.*

No, no. A particular one. You bought him from the Shaved-heads,
they said.

Oh, that one. Crazy. Yes, too bad. He died.

Died?

*Yes. It is seldom to have such bleeding just from castration, but
sometimes . . . Too bad.*

There was nothing to do. They camped, well out of sight of the
other party, and a discussion was held around the fire. Woodchuck,
sick at heart, was in no condition to lead. The argument rambled,
and various irrational suggestions were made. Kill all the traders and
free their slaves . . . Go back to the Shaved-heads' town and attack
them . . . Catch individual hunters and kill them . . .

Everyone remembered what a good friend Big Dog had been to
him, whether or not it had actually been true.

Finally Woodchuck held up a hand for silence, and the group
quieted.

"There is only one thing to do," he said. "We are at war with the
Shaved-heads. Let us go home, hold a council, and make our plans."

2

$\mathbf{T}$he council was hot and heavy. Though the People were not warlike by tradition, there was a cry for justice, a need to avenge the loss of one of the finest of their young men. It was not a question of whether to retaliate, but *how* and *when*.

There was one school of thought that suggested a quiet vengeance. . . . An occasional ambush of a lone hunter, maybe. That suggestion was hooted down in scorn. There must be a decisive event, an open defeat of the hated Shaved-heads. They must be taught a lesson!

The council discussed at some length how to organize such an attack, and a plan evolved. There could be no greater impression on the enemy than to attack them where they lived, to destroy their town. Someone called attention to how well the pole structures with grass thatch would burn, and there was a flurry of excitement. Yes . . . An attack at dawn, when everyone was not yet fully awake . . . Fire a few of the houses on the upwind side of the town and watch it spread . . . Kill everyone as they came out, by the light from their own burning homes. When? The sooner the better . . . With more enthusiasm than judgment they began the ritual dances and chants, the fasting and ceremony that would lead to the attack. The fires burned all night, and the next day was occupied in readying weapons. The war party would depart at dusk and travel under cover of darkness.

The first streaks of yellow-gray were showing in the eastern sky when the men of the People crept silently toward the enemy village. There was no sign of activity. Carefully, the warriors spread out around the shadowy structures. Those who had brought the hot coals in pots of sand brought out their tinder and kindled small fires for torches. There was still no stirring in the sleeping town. This was going well. . . .

The first of the grass-thatched dwellings burst into flame, and there was an eagerness that could not be contained. Someone voiced the full-throated war cry of the People, and the warriors rushed among the houses. And nothing happened. . . . There was no response.

In the growing light, they ran from one structure to another, and it was the same. The enemy was gone. There were a few fires, carefully laid to burn long and slowly, to give the impression that the town was still occupied.

"Ah!" exclaimed a young man. "We have shown them the strength of the People! They have run away!"

There was silence for a few moments, broken only by the crackling fires of the burning houses. Then the realization began to dawn. . . .

"But where are they?"

"Could they be . . . ?"

"*Aiee!*"

Those whose thought processes moved a bit faster than others were already turning, hurrying along the back trail. There was no organization, only men who feared for the safety of their families. Men who had not slept and whose excitement had been drained by fear. Men who stumbled in their efforts to hurry and whose hearts were heavy with the realization that they had left their families unprotected. They were also men unskilled in war, by a generation of peace, and they were opposed by experts in such conflict.

Thus, the People were easy prey for an ambush. They were strung along the trail for some distance, the more fleet of foot well in advance. The older and slower warriors lagged far behind, panting and puffing.

They were attacked in the worst possible setting, a narrow pass between two hills. The first of the warriors, the most able, were allowed to pass unchallenged. When they were already through the pass, and the main body of the party hemmed in by the hills, the enemy struck. There was a shower of arrows, followed by war cries from the attackers. . . . High-pitched, quavering sounds that seemed not to come from human throats mingled with screams from the wounded and dying. There was another shower of arrows, and then the enemy came bounding down the hillside, swinging heavy war clubs or wielding spears.

The battle was short and decisive. Before the sun had risen high enough to really begin the day, most of the men of the Forest Band of the People were dead or dying. Woodchuck had been one of the first to fall, transfixed by an arrow.

Those few warriors who had been in the lead had turned back when the attack came, to try to assist. They, too, were at a disadvantage. The enemy had known their number and their position before the first volley of arrows. They never reached the main battle.

Now, the Shaved-heads moved with gruesome deliberation among the wounded, clubbing or spearing those who still moved. A few of the uninjured were spared, and their hands quickly tied behind their backs. They could be sold as slaves.

There had been two, however, the fastest of runners, who had not turned back to the fight. They were well ahead, and out of concern for their families had continued toward the village of the People. Striker and Red Owl stumbled into the camp well before midday, to spread the warning, and to try to organize a defense.

There was no time for mourning or to try to learn who had been lost. That could come later. For now . . . A few of the older women rounded up children, assisted by the adolescents, to hide in the rocky glens and caves along the ridge behind the camp. The other women, those in their active years, now prepared for the fight that was surely coming.

Among the People, the education of the young was the same for boys and girls until the approach of puberty. Both sexes received instruction in the Rabbit Society, the same stories, dances, the use of tools and weapons. It was necessary for women to be able to hunt or to help defend their families. It was not unusual for an unmarried woman to participate in a hunt with the men. Or, in fact, for a young wife to hunt with her husband, until her lodge was blessed with children. The women of the People were far from helpless. But, they too had no experience in combat. In addition, most of the better weapons had been taken by the men.

"When will they come?" asked young White Moon.

"There is no way to tell," said her husband, Striker, "but I am made to think it will be before night. They will not want to fight in a strange place in the dark."

"Let us talk to Spider," suggested Red Owl. "He is too feeble to fight, but he may remember things that would help us."

Spider had been in his prime the last time there had been fighting. That had been with the Panis, the Horned-head People. The three approached the old man.

"Uncle," began Striker, using the term of respect. "We are in need of any help you can give us."

"*Aiee,*" said Spider. "These old hands cannot even hold a spear!"

"No, no, Uncle." Advice . . . How can we defend our families."

"Oh . . . Yes . . . I do not remember . . . The Horn People . . . Very dangerous.

His mind is gone, thought White Moon. She pulled at her husband's sleeve. "Come away," she whispered. "Thank you, Uncle. We will be careful," she said aloud to Spider.

"Is there anyone else?" asked Red Owl.

The three looked at each other helplessly.

"There was Lean Wolf. . . . His mind was good, but . . ."

"He died last winter . . . ."

"Yes . . ."

"Let us call together those who can fight," suggested Striker. "Now, at the council ring." He raised his voice. "Let us meet now!" he yelled. "Hurry! A council. Anyone who can fight."

The women poured toward the council ring. Young, old, any able-bodied girl or woman. There were a few teenaged boys and a few old men, carrying makeshift weapons.

"I am made to think," said Striker, "that they will come soon. We should scatter in the woods and attack them after they enter the camp, no?"

There were nods of agreement.

"Then let us . . ."

"They come!" called a breathless young woman, sprinting into camp from her position as lookout.

"Scatter, then! Now!" Striker yelled. "Make every arrow and every blow count!"

"Do not let them capture you," White Moon whispered to her husband as they crouched in the hazel bushes. "You know what they did to Big Dog."

That had not been the Shaved-heads but the slave traders, of course, Striker knew. And, the reason for such treatment was that Big Dog had fought instead of cooperating. Yet, even with such a choice, it would be preferable to die fighting. . . .

"Of course," he told her.

Now there were quiet shadows flitting among the trees. They could see from their place of concealment that nearly every tree and shrub partially concealed a warrior. A dog barked. . . .

There was a signal of some sort, and all at once the enemy warriors burst from cover and rushed into the clearing. Three old women, who had volunteered to move around among the lodges to make the enemy think they were unexpected, now screamed and ran. The first of the warriors to pursue them were cut down by a surprise flight of arrows from women hidden in the lodges. But more came, and more yet. . . .

Striker, Red Owl, Moon, and another few women attempted a flanking attack from the woods. They wreaked havoc for a moment, but the People were badly outnumbered. Owl fell, an arrow in his flank. He was still trying to nock another arrow to his bowstring when he was struck down from behind.

A big man rushed Striker, and met Striker's arrow, but his momentum carried them both to the ground. Striker struggled to reach his knife and to escape from the weight of the dying warrior. He was still not freed when a war club descended from behind, and the darkness of death with it. White Moon screamed in rage as her flint ax crushed the skull of her husband's killer. Before she could turn, she was overpowered and thrown to the ground by a rush of other warriors. She did not much care. Striker was dead.

It was nearly dark when the killing and looting and burning ceased. The invaders had methodically killed all of the elders and the wounded. They had rounded up the children from their hiding place, killing the women who had tried to hide them and any children who resisted. There were no more than twenty prisoners, mostly children. White Moon's spirits sank as she realized that those spared, including herself, were those who would be most desirable to sell as slaves. It was the end of the Forest Band of the People.

"Wait!" someone said to the storyteller as he finished. "Then how is it that you are here, claiming that seat in the circle?"

The stranger smiled.

"Ah!" he said. "That is not the end of my story. . . . It is the *beginning!*"

3

It took some time for reality to descend on the survivors. The People, at least the Forest Band, had been engaged in a war, and had lost. The prisoners who huddled together, wailing softly the Songs of Mourning, were the only survivors.

At least, White Moon believed it to be so. Shaved-head warriors had straggled in for half a day with more prisoners. A child or two, a woman with an infant . . . Most of the captives were women and children. There was an occasional youngster just approaching manhood, but physically no match for a mature warrior. Potential slaves . . .

Moon began to wonder if the entire plan of the Shaved-heads, the move into the territory of the People, was designed to capture slaves to be sold to traders. She had heard the discussion in council, and the references to the slavers who had been responsible for the death of Big Dog. Had the whole thing been a plan to prey on the People from the beginning?

But her main thoughts, as she sat, her hands tied and one ankle tethered to that of her friend Turkey Hen, were of Striker. He was dead. Moon knew that, for she had seen him killed. She had in turn struck down his killer, but that was no comfort. Her life was empty. . . . It was over. She did not care, now, what happened to her.

She had sung her Song of Mourning for Striker, and would again, for the traditional three days, until his spirit had crossed over. For a little while, she thought of trying to find a way to join her husband. She rejected that, realizing that Striker would not want it so.

Probably the thing that gave her a determination to go on was the sound of the children, mourning their own losses. Most of these had been orphaned in the frenzy of killing. They were terrorized, confused, crying softly. Any louder crying brought cuffs or kicks. The older children tried to comfort the younger.

Her attention was drawn to a small girl of perhaps five summers. The child was sitting, wide-eyed and numb, staring emptily into space. A small ankle was tied by a thong to that of another child, whose face was streaked with tears. White Moon held her trussed arms toward the youngster.

"Come, little one!" she whispered. "Let me hold you!"

The little girl crept into her embrace, and Moon sat rocking her. The feeling of helping a child, the mother instinct, could partially replace her grief, she found. *Yes . . .* That might be the answer to this situation. . . . If she could focus on the needs of these others, maybe she could survive the pain in her own heart. She began to hum softly to the little girl, a combination of lullaby and words of comfort where there could be no comfort.

"What is your name?" she asked.

"Fawn," the child sniffled. "Spotted Fawn."

"It is good. I am White Moon."

"Where is your little girl?" the child asked.

"Ah, I have none! Will you stay with me?"

The child snuggled against her, and somehow both were comforted.

Sleep, little one, gather your strength, for we will need it tomorrow, she whispered, mostly to herself.

The next morning, after a sleepless night, she began to try to communicate with their captors. They had remained near the sacked camp of the People, still rummaging among the personal property of the dead or captives. This added to White Moon's thought that the whole series of events had been planned from the start. The Shaved-heads had set out to exterminate or enslave this band of the People. Odd, that the Eastern Band, known for foolishness and poor judgment, had not been the target for extermination. Or had they? Had the other bands, too, been subjected to this destruction and enslavement? There was no way to know, but . . .

Well, as she understood the events of the past few days, the Shaved-heads had released Black Snake so that he *could* tell of the power of their people. This time, she had the impression that no one had been spared. All of the People had either been killed or were captives. At least, she thought so. This reinforced her idea that it was a deliberate extermination.

But she must establish communication now. She caught the eye of one of the warriors who had been assigned to watch the captives, and beckoned to him. She managed to indicate, even with hands tied in front of her, that she must empty her bladder. The man nodded and motioned her to follow him. She rose, and the two little girls did also, holding to her skirt and whimpering. Turkey Hen, tied to Moon by the ankle, followed. The warrior led the way to a more private area and motioned for them to go ahead. White Moon nodded thanks, but held out her bound hands, with a helpless expression on her face and a glance at the child. The man nodded, untied the thongs, and motioned again.

Ah! It is good! Moon signed, rubbing her sore wrists. *Her, too?* She indicated Turkey Hen. The man nodded and released the other woman's hands. They attended to themselves and the children. White Moon turned to their captor with a smile of thanks. He glowered and motioned with the waiting thong. But now she could communicate.

Leave them free? she questioned. *We can help with the children better.*

The warrior was suspicious.

I will not run, she signed.

If you do, I will kill you! He shook his heavy war club.

Agreed! White Moon signed. *Her, too.*

Turkey Hen's eyes widened in surprise, but she said nothing.

"This will make it easier," Moon told her.

"Make *what* easier? Are you crazy? You'll get us all killed, trying to escape!"

"No, no. We couldn't try to escape and leave the children. Don't be silly."

Stop the talking! signed their captor. *Now! Back where you were!*

They retraced their steps to the area where the other captives were confined. White Moon did not fail to notice the seductive sidelong glance that Turkey Hen gave the Shaved-head warrior, or the smile that he gave her in return. Well, Turkey had always been a flirt, and had not yet taken a husband. Why should she be expected to change now?

When they returned to the camp, preparations were under way for departure. Those warriors not directly concerned with care of the captives were burdened down with plunder. Everything usable was to be carried off, it seemed, or burned if there was too much to carry.

There was a considerable amount of shoving and slapping the captives, to show the authority of their captors. The children appeared bewildered. Among the People, there was none of that. Even in games and contests of strength and athletic ability, or in the heat of anger, it would be inappropriate. Wrestling, yes, but none of the People would strike another of the People. Likewise, a parent would not strike a child. White Moon knew that it was not so in some other tribes, but even she found it disturbing.

"Do as they tell us," she called to the others. "Their ways are different. But keep our pride. Remember, we are the *People!*"

For this effort, she was rewarded with a blow across her shoulders from a stick in the hands of one of the Shaved-heads. She moved on, head still high.

The captives were tied by twos and threes as before. A thong no more than a pace or two in length bound each to the ankle of the next. Some had their hands tied, mostly women and older boys who had shown indication of resistance. The hands of White Moon and Turkey remained free, which made walking considerably easier. The pace was steady, but not hurried or urgent. It was apparent to Moon that their captors were completely unconcerned that they might be pursued. This could mean only one thing. The defeat of the People had been so complete that there were no other survivors.

That thought now descended on her like the stillness in the air before the attack of the Big Whirlwind in the summer. Gloom enveloped her. As if the death of her husband, her parents, her brother were not enough, there was this. . . . In any other loss or tragedy in her life, she had been able to depend on the support of her extended family, the Forest Band of the People. Now, that too was gone. The pitiful survivors who now staggered along the trail as captives of the Shaved-heads were all that remained.

It was easy to allow herself to sink into her grief and depression, and to abandon all hope. She came very near to doing that, on that first morning of her captivity. But during one of the infrequent rest stops, she began to think along different lines. *I must not do that,* she told herself. *We are still alive. Those who are still alive owe it to our dead to live with honor and pride.*

She thought of Striker, and tears came to her eyes. But at the same time, she felt a new strength, as if she were somehow being given some of her husband's stamina and strength. Striker had fallen bravely in battle, defending her and the others of the People. Yes, it would dishonor his memory to do other than her best. A sort of peace, a serenity of understanding began to settle over her. She prayed quietly for a few moments, asking the help of those who had gone before. . . . The Grandfathers and Grandmothers . . .

Up! Move, now!

Her reverie was interrupted by the yells of their captors, along with hand signs and the occasional whacks with the sticks, which the Shaved-heads seemed to enjoy.

"Thank you, Grandmother," she murmured as she rose.

She took a deep breath and stepped into the trail beside Turkey Hen. She smiled at Fawn, who returned a shy grin.

"Come on, Little One," Moon said. "Stay with me."

She began to plan, realizing even as she did so that there were those who would think it ridiculous. She would learn all she could about the Shaved-heads. . . . Their customs, their language . . . Already, she had recognized the meaning of a word or two in their tongue. *Up . . . Move . . . Be still!*

She would continue to listen and learn, but would conceal such knowledge. In that way, she could begin to understand the conversations of their captors, unknown to them. That would give her an advantage. Then, even under the circumstances, it struck her has amusing that she should be thinking in terms of *advantage,* where there was little good to be seen.

But we are alive, she thought, *and we are the People. Is this in itself not an advantage?*

She straightened her shoulders and walked with pride.

4

White Moon was startled at one of the brief rest stops during the day to see Turkey Hen conversing in hand signs with one of their captors. . . . He was the one with whom she had flirted earlier in the day.

"What are you doing?" Moon demanded.

Her friend shrugged. "I think that one likes me."

White Moon was furious.

"*Likes* you? Turkey, these are the people who killed my husband . . . your family. . . ."

Turkey Hen dropped her eyes for a moment, and then looked up.

"Moon," she said seriously, "I know that. I also know that, like it or not, we will be warming the beds of these men. . . . Sooner or later, probably sooner. Otherwise, they would have killed us already. We will be slave-wives, of these or some other men. Would it not be better to be the slave-wife of one who likes you?"

"But . . . But . . ." White Moon sputtered, "I could not . . . would not . . ."

"They will force you, then."

"And I would cut his throat in his sleep!" White Moon raged.

Turkey Hen smiled tolerantly. "Of course you would. Then they would kill *you,* and who would look after your little Fawn, there? No, Moon, I think it is better to try to be friends with the man who takes you. So, I am working on it."

Here! Be still, you two! a warrior signed. *Up, now! We go on.*

They rose and continued on the trail, prodded along by their captors. White Moon was burning with anger and frustration.

What was most infuriating was that Turkey was right. She could not deny it. Her hatred for these men burned deep inside her. How could she overcome the loathing that flared up at the mere touch of the Shaved-head warriors' hands. How much worse . . . . *Aiee!* Her heart was very heavy.

During a midday halt the captives were given a little food in the form of dried meat and smoked fish. Moon thought to refuse at first, but quickly realized that such an attitude was self-defeating. She must keep herself in good condition, because in the back of her mind one goal was beginning to form. . . . Someday, somehow, she would escape. And, to do that, she must keep herself in the best of condition, physically and mentally.

She took a piece of the unfamiliar smoked fish and chewed it. . . . Different. . . . Not bad, actually. She had eaten worse, during the Moon of Hunger in some years. She realized only now how long it had been since she had taken any food. In her grief she had not realized her hunger. She would continue to mourn, humming the songs for the loss of her husband and parents. Normally that would include a time of fasting, anyway. But it would not have included travel. Now, she was being forced to travel, and to more indignities yet unknown. There would be little accomplished by proving that she was stubborn enough to die from lack of food. No, she would stay in good condition, to be ready for escape whenever the opportunity offered. Meanwhile, she must also watch over little Fawn.

It was nearly evening when they approached a town of log and thatch houses similar to the one the People had attacked. Moon wondered why they had been brought here instead of to the nearer of the Shaved-heads' towns. Of course, it had been partially destroyed, Striker had told her. Maybe it would be abandoned. Who knows what a Shaved-head thinks, anyway? Maybe this was simply an opportunity to show off the captives to more people.

The travelers were met by cheering people and barking dogs as they paraded through the town. An old woman hobbled alongside the captives for a little way, screeching at them in a strange tongue with apparent rage. Finally the woman spat at the procession in general. A fleck of phlegm struck Moon on the cheek, and she wiped it away with the sleeve of her buckskin dress. For an instant she was tempted to attack the old crone, but thought better of it. Her ankle was sill tethered to that of Turkey Hen, and little Spotted Fawn was clinging to her skirt in terror. No, she must at least appear to be cooperative, for now.

The captives were herded into a house that appeared to be a meeting place. There were woven mats on the floor, and their captors made signs that they were to sleep here. It was also made plain that there would be guards present.

It will be cold, White Moon signed, indicating the children. Nights were becoming cool with the shorter days of autumn.

After a moment of thought, one of their captors nodded and spoke to the others. A couple of them left the house and soon returned with armfuls of robes and tanned skins. Moon recognized some of them as loot from her own town. The men tossed them to the floor and departed.

She slept hardly at all, between the restless crying and whimpering of the children and her own grief at the loss of her husband. She was sure that she could never love another man.

Morning came, and with it a sense of apprehension.

"What will happen now?" whispered Fawn.

"I don't know," Moon answered, "but I will try to keep us together. Be brave. Remember, we are the People!"

Then she raised her voice for the rest to hear.

"Hear me, now! Let us all do what they want, but remember to keep our pride. Keep our customs as we are able."

"We are able to do nothing," sneered one of the women. "We are finished. It is over, White Moon. Accept it!"

"No! I will not! Someday, I will escape. You should try, too. But in the meantime, we must teach these children what it means to be one of the People. Teach them our ways, our songs, our prayers, and our pride . . ."

As she finished that sentence, she saw alarm in the eyes of those who looked past her. She started to turn, but just then felt a hard blow from a stick across her back and shoulders. She nearly fell forward, but recovered and turned.

Be still, you! the man told her, using signs as well as what apparently amounted to the same message in his own tongue.

She lapsed into silence, with only a reassuring glance around the group of captives. Then her message and its importance overcame her again.

"Remember!" she admonished them again. She was rewarded with another whack from the stick.

About midmorning the captives were herded outside, and a crowd gathered. Moon was uneasy, because this seemed to be a formal gathering of some sort. The alarming thought crossed her mind that the Shaved-heads might be choosing one of the captives for torture and sacrifice in some public ritual or ceremony. At least, she felt that they were being evaluated and sized up by the onlookers. She was very uncomfortable with the leering, sensual looks from some of the men.

It developed, however, that the purpose of the gathering was somewhat different. The warriors who had participated in their capture began choosing individual captives and taking them aside.

There was no mistaking the attitude of possession on the part of the Shaved-head warriors. *This one is mine. . . .*

Quickly, White Moon looked around, trying to account for the captive People before they were split up and taken away. A quick count . . . About a dozen adults or young women nearing marriageable age. There were six boys who appeared to be approaching manhood, but who had been too young to fight with any serious threat to the enemy.

The rest were younger children, both boys and girls, from two or three summers of age on up. Some were family units, two or three siblings clinging together for protection. Moon knew most of them, had known their parents all her life. . . . Parents now dead, having defended their homes with their dying breath.

She felt a wave of guilt that she was still alive and had not been able to fight to the death. She wondered if the other adults of this pitiful group felt the same.

The young warrior with whom her friend had flirted now strolled among the captives. He was followed by a young woman who by her action and attitude must be his wife. As the woman turned, Moon saw that she was in the latter stages of a pregnancy.

The couple strolled among the captives, and then the young man appeared to locate Turkey Hen. He motioned to his wife and they approached, the husband talking rapidly and pointing. The woman looked the captive girl over with a critical eye, and they conversed for a short while.

You speak our tongue? asked the woman in hand signs.

Turkey Hen shook her head.

There was another short conversation between the man and wife, and then he bent and cut the thong around Turkey's ankle. He glowered at the girl.

You will come with us, he signed. *You will do as my woman says. If you try to escape, we will kill you.*

Turkey nodded as she turned to follow them, glancing back over her shoulder at White Moon and Fawn. There was anxiety in her face, and a silent plea for help that White Moon was not in a position to give.

"Remember what I said," Moon called after her.

She wondered if she would ever see her friend again. There was a lurking suspicion in her mind that many of the captives would be sold to traveling slave traders, as poor Big Dog had been. If so, Turkey Hen, having been chosen by the young husband as a servant for his pregnant wife, would stay here, while she, White Moon. . .

A man touched her roughly, and she turned to face him.

Is this child yours? he signed, pointing to Spotted Fawn. The little girl clung tightly to her skirt.

Yes, she is mine, Moon signed, putting a protective arm around Fawn's shoulders.

There was an expression of doubt on the man's face, and he called to a woman who was looking at a group of the children. The woman approached, and White Moon guessed that these two must be man and wife. They were a bit older than the couple who had claimed Turkey Hen.

They were conversing now, both looking at Spotted Fawn. Then the woman turned and swept her eyes over Moon's lithe body. She spoke to her husband with what might have been some sarcasm in her tone, and he shrugged helplessly. Then the woman turned back, and Moon saw a twinkle in the eye of the other. . . . Just for a moment . . . Then the stern expression of disapproval returned. She turned back to her husband, talking rapidly.

White Moon was unsure what the argument was about, or if there really was one. It was possible that this was merely friendly bantering by a married couple. Regardless, it was not reassuring, since any disagreement, or worse, was very closely connected to the future of White Moon and the child she had chosen to try to protect. She did not know what she would do if the Shaved-heads decided to separate them.

But now the woman spoke to her in hand signs.

Well, come on. . . . Both of you.

White Moon picked up another. stick and added it to her armload. A few more . . . She was several bow shots from the town, because there was always a need for firewood. In this area of heavily timbered forest, dead wood was plentiful, but also in great demand.

As usual when she was a distance from the town, the thought came to her that she could run. Escape was always in the back of her mind. She would have tried it, even under the threat that she would be killed. Two of the older boys had tried it and had been captured. One was killed on the spot, the other dragged back and kept tied until he was sold, with a dozen others, to a passing trader. Moon had confidence that she could evade pursuit, but she must think of Spotted Fawn. She had assumed responsibility for the child and could not abandon her. And, it seemed unlikely that she could manage an escape while hindered in her mobility by the presence of a child. Green Turtle and his wife, Maple Flower, who had no children of their own, had taken the little girl into their hearts. This further confused the situation. Moon knew that if she escaped herself, leaving Fawn behind, the girl would receive loving care. But she would be raised among the Shaved-heads, and would never know her own culture.

That, Moon found unacceptable. The most important thing in her now limited world had become the preservation of the Forest Band of the People. It had replaced her grief, after the traditional period of mourning. It had overcome her somewhat irrational desire for vengeance against her husband's killers. Even her deep-seated determination to escape was set aside in her vow that the story and the customs of the People should survive.

Among the other captives, she had not found much support for this dedication. There were only a handful of the People left in the Shaved-heads' town now, nearly two moons after the destruction of the People. A few had been killed, like the boy who had tried to escape. One woman had died from a wound that had appeared minor but that festered and spread. Moon personally thought that the shock of the surrounding events, of having seen her husband and sons killed, had been as great a factor as the wound in the woman's death.

Most of the captives had been sold or traded, however. This seemed to be a common practice among their captors. The ownership of slaves was not unknown among the People, but was not as common as it was here. A few of the children had remained as personal slaves to their captors. She hoped to find an opportunity to teach those the old ways of the People.

Turkey Hen was still with the couple who had claimed her. Her flirtation with Short-tail Dog had been successful for Turkey. She was now second wife to the young warrior. She was ordered around by the first wife, which was only right, but Bluebird Woman, with her new baby, did seem grateful for the help with the house.

"And he's very good in the robes," Turkey told her friend, with a suggestive lift of the eyebrow. "They have a custom, it seems. . . . None of that after the baby's birth, until it is able to sit up. I can fill that need in Bluebird Woman's lodge."

They had little opportunity to talk, except an accidental meeting while gathering wood or carrying water occasionally. They were watched closely.

"Do not forget, Turkey, that we must follow the ways of the People as much as we can," White Moon had reminded her.

"Yes, yes, of course," her friend replied. "How is yours in bed?"

Moon was somewhat offended. Not by the question, which was quite appropriate, but by the careless way in which Turkey Hen brushed off the serious mention of the People.

"I don't know," she said irritably. "I think they wanted me for Fawn. They have no child, you know."

"But . . . They aren't much older than we are, are they? Maybe something is wrong with him. . . . Or with you!" Turkey Hen giggled.

"There's nothing wron. . . ." Moon started to defend Green Turtle and herself against the remark, but stopped short. She should not dignify such an inappropriate comment with an answer.

Actually, her friend had struck very close to home with her joke. Moon had dreaded the touch of any man. She doubted that after Striker's death she could tolerate such a thing, especially from those who had killed her husband. Yet she had known that it was probably inevitable, with her captive status. It was still so, but it had not happened. Despite herself, she wondered . . . *Was* there something about her that Green Turtle found undesirable? She shoved such a thought aside. Maple Flower was basically a good woman. She was a strict overseer, and demanded efficiency and good work, but demanded it of herself as well.

From what White Moon had seen, this was a devoted couple, whom she might have liked under other circumstances. Flower had wanted a child badly, and had none, it seemed. Her husband had seen this opportunity to obtain one, and at the same time, a servant for his wife. Moon had let them believe that Fawn was her own, hoping there was less likelihood that their captors would separate them. She had seen no reason to tell them otherwise.

Moon was learning the language of their captors rapidly, but still concealing that fact by using hand signs almost entirely. She had resigned herself to the fact that with winter coming soon, there was little chance of escape. It would take more planning and much better weather than could be expected in the near future, the Moon of Long Nights and Moon of Snows. She could see no alternative to spending the winter in the lodge of her captor and his wife. But she could bide her time. When the moment was right, she would make her move. Meanwhile, it was to her advantage to appear docile and cooperative.

As for the likelihood of her becoming a wife to Green Turtle, there was nothing she could do about it. As a slave, a captive of the brief and disastrous war, she would have to submit, be forced, or be killed. Her friend Turkey Hen seemed quite content with her lot. . . . *Well,* Moon thought, *I'll face that problem when it comes.* And it had not. . . . Not yet.

Meanwhile, she took advantage of the fact that their captors did not understand the tongue of the People. She talked to young Spotted Fawn. Day after day, stories of the People. The Creation story, the tales of the olden times when everybody, people and animals, could speak the same tongue. Whimsical tales, such as how the bobcat lost his tail, and how the People were given the buffalo.

When they were alone, she repeatedly demonstrated the hand sign for the People.

"When you are grown," she explained to Fawn, "this will help you to know who you are. We should not use it except to ourselves for now, but someday we will find others of the People, and by this they will know us. But it is our secret."

"We do not use it for Flower and Green Turtle?" the girl asked.

"No. They are not of our People."

"For Turkey Hen? She is. . . .

This began a dilemma for Moon. She was uncomfortable with the way Turkey was fitting so well into the lodge of Short-tail Dog and adopting the ways of the Shaved-heads. Each time Moon tried to remind her, Turkey would give the same response. *Yes, yes, of course,* and then change the subject. Moon was becoming quite concerned that of all those left alive, she, White Moon, might be the only one left who could carry on and teach the ways of the People.

But she would try to do that. She could be compliant to the extent that she must. She could endure whatever was needed, could seem to cooperate as much as Turkey Hen, for the purpose that was becoming more and more important in her mind.

Initially, it had been for the protection of little Fawn, who had no one else. That and her own survival, to keep herself in good condition for a time when escape and possibly vengeance could be carried out.

Her thoughts were changing, though. She could not envision vengeance now against Green Turtle and Maple Flower. They had been good to her, and especially to Fawn. Moon had been beaten very little, and then, not sadistically. It had not been Turtle who struck down her husband. Both of them had understood her need to mourn.

Gradually, as the other captives had been taken away, her concern grew that there would be no one left. Personal survival seemed less important than that of the People, their place in Creation and in the world. . . . Their *identity*.

Possibly there were others among the captives who felt this, too, and would carry it with them as they were dispersed and scattered. But among those whom she knew very well, she could think of no one who could be depended upon to accomplish it. Either they were too young to have the understanding, or had not seemed to care enough. Well, she would hope that some of them would realize and begin the teaching of the young as she was doing, herself.

For the present, she would defer plans to escape. They would winter here, and then . . . Well, she would see what the Moon of Greening might bring.

6

The Moon of Long Nights, the start of winter for the People . . .
Each day grew shorter, Sun Boy's torch weaker.

It had been nearly three moons since the destruction of the
Forest Band and the capture of White Moon and the others. The
captives were scattered now, and she knew little of the fate of most
of them. Turkey Hen had assimilated so quickly and so well that
now Moon felt that she hardly knew her former friend. Turkey
seemed almost happy in her status as second wife to Short-Tail Dog,
her captor. She had confided to White Moon that she was pregnant,
and expecting the child in the Moon of Ripening. Turkey seemed
excited about that. More interested in her expected child, in fact,
than in Moon's reminders that they must not forget their heritage.

"That is over, Moon," her friend finally snapped. "It is for us to
make a new life here. My child will be a Shaved-head, not one of
the People, anyway."

From that day, the two surely and steadily drifted apart.

At least, White Moon thought, *I have Fawn. I can teach her.*

There were very few other captives who were of the People.
Moon knew of two, but had had little opportunity to contact them.
She suspected that there might be a third, but was unsure.

She was thinking ahead to the time of the Sun Dance and the Big Council. Six moons ahead, the Moon of Roses . . . Sycamore River had been selected as the site of the gathering. The bands would gather and the chieftains of each would tell the story of the year's activities. But the place in the circle of the Big Council reserved for Woodchuck, chief of the Forest Band, would be empty.

She did not know whether there might be any survivors who had escaped the massacre to tell the tale. It was possible, of course, but the attacks of the Shaved-heads had seemed well planned, and coldly thorough. They had seemed so intent on killing or capture, and had tracked down every survivor, as far as she knew. Those who had been sold as slaves had little chance to escape and return to the People. She herself was a slave, though she did not feel so. Yet, how is a slave expected to feel? Moon did not, and would never feel that she was *owned* by anyone. This was a temporary situation, and she must make the best of it. She was being treated well, all things considered.

It was possible, of course, that when the time came for the Big Council, someone *would* show up to tell their tale of tragedy, but she could not count on it. Gradually, she came to think that this was *her* responsibility, because there might be no one else to do it. She would time her escape to allow herself to arrive at the Big Council to represent the Forest Band.

In all of this thinking and planning there were a few factors that kept recurring to her as she reviewed the details of her plan. One, of course, was the child whom their captors presumed to be her own. Fawn was relating well to her status as the child that Turtle and his wife had never had. She was pampered and doted on, and responded with pleasure, as a child would. This in turn resulted in better treatment for White Moon.

Moon realized that when the time came to make her escape, it surely would be much easier to accomplish what she must without a child. Moon could travel faster, farther, and with less concern for comfort if she were not encumbered. . . . But no, she refused to consider leaving the girl behind. Fawn had become not only *hers* but a part of Moon's plan to preserve the story of their destroyed Forest Band. She, Moon, must teach the story so well that Fawn could tell it later, when she was able to do so. Moon hoped that if she herself was not successful in the escape and return, little Fawn would be, someday. It was a nebulous idea, but it was all that she had. There was time for planning the details later.

There was yet another factor that nagged at her. In spite of herself, she sometimes felt attracted to Green Turtle. She could not imagine that this could be, and fought such feelings even more because of Turkey Hen's flaunting of her own conquest. But it was there, though she tried to deny it. Moon was his captive, yet he had not abused her. He was kind and gentle to Fawn. The child had quickly grown to love him, even to the extent that White Moon resented the relationship of the two. The thought crossed her mind that some men are attracted to children, but Turtle did not seem that way. It appeared to be merely the love and affection that a father or grand-father would bestow on a child.

Turtle and Maple Flower were somewhat older than Moon, she thought, maybe ten or fifteen seasons. Someday she would ask, maybe, out of simple curiosity. For now, living in their lodge, she observed their comfortable relationship. They seemed happy with each other. Turtle was considerate and kind to his wife, and the two seemed to enjoy each other's company at all times. They laughed together, and this sometimes tugged at her heart, as she thought of her own lost husband.

Maybe the worst times were those when Turtle and Maple Flower were making love in the darkness. They were not noisy, but the subtle sounds of motion in the robes across the lodge, the soft murmurs of love and ecstasy, were unmistakable. The next morning, she would find herself envious of the relaxed, contented smiles on their faces and the warm glances at each other as the day's activities began. She would think of her own marriage, and all that could have been. But her unexpected reaction was one she could not understand, much less accept. She found herself stimulated by such episodes. That part, she assumed, was normal. But she also felt a physical attraction, and Turtle's nearness in the confines of the lodge as winter approached was sometimes exciting. She could even understand, in some degree, Turkey Hen's acceptance of what must be. Moon did not necessarily have to *approve,* but . . . Well, Turkey did have a point, and Turkey had not had a husband killed before her eyes, so had been able to adjust faster. Maybe she should talk to Turkey again. . . . Such thoughts were always followed by guilt feelings, as if she were disloyal to Striker's memory. But life must go on, no?

The greatest confusion of all was that she wanted to hate Turtle, and could not. When she was first captured, her escape plan had included cutting the throat of her captor as she made her departure. Now, that seemed like a foolish thing. Especially since Turtle had proved to be a kind man, good to his family. And, apparently quite romantic in the robes, judging from the contented expression on the face of Maple Flower on some mornings. Moon could not harm these two as she made her escape. She might even feel sympathy for their loss as she took Fawn from them to leave them alone again. Then, she was startled at such a thought. . . . Sympathy for her *captors?*

It was on a night that held the threat of a hard freeze. There had been several nights of light frost, when they had looked out next morning to see the world dusted with silvery crystals. But these soon dissolved in the sun. The coming night, however, held a threat of real cold. The previous night had been clear and still, with a full moon that lent an eerie, ghostly quality to the scene. During the day the wind had risen, and there was a bite to it. *Cold Maker is almost here,* thought White Moon as she gathered extra firewood.

They ate and prepared to retire to the robes. There had been many suggestive glances between Turtle and Maple Flower, which

Moon observed with interest. Maple Flower had just finished her moon time, and for the past few days had slept apart from her husband. That appeared to be the way of the Shaved-heads, and was well understood by White Moon. A woman of the People avoided touching her husband's weapons at such a time, too. Her power during menstruation was not to be ignored. In some nations, she had heard, a woman would leave her lodge entirely for the duration of her moon time. Moon thought that a bit excessive, but understood.

Here, among her captors, they slept apart for the few days involved. She knew the frustration that a devoted couple such as Turtle and Maple Flower must feel. She had felt it herself, the separation from Striker and the thrill of being together again. . . . Feelings that she would never have again, now. Striker was gone.

Still, she found herself stimulated by the fact that this would be the night when Maple Flower could return to Turtle's bed. She heard them talking, the suggestive, teasing remarks and sidelong glances. She listened intently. They did not realize how much of their tongue she understood now, she believed. She was happy for them, but confused and frustrated with her own reaction to the prospect of listening to the sounds of their lovemaking when there was none of her own. She knew that the rest of the village must assume that she occupied the position of a second wife, slave-wife though she might be. Turkey Hen had assumed so, long ago, and had even teased her about it.

The fire was dying and the time to seek the robes was near. Little Fawn was already asleep. There was a knock at the door, and in answer to invitation, a man pushed aside the doorskin to enter. His eyes sought Maple Flower, but he spoke to Turtle.

"Bluebird . . . ," he said. "It is her time for birthing. She asks for Maple Flower."

"Of course," Maple Flower said quickly. "I will come."

The man withdrew, and Maple Flower turned to her husband, a frustrated look on her face in the light of the dying fire.

"My heart is heavy, my husband. I had hoped . . ." There was a teasing, provocative look on her face. "I will be gone all night," she said with a sad smile.

She gathered a robe around her shoulders and turned back for a moment, with a tilt of her head toward White Moon.

"Maybe she can help you."

It was said in a half-teasing way, but was a shock to Moon. She wondered if Maple Flower realized that Moon might have understood. Whether Maple Flower realized that or not, it appeared that the suggestion was genuine and serious. This was an accepted custom among these people. Among her own, too, now that she gave it thought.

The doorskin fell back into place, and Moon looked across the fire from where she sat to Turtle, sitting in his own robes. Neither spoke. The fire sputtered, and one of the brighter flames flickered out, leaving only a soft glow in the lodge. She could barely see Turtle's face. She glanced at Fawn, who had slept through the intrusion.

"You knew what Maple Flower said just now?" Turtle asked.

"Yes."

"I have had respect for your loss."

"I know. I thank you."

"Will you come to my bed?"

"Do I have a choice?"

"Of course."

"Then I *choose* to come." Her voice was a little more than a whisper.

"It is good," he said softly.

White Moon had thought that she could never feel like a woman again, but that theory had certainly been proven wrong. As she had expected, Turtle was gentle and considerate. And, experienced. He had seemed to know her needs and desires, and skillfully fulfilled them. Moon wondered if Maple Flower appreciated her incredible good fortune, her status as first wife to such a man.

Flower returned to the lodge just as the blackness of the smoke hole in the roof was turning to yellow-gray with the approach of dawn. Moon had risen from the bed she shared with the child and was blowing life into the coals of the fire pit, adding twigs to rekindle for warmth. Turtle was still asleep in his own robes. A brief glance passed between the two women, which exchanged more meaning than conversation could have. Flower looked from her sleeping husband to Moon, an eyebrow cocked in question, and Moon nodded nervously, ever so slightly. Flower said nothing, but a quick smile of satisfaction flickered across her face and was gone.

"The birthing is finished," she signed. "It is good."

Moon nodded.

Flower dropped the robe from around her shoulders and crept into Turtle's bed. He stirred sleepily and gathered her into his arms without fully wakening. Moon added another sizable stick to her fire and crept back to bed with Fawn, waiting for the lodge to warm before rising.

How long had it been? She tried to count, but the time since the lives of the Forest Band had been destroyed was a meaningless blur. One day, they had been preparing their camp for the coming of winter, and the next . . . The unfortunate young men had been killed, and their world had disintegrated into warfare and genocide. The tragic loss of her husband had brought on a dreamlike sense of unreality that had no relation to time. She had stumbled through miserable days and nights that she could now hardly remember. She suffered nightmares, reliving the horrors of the massacre, and would waken in a cold sweat. She wondered, sometimes, how she had managed to look after the orphaned child. Possibly, though, that necessity, the responsibility, had forced her to keep her sanity. But there were blank spots in her memory. There were days and nights that she did not even recall. The Moon of Madness had been very nearly that in truth, for her. There were many things that she did not remember, terrible moments that were too painful for her mind to allow her to relive.

Nature is kind, giving a better memory for those times that are pleasant, the sounds and sights and especially the scents of happy times. Nothing stimulates childhood memories like the smells that are associated with the good times. The fragrance of the blossoms of a plum thicket, or the blooms of a large grapevine . . . The musky smells of warm autumn days . . . Ripe scents associated with the People's preparation for winter.

There is less association with the unpleasant. The mind is encouraged to forget, and the memory of pain and deprivation is blurred and disconnected. Except, of course, for the few individuals who choose to wallow in it for the scant comfort of whatever sympathy they might glean. Even that fades with time.

Moon had also talked to Striker in a dream. It was as if she knew that it was a dream, and that her husband was dead, but talking to her from the Other Side. In her dream, she was sitting and watching flowing water, enjoying its song and those of the small creatures around her. Striker was with her, and they talked. She had hesitated to bring up the subject of his death, but he initiated it himself. She had remarked that he looked well, and he seemed pleased.

"Yes," he assured her, "this crossing over is no great thing. Do not be concerned with it."

When she woke, she found that she did have less concern. It was as if she had been given permission to go on with her life. The nightmares lessened in frequency and severity, and soon ceased to bother her.

All of these events, along with Fawn's rapid adjustment and her own new relationship with Turtle, allowed her to think more of her own status, her feelings and needs. In short, her womanhood. Along with this, she began to wonder about her own moon time. When had it been? She had not experienced menstruation since her capture, she was certain. That was not unexpected. In times of stress such things can simply fail to happen. Now, she remembered a friend of her mother's. . . . Badger Woman had had a good marriage, but no children. Her husband was killed, during her moon time. She finished her flow and then never menstruated again. Badger could not be a woman for anyone else, it was whispered, and she never remarried.

Now, White Moon began to wonder. Was she to be like Badger Woman? That idea was short-lived. Her womanhood had not only returned, but had been admirably proven in the robes of Turtle. So, would her moon time now return? She realized that she had been experiencing some of the feelings that she would expect. . . . A bloatiness in her hips, fullness and tenderness of her breasts . . . Ankles a trifle thicker . . . Then why had she not started? In her condition of captivity and her time of mourning she had not paused to notice these signs, but now . . . It had been three moons with nothing. . . . Well, she had gone this long before, the time when she fell from the horse and broke an arm. *And I was never as regular as some,* she told herself irritably.

But . . . In her robes that night, after the soft snores of the others in the lodge signaled their repose, she lay on her back and tried to palpate the flat softness of her abdomen. It was firm, but she could allow her muscles to relax and feel with fingertips. . . . *Aiee!* Theré, just behind her pelvic bone, a firm round ball, the size of her clenched fist! It lay deep, but the finding was unmistakable.

That would account for many of the symptoms that she had been trying to ignore. Slight nausea in the mornings, now better already . . . The heaviness in her hips . . . The irritability, sudden burst of tears and anger . . . She had attributed these things to her captivity and her bereavement, but now . . .

When? She remembered, a night or two before the horrible events, when she and Striker . . . *Aiee,* it was always good, but that night had been near perfection for both! But then it was over, forever. She had not even thought of it, but that must have been . . . *I am carrying Striker's child!* she told herself. Her heart soared like the eagles.

But wait . . . She did a rapid count, verifying her calculations on her fingers. Ah! All thoughts of escape and return to the People for the Sun Dance must be abandoned. That would be very near her time for birthing the child of her husband. It was a mixed feeling. She still felt that it would be necessary to return to the People sometime. She could not, now, with winter coming, and then the birth of her child . . . Maybe the following year. Whatever, her escape and return to her own people must be postponed for at least a year, possibly more. It would be very difficult to travel with an infant as well as a small child. Maybe she would be able to leave Spotted Fawn with her adoptive parents while she and the baby . . . Such thoughts usually ended with feelings of guilt that she would even have considered such a thing.

Overall, though, her feelings were of joy. She would now have a child of her own, hers and Striker's, to whom she could teach the ways of the People. No matter when she was able to make her escape, even if it took years, so be it. She would have *her* child to teach. In her mind, the escape and return was not to be abandoned, only deferred.

Now . . . How and when would she reveal her discovery to Turtle and Flower? She did not know why that step should concern her, except that it was now the one thing that was her own. Very nearly, the only thing. Though they had been relatively kind to her, she was still a prisoner, her life completely controlled by her captors. Even with her affectionate relationship as Turtle's second wife, it was not the same. He could have taken her by force, and might have done so if . . . No, she could not imagine Turtle treating a woman so. Now she was becoming completely confused. How could she have such feelings? She had actually had a moment when she felt that she must *defend* Turtle's actions. *Aiee,* so many conflicting emotions!

The most important thing in her life, though, was the baby she was carrying. That would supersede all other decisions. But it was only fair to share that information with her captors. Maybe there was a slight temptation to flaunt it. After all, Turtle and Flower had wished for many years to achieve a pregnancy, without success. Now, she had successfully bested them at that.

She thought about it for a long time, and planned several alternate scenarios in which she might reveal her secret to Turtle in bed when that time came again. Or, to both of them, so that she could watch their reactions. It was some time before she decided just how it must be. She would tell Maple Flower, alone, and then consider the reaction.

It was several days more before the occasion arose. Turtle was visiting and smoking in the lodge of a friend, and Fawn was playing with some other children outside. Moon and Maple Flower were alone in the lodge.

"Flower?" she began, using the Shaved-heads' tongue.

"Yes?"

Now Moon reverted to hand signs. She still wished to keep her understanding of their language as quiet as possible.

I have something to tell you, she signed.

"What is it?" asked Flower aloud, signing at the same time.

I am with child, Moon answered.

A wave of mixed emotion washed over the face of Maple Flower. A hint of anger and resentment, maybe.

It is not possible! It is too soon! You were with Turtle only half a moon ago. . . . Her eyes fell to Moon's abdomen and the expression changed. "Oh! I . . ." *It is not Turtle's, then?*

Flower was still using both words and signs.

No, Moon signed. *My husband's.*

"Ah!" There was a long pause, and then Flower signed again. *I . . . I am happy for you, Moon.*

What a strange situation! The two women stood staring at each other in confusion, and finally, Maple Flower began to giggle. Then both of them broke into laughter. Finally, they paused, and Flower wiped her eyes.

"When?" she asked.

I am not certain. Maybe in the Moon of Roses or of Thunder.

Flower nodded, but there was still a question in her face.

It must have been only a night or two before . . . Moon paused.

Ah! My heart is heavy for you, for that. But you are my sister, now. I will help you.

Moon did not know what to say or do. Here was a woman who should be a hated enemy, but who was now ready to support and help her. She had had no one at all for support since the defection of Turkey Hen, and had not realized how much it was missed. She had tried to carry the weight of the world alone. It seemed incredible to her that her help would come from this woman, with whom she now shared a lodge and a husband.

"Thank you," she whispered in Maple Flower's language. There was a large lump in her throat, and tears in her eyes.

White Moon had mixed feelings about her pregnancy. There was joy that she carried the child of Striker, the love of her life. She was proud to have a part of him. The bad part was that Striker's child would be born among the people who had killed his father. . . . His or *hers* . . . Moon found that she was thinking of this baby, yet unborn, as a boy, a man who could live the life denied his father.

Well, it would be up to her to get him out of this unacceptable situation, along with herself and Spotted Fawn. She finally became resigned to the fact that there was nothing she could do now. Not until after the baby arrived. And even then, until after he was old enough to travel. She was not sure how long that might take, but a few moons would bring the next winter, and yet another delay. It was too much to think about, and too far ahead to plan. It was always a day-to-day life anyway, comfort and even survival itself depending on the whims of nature and the success of the hunt. And in her present situation, the whims of her captors, of course.

Yet that status was also changing. Moon quickly realized that Maple Flower, too, had many mixed feelings about their situation. Flower had almost instantly become like a sister, offering help and comfort that seemed above and beyond any that could be expected. There

It was nearing the longest nights of the year when Cold Maker came roaring across the earth, his icy breath chilling all creatures to the bone. Those who have bones, of course. Some were already in their winter sleep, and did not notice. The bear, woodchuck, the little squirrels who live in the ground . . . All of the snakes, frogs, lizards, and turtles . . . They would not be seen until spring, the Moon of Awakening. Many of the birds, knowing of Cold Maker's coming, had already gone south to warmer places.

Insects contrived their own winter defenses, some in eggs, others in shiny brown chrysalides in the earth, a few even in furlike cocoons.

Those who would remain active grew thicker garments of fur or feathers, and ate almost frantically to build up layers of fat for warmth. Raccoon, beaver, and otter fattened and thickened their fur, increasing its desirability for garments and for ornament or for ceremony.

Human beings, too, prepared for winter in a variety of ways. Like the squirrel, they stored food. The Shaved-heads among whom White Moon would winter did so, much as the People did. They dried meat, processing some of it further into pemmican, a mixture of pounded meat and dried fruits or berries. It was mixed with melted tallow and stuffed into casings or rolled in balls for storage. This nation stored more vegetables than Moon's People, since they did more planting, less hunting. There were large supplies of dried corn of several types, bags of beans, and great quantities of pumpkin, cut into slices the thickness of a finger and dried as rings to be threaded on a string to form bundles.

Preparation of the houses was considerably different, however. Among the People, who lived in skin tents, it was a matter of moving to a sheltered area and winterizing with a windbreak of brush. Dry grass would be stuffed between the lodge lining and the cover skin. Snow, when it came, could be piled around the outside to keep out Cold Maker's probing icy fingers.

For her captors, it was a process of repair and maintenance of their more permanent dwellings of logs and poles. The chinking of openings in the walls with mud and clay had long since taken place, and quantities of firewood gathered.

Even so, as always, the first bitter onslaught of the season seemed to come as a surprise. Cold Maker struck with his full fury, from one day to the next. He flew in on a wind that clawed and bit and snarled like a living thing with its own intentions. In truth, it was only a weapon of Cold Maker's, along with ice, snow, and freezing rain. People wrapped themselves tightly and hurried back inside as quickly as possible when it was necessary to go out for more fuel or for bodily functions.

That first skirmish between Cold Maker and Sun Boy lasted for three days. The sky was so dark that some felt that maybe this time Sun Boy's torch really *would* go out. It never had, as far as anyone knew, but maybe . . .

But then the clouds drifted on and the sun's rays were seen again. Everyone had settled in and taken the necessary steps to prepare for even colder and longer onslaughts. It was a time to appreciate even the pale watery light of Sun Boy's fading torch, and to make final adjustments. A bit of extra chinking in the outside wall on the north side of the lodge . . . A few stitches under the arm of a warm fur garment . . .

It was a cold and lonely time for White Moon. There was very little about which she could find anything but despair. Repeatedly, she had to remind herself of that which was still good in her life: *I am alive. . . . My captors are kind. . . . I carry my husband's child. . . . I have Spotted Fawn, to whom I can teach the ways of the People.*

That last was a mixed blessing and a terrible responsibility, which she often felt was too great for her. At other times, there was an excitement, a thrill in sharing the age-old stories of Creation and how the People came into the world from inside the earth. And sometimes, even, she would share the stories of the People with Turtle and Flower, in a traditional exchange of stories: "This is how our old ones say that Bobcat lost his tail. . . ."

Moon was not invited back to Turtle's bed again. She was not quite certain why. It was not because of disapproval by Maple Flower, she was certain. The number one wife had suggested it, and had seemed pleased by the success of that event. Turtle, too, had seemed to take pleasure in the result. Possibly, she thought, there were taboos among these people about what could be permitted during a pregnancy. Maybe, even, the fact that she, in the status of a second wife, carried a child sired by a previous husband. *Aiee*, it became complicated! Actually, she was a bit uncertain as to the rules in her own culture. She did not recall such a case among the People. She did know that there were many long nights when she lay awake, thinking of all the trouble and responsibility that had fallen on her. At these times, she would have welcomed the embrace of muscular arms, the feel of a strong body next to her. The reassurance of her own femininity and desirability would have raised her spirits. Just to be held, cherished, and reassured for a little while . . .

The Moon of Long Nights was displaced by the Moon of Snows, and the Moon of Hunger was approaching. Her wildly disturbing mood swings had stabilized somewhat. It was frustrating that she still needed more rest, but that was a minor annoyance. Actually, she was gaining confidence, and her outlook became more optimistic, in spite of the fact that her belly had begun to bulge a little.

Moon encountered Turkey Hen in the snowy woods gathering fuel one cold but sunny day. Their paths had not crossed for some time.

"I am with child," Moon confided, opening her outer robe for an instant.

"*Aiee!* You are bigger than I am!" Turkey exclaimed. "How can this be?"

"It is the child of Striker."

"Ah! Moon, I am glad for you."

They embraced for a moment. Now they once more had something in common, something to share. The friendship that had drifted apart could begin to right itself.

9

Little Striker was born near the end of the Moon of Thunder, just before the beginning of the Red Moon. The birth itself was uncomfortable, but not long in duration.

"My family has always had easy birthing," White Moon told Maple Flower as she watched the other woman wrap the squalling child. Even so, there was sweat on her forehead and on her upper lip. She was glad it was over. Glad, too, that the child had decided to arrive on a day that was cloudy and relatively cool. At this time of year, the oppressive heat of the summer could be very uncomfortable. She longed often for a breath of clean fresh prairie air, whispering through the tents of the People. They would roll the skin lodge covers like lifted skirts in the moons of summer. This could not be done in a permanent house of logs, poles, and thatch, such as the Shaved-heads used.

But it *had* been a cool day that Striker's son selected for his entry to the world. *Maybe he will be kind and considerate like his father,* she thought, as she put the babe to breast. *Of course he will,* the thought came back at her. *He is mine. Mine and Striker's.*

The discomfort of the birthing was behind, now. The stimulus of the child's sucking quickly caused a tightening in her belly that expelled the afterbirth. That was a great relief, and the rhythmic cramping that followed was reassuring. Yet, during the entire pregnancy, once she had realized that she was with child, the greatest pain had been that of her heart, not of the body. She had so looked forward to sharing her lodge with Striker and watching together the development of their children. She shed a tear, and felt a moment of self-pity and a hatred for those who had taken Striker from her. But that was quickly replaced by the warm glow of satisfaction and gratitude for the child at her breast. *Life is good,* she decided. *It only has bad times.*

Moon's second winter as a captive passed, and during the following summer Little Striker learned to walk. He was a beautiful child, and filled her heart with gladness.

She had not abandoned her ideas of return to the People, only deferred them. She still worked at instructing Fawn whenever occasion offered. Striker was too young to understand, and she would begin his secret instruction later. When, she did not know exactly. When he was three? Four? It must be certain that he was old enough to understand the meaning of the required secrecy. Maybe it would not be necessary to begin such secret teaching at all. Maybe by that time they would be back among her own.

Meanwhile, Turtle and Little Striker seemed to relate well. Moon was glad for this, yet concerned a little. Among the People, it would have been her own brother who held the responsibility of teaching the boy. The "uncle," the male relative with authority, would have provided a role model. But in this situation it was not possible. She assumed that her brother was dead anyway. But in the end, was not Turtle a good man? Kind, generous, a good provider . . . What better uncle could the boy have? She could complete his instruction later. And with each passing moon, it became easier to set aside that thought, because it was not yet time. Someday . . . But the urgency was gone.

True, she did consider simply asking permission to go home. There was a time when she almost brought up the subject, and felt certain that Turtle and Flower would allow her and the children to leave. About that time, an odd stretch of weather occurred, lasting nearly half a moon. It was dark, damp, and gloomy, with drizzling rain nearly every day. . . . Very unusual weather for the Moon of Roses, and an atmosphere in which one did not even want to think of traveling. Then, when the weather cleared, she became busy with other things and other thoughts.

There were many distractions. One or the other of the children would have a slight cough or an unsteady stomach, and a major travel could not be considered. *Maybe after this little cough clears,* she would think. But each time, there was less urgency. Someday . . . She would know when the time was right. . . .

When Little Striker was two and was eating well, he began to lose interest in breast-feeding, except for comfort. Moon had already resumed her menstrual cycle. She had felt little interest in romance for several moons after the child's birth. Those feelings had been eclipsed by her mothering instincts. Somewhat later, her physical attraction toward Turtle returned, a little at a time. He made no moves toward her, and she came to realize that probably marital relations were restricted among these people, as among her own. For some prescribed time after the birth of a baby, there could be no such activity. She was certainly not going to ask, but she tried to think of some of the restrictions that she knew were practiced among other tribes. . . . No marital activity until after the child sits, or stands, or walks . . . These were methods of spacing children. . . . Or, until breast-feeding ceased . . .

It occurred to her that among these people, that might be the deciding factor. She mentioned it to Turkey Hen.

"Something like that," her friend agreed. Turkey had made no bones about her desire to resume activity after the birth of a daughter in the Moon of Ripening.

"You're finding," Turkey went on with a suggestive leer, "that it's not all bad?"

"Something like that . . ."

White Moon no longer talked to Turkey Hen about escape, or even of the needed instruction of their children. Turkey was apparently quite comfortable with her present status, and saw no reason to change it. Moon resented this deeply. It suggested a disloyalty to their own heritage. It was doubly irritating, then, when she found herself falling into the same trap. . . . A considerate and gentle husband . . . His First Wife who was now more like a friend . . . It was easier to adjust to such a situation than to try any plan to change it. Constantly, it became easier to defer whatever action she might decide to take. Someday . . . Once, there had been detailed plans and schemes for escape and vengeance. Now there was only a vague, deeply submerged idea that eventually she must do something about it.

This change in her goal was helped along by Turtle's attitude as Little Striker ceased breast-feeding. *That must be it,* Moon told herself. She was certainly not prepared, however, for the manner in which marital activity was resumed. It seemed as if she was actually courted by Turtle. There were kind and thoughtful gestures, smiles and touching, and she felt herself responding. It was flattering that he found her desirable. By the time that she was invited back to his bed, she had no hesitation at all. Largely, because it was an invitation and not a demand.

It was also at this time that she sensed a change in Maple Flower's attitude. Sharp glances of disapproval, a word of criticism, a demand . . . It was plain to White Moon that here was a potential danger. . . . Jealousy. She did not know what to do about it. There was nothing that she could change in their situation. She could not control the feelings of Turtle, or her status as a captive second wife.

She tried to understand how the other woman must feel. Flower was still attractive, but aging, and must be looking toward the end of her reproductive years. These had already proved unsuccessful in producing children for Turtle. Now the woman must feel threatened by the presence of a second wife who was unquestionably fertile.

This uncomfortable situation came to an abrupt end when Flower announced that she, too, was with child. White Moon rejoiced with her, and the warmth of friendship that had once been enjoyed began to return.

"Surely this time it will go well with you," Moon told her. "I will help you in any way I can."

"I know . . . Thank you!"

Once again, they were sisters.

The pregnancy of Maple Flower proceeded uneventfully, and a healthy boy was born in the Moon of Falling Leaves.

"It is because your children have shown him the way to our lodge," Flower told White Moon a few days later. "My other ones were unsure of the trail."

"Maybe so," said Moon, smiling, "but I am made to think that this one can find his way. He is strong!"

"Yes, and hungry, too," agreed Flower, shifting the baby to the other breast.

Moon wondered, though . . . Is it not true that once there is a child in the house, it is easier for others to find their way there? She thought of Tall Willow, a woman among her own people. Barren for many years, Willow had adopted the motherless child of a relative. Almost at once, she became pregnant herself. The first one showed the way, the old women had said.

"What will you call him?" Moon asked.

"I do not know. He has much fur on his head, no?"

"It sticks up like that of a possum," laughed Turtle.

As chance remarks sometimes do, this one provided a memorable event that remained in the family tradition. Soon the child was called "Possum." In later years, it was forgotten why, and the growing boy was called Possum simply because that was his name.

Little Striker had seen two winters when Possum arrived. They were, for all practical purposes, brothers. Little Striker was protective in a brotherly way, and as they grew, there would be less and less difference in their relative ages.

White Moon had not yet begun to teach him his own background and that of the People. He knew only that Turtle was not his father, and that his own father was dead. That would do, for now. She continued to tell the stories of the People to all of the children. There was no harm in that. Exchange of stories was the custom among all of the tribes and nations. . . . Stories of Creation and of a time when all creatures, human and animal, spoke the same tongue. In this way, she hoped to instill a framework of information that could be used later when she began to teach Little Striker of his true heritage.

Turtle and Maple Flower not only approved of her storytelling, but were interested, themselves. These, the stories of the People, were new to them, and they began to look forward to her tales. Neighbors and other children sometimes visited, and by the time Possum was walking, Moon had an audience whenever she started her stories.

She took advantage of this, teaching her own, waiting for the right time to come. Then, she would reveal to Little Striker and to Fawn the information that they must know to perpetuate their heritage from the People. That had become her primary goal.

Sometimes, in the Moon of Roses, she would think of the People, gathering for the Sun Dance and the Big Council. She would think of the thrill and excitement of the festival, most important of the year, and wonder . . . Was there anyone left to represent the Forest Band? When the Real-chief called on the band chieftains to relate the happenings of the past year, would there be anyone to answer? Or, would there be an empty place in the circle at the Council?

It was a depressing thought, but Moon could always overcome it by replacing it with another. Someday, she would go back, to attend the festival and the Big Council, and make sure. Meanwhile, she must educate the children entrusted to her. If it became impossible for her to fulfill the responsibility, one of them must do so.

It became easier through the years to defer any action on her own part. Gradually, her vague ideas of escape and return to the People were modified. Finally she came to realize that Striker would be the one to carry on the secret. She would teach *him*. Then, someday, he could return to claim his heritage and to claim the empty space at the Council fire.

Part Two
Striker

10

Young Striker had seen fourteen winters now, and was ready to become a man. The past two seasons, his growth had progressed remarkably. He was taller than his mother, and she was considered tall by the standards of the town. Most of the people he knew were of slightly different build than he and his mother. His sister Fawn was tall, of course. . . . She had taken a husband four or five summers ago, and now had her house and two children of her own.

Striker sat on the crest of the ridge, deep in thought. He was hunting, presumably. But the still-hunter has much time on his hands. He must watch, wait patiently, unmoving, and trying to think like the creature who is to become the quarry. *If I were a deer, where would I be?*

Today, he had placed himself at a spot where he could watch the ancient game trail. It was a trail used by the People sometimes, though not the main trail. This one was dim and narrow, made by centuries of cloven hooves and padded paws over the rocky slope of the ridge. From where he sat in the warm afternoon sun, he could see the trail in both directions. It was the Moon of Falling Leaves, except that the falling part had not yet occurred. The foliage had begun to change in color, all the warm shades of a ripening forest.

Yellow, gold, all shades of red and pink . . . The smells of autumn were as interesting and as varied. It was a season that he loved, even though it suggested by its very nature that next would come winter.

Today, though, was warm and still, and his mind wandered. It had been three summers . . . no, four, maybe, when his mother had taken him aside and revealed to him the secrets of her past.

"Then Turtle is not my father?" he had asked in amazement.

"No, he is not. He is my husband now, and he has been good to us. He is the father of Yellow Bird, your sister."

Striker could remember the birth of Yellow Bird. He had been five, and his brother Possum, three. Possum's mother was Maple Flower.

"What about Fawn?" he asked.

"Fawn came with me from the People. *Our* People."

"Does she know?"

White Moon hesitated.

"I . . . I am not sure how much she remembers. You see, there was much killing. But let me go back to the beginning. . . . The end of my other life. Our People."

He knew that in nearly every tribe and nation, the word for one's own has the same meaning: *the People.* But that his mother's People were different . . .

"The Prairie People are your people, too, my son. You have grown up listening to my stories, no? Those of the Old Times when all people and animals spoke in the same tongues?"

"Yes, mother . . ."

It was well known that White Moon was one of the best story-tellers in the town. She knew at least four accounts of how the bobcat lost his tail.

"Many of those stories are from our people. . . . The People."

She had then told him every detail of her previous life as one of the Prairie People. They were hunters of buffalo, and moved their skin tents instead of staying in more permanent towns. Part of this story he had heard before, but it had been told in an impersonal way. Now, it became real. His mother spoke with a burning intensity. She told of her husband, Striker, the love of her life, and for whom she had named her son.

"How I wish that you could have known him, my son. And that he could have known you."

"I wish this too, Mother."

His heart was heavy for her, and he had wished that he could do something to lift the heaviness of her heart as she told him those things.

"It falls to *you*," she had told him "to return to our People and tell them what happened."

Striker had not been certain that he wanted such responsibility. It would have been much easier to simply be like the other boys in the town. They hunted squirrels and rabbits, swam in the stream, and worked in the gardens. His mother had cautioned him that he must tell no one of his secret heritage.

"Even now, there might be some who would want to harm us if they knew," she cautioned.

Striker thought that was unlikely, and wondered if his mother had become a little mad. But she seemed no different than ever, except for this secret thing, her other life before she came to live with Turtle and Flower. All in all, though, the wonder of it . . . There was a delicious feeling of conspiracy that stirred his blood when his mother took him aside to talk of it. This drew him in, fastened his attention on her every word.

"The Big Council circle is like this," she related, drawing a circle in the sand. "There are five other bands, besides ours. Here, the Northern Band, here, Eastern, next to the entrance to the Council ring. That faces due east, of course, like a lodge door."

She told him the jokes about the foolishness of the Eastern Band, which made him chuckle.

"Here, at the other side of the entrance, is the seat reserved for the chief of our Forest Band," she went on. "Then, the Southern Band . . ."

Each time they had a chance to share one of these instruction sessions, he learned more.

"No one else in all the town knows of this?" he asked her one day.

His mother paused in thought for a moment, apparently searching for an answer.

"Everyone knows that I came here as a captive," she said finally. "There are a few others."

"*Aiee!* Others like *us*?"

"Yes . . . I am made to think that they do not feel this is as important as we do. They cannot be counted on to be of help," she said sadly.

"Who is it?"

She paused again. "I . . . Maybe it is better not to know, my son. We want it to remain a secret that I am teaching you."

This lent a further air of conspiracy to their private sessions, which he found exciting. He began to learn the language of his mother's people. When they were alone they used only that tongue, and he had become adept with it. He longed to confide in Possum, but White Moon constantly cautioned him. *No one else must know.*

Over the years since, he had gained a tremendous amount of knowledge and information about his people. He could speak their language fluently, he knew their customs and beliefs, the ritual and ceremony of the annual Sun Dance, the pattern and construction of their garments and their moccasins. Much of that part was not secret. His mother's sewing was a little different. The shirts and leggings that she made were not quite the same as those made by Flower, the other mother in their lodge. He had never wondered why, but now, with the great revelation now opening for him, he began to notice.

"Mother, there is another boy with moccasins like mine. Is he one of us?"

A look of alarm crossed his mother's face for a moment.

"Who is his mother?" she asked.

"I think she is called Turkey."

White Moon nodded.

"She came at the same time as I. I am made to think that she has forgotten who she is . . . or, *was*. . . . Look, here is a way to tell. . . . Say a few words in our tongue, yours and mine. If he understands, he will answer in our same tongue. That is how to learn whether he knows."

Striker tried it, and got no response beyond a quizzical look and a superior attitude. It was a very satisfactory feeling, that of knowing something that the other boy did not. He had smiled to himself and shared the incident with his mother, who chuckled over it.

"You see? This gives us power. It is good! Now, you can test anyone, find whether you are kindred. Not all who came to these people when I did will be teaching their children."

"Mother, does Fawn know our tongue?"

"Yes, a little. But she is busy with her family. It falls to you to be the keeper of the secret."

"Could I speak the words to her?"

"Yes. It should be in private, of course."

It had been some time before the opportunity offered, but when it did, the response was gratifying. After a startled look, Fawn smiled broadly.

"She taught you, too!" Fawn answered in their mother's language.

"Yes. Fawn, do you remember when this all happened? The war?"

The young woman sobered. "Some. It was very bad, Striker. I have been made to forget a lot, maybe. I am glad that Mother teaches you, too. I feel sometimes that I neglect what I should teach my children."

"They are not old enough to share this, Fawn. When they are . . . *Aiee!* I am their uncle. This is part of my duty!"

They laughed together, and it was good.

Striker was pondering all of these things. He had tried a few words of the language of the Prairie People on several others over the years, and had encountered a variety of reactions. One, of course, was a blank look of nonunderstanding. This indicated that his suspicion that the individual might be a kinsman was probably wrong. Another time, a woman had flown into a rage.

"Do not talk so, boy!" she hissed. "You will get us killed!"

It was significant, however, that she had scolded him in the tongue of the Shaved-heads, not that of the Prairie People. *She understood, but was afraid,* he thought. He would not bother her again.

The reaction of Turkey Hen, known to be of the Prairie People, was unique.

"Good morning, Mother," he greeted her, using the Prairie People's term of respect.

There was a startled moment of surprise as she began to answer, then paused. A look of amusement came over her face, and she laughed aloud. "You are White Moon's boy, no?"

She used the Shaved-heads' tongue.

"Yes," he nodded.

"So, she is teaching you. . . . She said she would."

"You do not teach your children?"

Turkey Hen laughed again.

"What is the use? We live here, now. Your mother once had a dream of returning. . . . *Aiee,* I supposed she had forgotten. . . ."

In all of this, the woman used the language of the Shaved-heads, not her own. Striker was irritated by her flippant manner.

"I am made to think," he told her in the tongue of their fore-fathers, "that it is you who have forgotten!"

Turkey Hen gave him a startled look, then laughed even louder.

"*Aiee!*" she chortled. "You *are* your mother's son!"

Then she became serious. "Look, boy . . . Striker, isn't it? Named for your father . . . Striker was a good man. But, be careful who you talk to. There are still those whose hearts are hardened against us."

This last advice was completely serious.

"I know. My mother has taught me," he answered. "Do you know others of our People?"

The woman shrugged. "There are some, I suppose. I do not think about it much."

Striker was offended by her disinterested attitude.

"My mother does!" he said harshly.

He was surprised by her reaction, a winsome smile with a bit of sadness and regret.

"Yes," she said slowly. "Your mother *does*, and you are her son. May it go well with you, young Striker...."

This last was spoken in the language of the Prairie People.

She does understand, he realized, *but feels a need to hide it.*

"Thank you, Mother," he said. "It is good to know you better."

He thought, as she turned away, that he saw a tear in her eye.

All of these things drifted through his head as he sat on the ridge, watching and waiting. It was good to be alone sometimes to think, away from the confusion of other people, barking dogs, and the constant stir of activity in the town.

Striker was looking down the slope, absorbed in his own thoughts, when he realized that he was staring at a magnificent buck deer. The animal was no more than thirty paces away. Its head was raised and it was staring directly at him. At least ten points on each antler . . . How had this happened? One moment it was not there, and now, it was. He had not been aware of any motion. But now . . . The slightest move on his part would send the animal into instant flight. His palms were sweating, and he was not ready. The arrow was nocked on the bowstring, but he must raise the bow. . . . He debated for a few heartbeats. . . . Would it be better to move quickly and try to shoot as the buck whirled away? No, the deer could move faster than he could shoot. That would never do. He must move so *slowly* that his motion would not be noticed. He began to lift the bow, holding himself in check with great difficulty. But not slowly enough. With a flash of the white tail-flag, the buck whirled and leaped over a clump of dogwood and out of sight among the trees.

Striker jumped to his feet, tempted to run after the fleeing deer, but he knew that such a move was useless. He was disgusted with himself. What a great occasion if his first deer kill had been such a noble trophy!

He glanced at the sun. . . . Growing late . . . He hated to go home empty-handed. Well, he could try for a rabbit, or a squirrel or two. Maybe a turkey. His deer kill would have to come later.

11

The woods were full of busy squirrels, gathering and storing nuts
for winter. He took a position next to a large hickory trunk, waited
and watched. Overhead was a bushy-tailed sentinel, barking its
strange birdlike call. He knew where it was, but did not want to
disturb it.

"Never shoot a barking squirrel," Turtle had taught him. "Watch
him, wait, and others will come to join him."

He had found that to be true, though a lot of patience was
required. In that one stand today, he had seen six of the flitting
shadows. He tried to make every shot count, but even so, lost one
of his best arrows and broke another against a mighty oak. To show
for it, however, he carried two plump gray squirrels and one fat red
prize, half again as big as the grays as he entered the town. He had
chanced on that one as he started home. The creature was on the
ground, in the open. It was feeding on the seeds from a fruit of the
thorny bowwood tree. Round and green, the fruit was as large as a
small pumpkin. Slivers and shreds from the inedible fruit were
scattered on the ground, while the animal dug out the desirable
seeds. One shot . . . He doubted that the squirrel had even seen him
before the arrow pinned it.

So, with three squirrels, one of them the big red one, he felt justified in strutting a little.

A young woman stepped out of one of the houses, glanced both ways, and her eyes fell on Striker. She smiled and moved toward him.

"Ah, the hunter returns," Pretty Moccasin chided. "What, no deer?"

Striker smiled. "I left it on the ridge," he joked. "It was too big to carry."

It was good to see his friend. They had been close since they were small. She had known that today he had hoped for his first deer kill. It was also plain that he had failed. If he had succeeded in killing a deer, he would not have bothered with squirrels.

"Maybe he will grow even bigger!" she suggested, and both laughed. They were close, had been since childhood. He thought back through the years. . . . When a group of children at play would be playing house, he and Moccasin had always paired off together.

"This is our lodge, between these two trees," she would say. "Over there, the lodge of Broken Knife and Little Bird. Now, let us visit them this afternoon."

The two couples would talk of the weather and the scarcity of game, and the girls would sew, or pretend to. The boys would scrape a straight dogwood stick for an arrow shaft, or pretend to, while they "smoked" toy pipes. Dolls received instruction, were fed and clothed and bundled in cradle boards. It was assumed by everyone that these two would someday carry out these activities in reality.

Moccasin was perhaps a year younger, but had shown signs of becoming a woman for some time now. The square body build of a child had first become lanky, and then blossomed into graceful curves. Her breasts were full, pressing most admirably against the soft buckskin of her dress. Her legs had become shapelier, too, and the sway of her hips as she walked was different, somehow.

She had reached the age of puberty, and began to outgrow her friend Striker. At one point, she was at least a head taller than he, with the natural process of earlier female development. Her face and changing form had attracted the attention of older youths and young men. A few older men, too. One lecherous old warrior who had lost his wife came sniffing around the lodge of Moccasin's parents, until the girl's mother indignantly told him to move on.

Moccasin herself was not above a bit of flirtation with some of the more eligible young men, all of them a few years older than Striker. He found himself burning with jealousy. He was frustrated that these would-be suitors had deeper voices, masculine muscles, and adult hairy places. Striker, on the contrary, still had the size, appearance, and the voice of a child. He felt like crying, sometimes, but that, too, would prove his childishness. Finally, he accused Pretty Moccasin of forgetting their friendship.

"You act like a dog in season, with those boys following you!" he complained.

She had been teasing him a little about his jealousy, but now realized that he was serious.

"This is driving us apart!" he protested.

"No, no, Striker. I did not mean it that way. They mean nothing to me."

"But I am still so short. I feel like a . . . a *child*."

"You will grow, as I am growing. I will wait for you."

He had not been completely convinced, and had been glad when his own growth began to accelerate.

IIis muscles were heavier, and he began to grow hair in places where there was none before. It was an exciting time, and he was anxious to accomplish some of the achievements that would qualify him to seek a wife. It seemed only logical to him, and to those who knew them, that it would be Pretty Moccasin to whom he would play the courting flute.

Just now, he dropped the good-natured banter to speak excitedly of the deer he had just seen.

"Moccasin, he was big. At least ten points on a side. I was made to think he saw me first, though. I could not get a shot."

"Ah! You were daydreaming," she laughed. She knew him well.

Striker smiled sheepishly.

"Maybe a little. But . . ." He held up the three squirrels. "Am I not a good provider?"

It was a good result to show for a day's hunt.

"Ah! A big red one!" she observed.

"Yes, that one is especially for you," he said impulsively, handing it to her.

She hefted it. "Heavy! It must be fat."

"Yes . . . The woods are ripe. The squirrels, busy."

"Preparing for a hard winter?" she suggested.

"Who knows? Have the elders said anything about that?"

"I don't know, Striker. But, the plums bore heavily. The nut trees, too . . ." She stroked the fur of the big red squirrel. "Thick fur, here, and on the dogs. That says cold."

"Do you believe that?" he asked.

"I don't know. Nothing much to do about it, anyway."

"Store more food, maybe. But I need to get home, now. My mother will wonder . . ."

"Of course. Thank you for the squirrel, Striker."

"It is my pleasure to hunt for you!" he said grandly.

Moccasin blushed and turned away. Then she paused and spoke, half over her shoulder.

"I have heard no courting flute yet!" she teased at him.

Now, a new problem had risen between them, one that made him very uncomfortable. It was his secret, that culture taught him by his mother. Pretty Moccasin, he thought, was completely unaware. It bothered him that he and Moccasin had never had secrets from each other, and here was one. He had longed to tell her, but his mother had so impressed him with the dangers of talking about it to anyone that he could not.

Like most women, Moccasin had the innate ability to know that something was wrong. She asked him about it, a few days after the fruitless hunt for his first deer kill.

"Striker, something concerns you. And, I still hear no courting flute."

She gave him a provocative look.

"Maybe after my deer kill," he suggested. "I have not been successful yet."

"It is the deer?"

"Maybe."

"Striker, I do not care. When the time comes, the kill will happen."

"But . . . I . . . I am not sure that it would be proper to court first. Maybe it is like a vow."

"You could ask . . ."

"Moccasin, I don't want to talk about it!" he snapped.

He rose and stalked away, not even noticing the tears that quickly formed in her eyes.

It was a few days later that Striker heard the sounds of a courting flute down by the river. He peered cautiously through the woods. He was still hunting his deer, and his luck had all been bad. Curious, he moved quietly in the direction of the music. It would be quite unacceptable, of course, to spy on a couple so engaged, but as long as the flute continued to play, privacy was not absolutely essential. Feeling only a little guilty, he shifted his weight to the other foot and leaned around a big cottonwood. *Aiee!* There on a log sat Pretty Moccasin, rapt in her attention to the young man across the clearing. Even worse, the man was Badger, one of the most disreputable in the town, a bully and a cheat.

"Moccasin!" Striker yelled at her. "What are you doing?"

Anger flared in her face.

"What is that to you? But as you see, I am listening to Badger's flute. No on else has asked me to listen."

"But you . . ."

"But what?" demanded Badger's deep voice. "You have interrupted our courting, boy. Run along to your mother."

Striker realized that he had made a big mistake. Badger was cruel and dangerous, and much heavier than he. A fight with this hulking brute might result in serious injury. He turned to Moccasin.

"This is not right!" he accused.

"You had not declared your intent," she flared, angry now.

"Please, Mocc—"

Heavy hands literally picked him up and threw him against a tree, knocking the wind from his lungs.

"Now, go on, boy!" Badger yelled, approaching again. The courting flute lay discarded now.

Striker scrambled to his feet, ribs aching. "This is not over," he said as he recovered his bow and scattered arrows.

Badger lunged at him with a snarl and Striker jumped back in alarm. The bully laughed.

"Run along, now, while you can."

Striker chanced one last look at the girl on the log. There was a look of concern on her face, but he was unsure whether her concern was for him, for Badger, or for the interrupted courtship. He was not sure that he knew her at all.

But, his heart was very heavy.

12

Striker was extremely dejected. It seemed that his life, his *world* was at an end. The taste of his shameful disgrace at the hand of Badger was like ashes in his mouth. He spent sleepless nights, tossing and turning with his hopeless thoughts.

How could he have been so stupid, to interrupt a courting ceremony? It had made him appear foolish, weak, inadequate. . . . *Aiee!* He cringed at how ridiculous he must have appeared to Pretty Moccasin.

His mother was concerned about him.

"You are not eating well, my son. . . . Are you sick?"

"No, no, Mother. I am just not hungry."

She knew better, of course.

"I think it is because of the deer," observed Turtle. "It must have been a fine one, and he feels that he failed. Probably he was not paying attention when it came."

"I am made to think it is more than that," White Moon pondered. "Striker has not spoken of Pretty Moccasin for some time."

"But his attention is on the hunt," Turtle insisted. "That is what he must do first."

"Maybe both," Moon answered, "but the girl is part of it. Don't you think so, Flower?"

"Of course," agreed the other woman. "When a man cannot eat, and looks as sick as that, there is a woman involved somewhere."

Both women chuckled.

"Maybe so," Turtle conceded, "but he still should finish his hunt. That will clear his mind, as well as make him a man."

Striker had come to much the same conclusion. With Moccasin lost to him, he must concentrate on other things. Life must go on. He thought with a great deal of sympathy of his mother's plight when she had been brought here. She had seen her husband killed, and was unknowingly pregnant. By comparison, his own loss was insignificant. Of course it did not seem so.

Eventually he determined to concentrate on the symbolic hunt. He must do that anyway.

He roamed the woods alone, tracking, watching, trying to note every disturbed leaf or twig. He began to recognize individual deer seen at a distance. The big gray doe with twin fawns still following her . . . A heavyset reddish female with the season's plump offspring . . . Another, a yellowish clay-colored animal with a long slender muzzle. There was no fawn with that one. Striker wondered if she had lost her offspring to wolves or other predators, or if she had simply failed to give birth this season.

As the season progressed, the bucks began to move around more freely. The Moon of Madness was approaching, when the lust of the rutting season would make all the deer a little crazy. On a clear quiet morning he could hear in the woods the rattle of newly hardened antlers. A young buck would rub them against a tree, testing, polishing, scraping the last shreds of velvet skin from the sharp tines. In a short while, they would be searching for the small bands of females with the season's young.

Several times, he could have tried for a kill. One young buck with only a spike antler on each side would have made an easy shot. . . .

The best of eating, too . . . Another time he encountered a fat doe, standing within easy range, still and unmoving. He actually raised the bow that time, but then lowered it again. The doe leaped away with a snort and a parting flip of her white flag. He should have tried, maybe. But only then did he fully realize that his task now was to prove himself. His first deer kill must now be not just a deer, but one far above average. The challenge was not merely a part of his coming of age, now. It was to regain his lost self-respect, and if possible, the respect of his lost love, Pretty Moccasin. He had carefully avoided contact with her . . . with most people, actually. He did not want to hear of the activities of Moccasin and Badger, or of the progress of their courtship. The hurt would be too much. There had been days at a time recently when he spoke to no one at all, leaving the town before daylight and returning to the lodge after dark.

"See . . . What else could it be?" asked Flower. "A woman . . . I am made to think that he mourns over the courtship of Badger for Pretty Moccasin."

"*Aiee!*" exclaimed Turtle. "That would make me mourn, too! It does, anyway. Has Moccasin gone mad?"

"They must have quarreled," said Moon. "Striker has not spoken of her for some time now."

Maple Flower shrugged. "To each, his own mistakes!"

"Striker worries much about his deer kill," observed Turtle defensively. "He has no time to court. He should not, anyway, until after that ceremony."

"Huh!" grunted Flower. "That should not stop a man in love. . . . It would not have stopped *you*, Turtle."

"That is true," admitted Turtle, with a trace of embarrassment. "But you did not have a rival suitor at the time, either, Flower."

Flower blushed, laughing. "Are you sure, Turtle?"

"Enough!" he said irritably, "I only meant, I can understand the boy's need for success. Let him alone!"

In her own mind, White Moon wondered whether these hunting trips were a part of something else. . . . Could her son be contriving a plan to leave, to try to return to their own people?

After some thought, she decided that whatever it might be that was bothering Striker, it was not part of such a scheme. He would have told her. No, Flower was probably right. It was the young woman, Pretty Moccasin. Moon had mixed feelings about this. A breakup of the romance would make it easier for young Striker to leave.

On the other hand, she liked Moccasin, and considered the girl a suitable partner for her son. Still, a permanent liaison might prevent either Striker or herself from ever returning to the big sky of the Tallgrass country, and she was unwilling to accept that possibility.

Well, it would be his to decide. . . .

Striker studied the tracks before him, in the soft mud where the trail crossed the stream. Yes . . . The big buck . . . He had seen it only twice, but had come to recognize its track. On the left hind foot, one of the toes of the cloven hoof had grown in a strange curve. An old injury, maybe. Whatever the cause, there was a characteristic curl to the tip of that toe, and he could identify it. That was not much of an advantage, because this was a wary, clever animal that had survived to become an outstanding specimen by that very cleverness.

Sometimes he wondered if the buck was real, or if it might be a spirit-animal, appearing and disappearing as it chose. On the occasions he had seen it, it had appeared suddenly, and disappeared in almost the same way. Well, the first time it had leaped gracefully over the dogwood thicket, but then had vanished. The other time, it had seemed to simply fade away like a gray ghost among the patches of early-morning fog along the stream.

A thought came to him. . . . Could this be his spirit-guide, attempting to make contact? After some consideration, he decided not. Such a guide would probably not have a crooked toe. . . . Might not even leave tracks . . . Or *would it?* Maybe Turtle would know.

On the other hand, would such a guide function in the same way for Turtle's people as it would among the Prairie People? Maybe he should ask his mother.

He had tracked the buck several times for quite a distance, and was beginning to understand the animal's habits. Most individual deer will follow a sort of routine, making it possible to guess where they might be at a given time. This wary old buck was different. Its pattern was never quite the same from day to day. Twice, Striker had waited in vain for its appearance, only to find its tracks later in a different area. Once he was startled to discover where the buck must have stood in concealment to watch *him*.

Gradually, though, he realized that the old monarch did follow a pattern. It was more complicated than usual, and consisted of three entirely different daily circuits, sometimes with a mixture of any two where the trails crossed, to lend even greater variety. But Striker knew each of the places where the animal went to water, or to browse, or where it bedded down for the night. He had located each spot, but avoided too close an approach. If the buck became alarmed, it would stop using that spot to seek another, and Striker must begin again.

Turtle had been able to give him much advice as he learned his hunting skills. He could have hardly imagined a better father. Sometimes he felt disloyal over the fact that he had the one part of his life, the secrets of his mother's people, not shared with Turtle. Yet he knew that it must be this way.

He estimated that very soon the rutting season would begin. Then, all the habit patterns of the whitetail bucks would be abandoned in the crazed frenzy of breeding. This lent an urgency to his hunt, and implied a couple of new factors. He had now decided that his kill must be this particular animal. The other, that he must do it soon, or the chance would be lost. He was not trying to guess which of the patterns the buck would use each day. He must attempt to be in a place at a time when the chances were most likely that his quarry would be there also.

Once, he narrowly missed an opportunity, as the tracks indicated later. In fact, he wondered how it could have happened that he did *not* see the big buck. Surely . . . The doubts about its possible supernatural qualities returned for a time, but there *were* actual physical footprints, not left by a spirit. Of course, a spirit-creature could leave tracks, maybe, if it chose. *Aiee,* it was confusing!

Today, he had a feeling that something was about to happen. He had planned carefully. He knew where the buck had been yesterday and the day before. This spot was the third in the animal's series of favorite locations. Striker had planned well, choosing his own spot from which to watch and wait. It was downwind from the narrow trail where he expected the buck to approach the spring to drink. If only the slight breeze would continue to blow in the expected direction, now . . . Any shift might carry his scent to the delicate nostrils.

Striker arrived just before dawn, his way lighted by the setting moon, a quarter past full. There would be a short while after moonset and before daylight when it would be quite dark. He had planned for this, too. It would be then that he settled into position, his bow already partly raised and an arrow fitted to the string.

Striker slid between the boles of a great oak tree and an equally large sycamore. There was just space for a man there. He had chosen it a few days ago, just after the buck's last visit. He must make sure it was a usable spot for a hunter's stand. He thought it a very unusual thing for two giant trees of different species to grow so closely together. The two had crowded out all other trees for several paces around. Their spirits, he decided, must work well together. Maybe this was a favorable thing for his purpose, too. He hoped so.

The sky in the east was lightening from black to gray-yellow when he heard the hollow cry of the great owl, *Kookooskoos,* who calls his own name.

"Good hunting, *Kookooskoos,*" he whispered, "to both of us!"

The breeze was still, and there were sounds of the awakening day-creatures. They would now become active, replacing the night-sounds as those who made them sought their dens and lodges.

Striker watched his chosen spot, the opening where he knew the buck had passed before as it approached the water. He must not be distracted this time. Even so, he did not see how it happened. One moment there was nothing there, and scarcely a heartbeat later . . . *Aiee,* he had seen no movement, but there stood his buck. Even then, the thought struck him that this might be a spirit-being, which could not be killed with an arrow. *We will see,* he thought. Slowly, even so much more slowly than he had ever moved before, he raised the bow and drew the arrow to its head. He knew, as he released it, that it would fly true. Sometimes a hunter feels this . . . It is possible to know where one's hands are even when the eyes are shut, is it not? In the same way, the hunter's projectile becomes an extension of his hands and arms. Not always, but sometimes. This was the time . . . Striker could see and *feel* the arrow strike, just behind the elbow of the left leg. The buck leaped high, whirled, and loped back up the trail from which it had come.

Striker was elated. He knew that this was a clean kill, and that the dash for escape was only the dying struggle. Even so, sweat damp-ened his body and his palms as he moved forward, fitting another arrow to the string as he did so.

The buck lay a hundred paces away, just over a slight rise. Blood trickled from the nostrils, and the large dark eyes were glazing in death. Striker was startled to find that he felt sorrow, as well as victory. He laid the bow aside and addressed an apology to the dying deer. It was a ritual, a ceremony taught him by his mother, a custom of her people.

"I am sorry to kill you, my brother, but on your flesh my life depends . . ."

13

It was a big buck, by any standards. Heavy, fat, and with the magnificent rack of antlers that he remembered. Striker bled it out and gutted it, and managed to drag it to a level grassy spot a little way from the stream. Even without the entrails, it was far too heavy to carry, or even to drag. He would have to go for help. He considered butchering out a hind quarter, to carry back in triumph. A quick glance at the sun's position in the west told him that there would not be enough time before dark. As it was, torch light would probably be needed to finish the job.

But, if he left to bring help now, with evening coming on, the carcass would be vulnerable to predators. The scent of blood would attract not only small meat-eaters, foxes and coyotes, but wolves, even bears, maybe. And someone had heard the scream of one of the big long-tailed cats a few days ago . . . He looked uneasily around him, but saw nothing in the shadowy glades among the trees. He had seldom felt afraid in the woods, but he had never before had a big kill to defend. For a moment he crouched over it, as he had seen a bobcat once, crouched over a freshly-killed rabbit to defend its ownership. Then the primitive reflex passed, and he was a planning, thinking human again. He must *mark* his kill. . . .

Something to produce a heavy human scent would be of help to deter scavengers for a little while. Or maybe . . . *Fire!* Of course! He would build a small fire upwind of the carcass. It would also guide the way back.

The thought had scarcely flitted through his head before he was gathering sticks and a handful of dry grass. His fire-sticks were in a pouch at his waist. It took only a little while to cut a stick for a fire-bow and fit to it a thong he carried for the purpose. The spindle twirled in the socket of the fireboard, producing a brownish powder, darker as he spun the spindle a little faster. . . . Then black. Now! A glowing spark. . . . Carefully, he lifted the handful of shredded cedar-bark tinder containing that spark, and breathed gently into it. When the flame leaped to life, he thrust it into his prepared cone of dry grass and twigs and fed a few more sticks. Then three larger pieces. *It takes three to burn properly,* his mother had always said. *It takes the spirits of all three.*

He stepped back for a look as he replaced the fire-sticks in the pouch and prepared to leave. Good. . . . The fire was growing, the tongues of flame licking up through the piled sticks. It would provide the needed sight, scent, and man-spirit as the smoke drifted across his kill. No predator or scavenger, large or small, would challenge his possession. Satisfied, he turned back toward the village, moving at a distance-eating jog-trot.

"I have made my kill!"

The words burst from his throat as he approached the lodge. White Moon, kneeling at the cooking fire outside, rose and turned in delight.

"It is good, my son! Today you are a man!"

She gave him a quick hug.

"Mother, it is the big one. The buck I have spoken of. Too big to carry back."

"Where is it?"

"North," he indicated with a wave of his hand.

"You left it?"

"Of course. I will need help to butcher it before dark. I bled and gutted it, and built a fire to keep animals away."

"Good. But we should hurry . . ." She glanced at the sun, and stepped to the door of the house. "Striker has made his kill," she called. I go to help him."

Maple Flower emerged, a pleased smile on her face.

"It is good!" she congratulated.

"Where is Turtle?" asked the young man. "He will be pleased."

"Yes, he will," agreed Flower. "But, I am not sure . . . Turtle went to smoke and talk with White Hawk, and has not returned."

"Should I go to find him?" asked Striker.

"No, no, it grows late," Flower noted with a glance to the west. "Look . . . I will stay with the children, and you two go on. Where is your kill, Striker?"

"North. Not far. I have a fire there. But, it may take us until dark."

"It is good. I will tell Turtle, and maybe he will join you."

Moon was already gathering her flint knives and a small axe to use on the leg joints.

"I will make you a shirt of the skin," Moon told her son as they approached the place of his kill. "*Aiee,* Striker, it is a proud day!"

They came over the slight rise in the trail and saw the fire and the deer carcass. Striker was startled. A man was kneeling over the kill, beginning to skin. He had slit the hide along the inside of the legs, and was stripping it away from flesh and bone. Now he rose and turned, and Striker recognized him . . . Badger!

"What do you want?" he growled.

Striker felt a cold chill up his back to his neck, where the hair began to bristle.

"That . . . That is my kill!" he said. His voice was tense and high-pitched, much to his embarrassment.

"Huh!" grunted the other. "You lie!" He turned to White Moon. "Take your little boy home, woman. I have work to do."

"If Striker says it is his kill, it is so!" she stated positively.

"Nonsense. I made the kill, gutted it out, and your boy must have found it while I gathered wood for my fire, here. Now, go away, unless you want to help with the butchering!"

He turned back to his work.

"It is my kill!" stated Striker, through gritted teeth. "I gutted and bled it."

Badger laughed, and only half turning, spoke over his shoulder.

"You are a nobody, boy . . . A son of a slave-wife. You have no claim to *anything*."

Moon started to step forward, but Striker held her back. "Do not try to fight him, Mother. Badger is too big." His voice sounded calmer now.

"And you are a coward, too, boy. You will not even let a woman fight your battles for you?" Badger sneered. "Even she is more of a man than you."

He turned back to his work.

"Ah! Here you are!" Turtle came down the path behind them. "Flower told me . . . Ah! What is going on?"

Now Badger rose again. "Ah, Turtle, it is good that you are here. This child of your slave-wife tried to steal my kill."

Turtle's face clouded as he turned to Striker. "Is this true?"

"No, Father. The kill is mine!" the young man insisted. "Badger came while I went for help with the skinning."

"Would you take the word of a slave-child over that of a warrior of the People?" asked Badger angrily.

"Maybe," said Turtle thoughtfully. "It would depend on who each one is."

"I have no time to argue," Badger snapped. I need to finish the skinning before night comes."

He returned to his task.

White Moon glanced at Striker. Her son seemed much calmer now, almost resigned. It worried her a little. It was not like Striker to give up so easily. He was very much like his namesake father in that regard. Why, then. . . ? Did he fear the bully so much that he would not insist on his rights?

"There is little we can do now," Striker said, almost sadly. "Later, maybe."

"Not later, not ever," Badger growled over his shoulder. "Now, go away!"

"No, no," Striker said quickly. "We will watch. You may need help when you turn the deer to finish skinning."

Turtle stared at the boy in amazement. *What . . .*

"I would never need help from you," Badger scoffed. "You would have to grow up first, anyway. And, I will show you how easily I can turn this deer."

Almost effortlessly, he rolled the stiffening carcass over on its back and onto the other side.

"Ah!" exclaimed Striker. "There it is! My arrow, the one that killed the deer. Exactly where I left it!"

There was no doubt about it. There in the grass, beneath the deer carcass, lay an arrow.

"Uh . . . That is my arrow!" snapped Badger.

"You lie," said Turtle calmly. "I know this arrow. I watched my son here put the feathers on it, and paint it. Your lie is unworthy of a warrior of the People."

Badger rose angrily, but it was obvious that he knew he had lost. "Your boy must have put it there when I went for firewood . . ." he began.

"No!" Turtle said firmly. "This is the end of it, Badger, unless you want the Council to hear it."

"No, no!" Badger said quickly. "It is not worth the bother. I will give him the deer."

"It is already mine," Striker said calmly. "But I thank you for skinning it."

Badger rose and shuffled away, still muttering to himself.

"I am afraid," said Striker, "that I have made a dangerous enemy."

"Yes," agreed Turtle, "but also a powerful kill. *Aiee, what a buck! Your medicine is good, Striker!*"

Moon was already completing the loosening of the skin and beginning to cut the carcass into manageable-sized chunks. The sun was setting as they divided the burdens and prepared to return to the town. Turtle set aside the severed head with its massive antlers for Striker to carry. Except for the tongue, there would be little meat to salvage from that head, but its symbolism would be powerful.

"This deer will be strong medicine for you and for our lodge," Turtle told the boy. "Ah, I can see it now, over our doorway! It will show *'a man lives here,'* that our boy is a man, a hunter whose medicine is good. Today we are proud."

Striker heard the call of a coyote, and knew that by morning this animal and its kind would have finished cleaning up the remnants of the kill. One of his mother's stories of long-ago times from their own people dealt with this. . . . Man and Coyote, who then, like all other animals, spoke the same tongue, came to an agreement. On any of Man's kills, Coyote would not interfere. But when Man has finished taking his share, the rest belongs to Coyote.

Turtle continued to celebrate, almost singing his joyful praises as they started home. Striker's burden was heavy, but his spirits were light, and his heart was good.

14

Most of the town rejoiced with the success of Striker's symbolic kill. Turtle was proud of the trophy that hung over the doorway, antlers heavy and wide, for all to see. The fact that young Striker was an outsider was all but forgotten to most of the people. After all, he had been born here, to Turtle's wife. His second wife, of course, but the manner of her arrival in the lodge of Flower and Turtle did not now seem significant. It was a respected family group.

Striker basked in the honor and recognition of his accomplishment. He was growing in stature, and now he seemed taller almost overnight in the way that he perceived himself. His posture was more erect and manly, and this, too, seemed to add to his height. Girls who had never noticed him before now smiled flirtatiously as they passed.

White Moon was occupied with the tanning, cutting, and fitting of the deerskin for a medicine shirt for her son. She would make it a little full around the shoulders, because his muscles were still growing and developing. *Aiee,* he would be a man of strength, and she was proud.

She was a bit concerned, as the days passed, that Striker was enjoying his notoriety too much, perhaps. There was a trace of conceit in his manner, a self-satisfaction that she considered inappropriate.

Ah, well . . . Let him have his moment. There would be occasions that would make him humble, she knew. She would regret it, but it is the way of things.

Moon was concerned, though, that his new status would distract him from his long-term goal, that of his preservation of their own traditions and culture. She had, by this time, realized that in all probability she would never be able to return to the prairie. This made it all the more important for Striker to do so. Just now, with his new prestige, he would probably be thinking of courting. *Aiee*, the young women would probably not let him do otherwise! That would present a new complication. If he had a wife and then children, it would be much more difficult for him to break the ties here to return to his own people. There was a threat, even, that he might forget . . . After all, he had known nothing else. It would be easy for him to think of *these* as his people.

That thought was so alarming that she resolved to talk to him about it. And, about the courtship. She was certain that Pretty Moccasin would be interested again, now that Striker had achieved his symbolic kill and was ready to enter manhood. The young woman had looked at other suitors in the meantime, of course, and . . . *Aiee!* Was not one of those the disgusting Badger, who had tried to steal her son's kill? *I must talk to Striker,* she thought.

"Moccasin?"

"What? Oh, it is you, Striker!"

She managed to appear surprised as if she had not planned the chance meeting and waited half the morning for it to happen.

"It has been a long time since I saw you," she said, lifting an eyebrow suggestively. "My heart is good for your success at the hunt."

"Thank you . . ." He brushed the compliment aside. "I . . ."

He was not sure how to begin.

"Moccasin, I . . . I must know . . . Are you . . . You and Badger . . . ?"

The girl blushed. That had been a mistake, and she should never have tried to make him jealous.

"Striker," she began, looking him straight in the eyes, "I was never interested in Badger. I was only teasing you, and for this, my heart is heavy. It was stupid of me."

"No, no!" he protested gallantly. "It was your right . . ."

"Let us not talk of it," she said. "That is behind us now."

She smiled, an open, friendly smile, and his heart soared.

"Then . . . I may play the flute for you?"

"I would be honored, mighty hunter," she said with an exaggerated motion. Then she became serious herself again. "Oh, Striker, I saw the head over your doorway. What a wonderful kill! Will you change your name? Killer-of-Deer or something?"

"I had not thought to. I am . . . Well, I am Striker."

He had nearly said "I am named for my father," but felt that it might be better to avoid such details. This brought on more confusing thoughts. It had been some time since he had spent much effort using the tongue of his mother's Prairie People. He had spoken it only to her, and had for some time seen her very little. His secret heritage had not been in his thoughts very much.

Maybe he should occasionally drop a few words to try to find others of his mother's people. He had had very little luck with it, though. His mother's friend, Turkey Hen, was mildly amused by his efforts, and was apparently not even teaching her own children any of their heritage. Other than Turkey, he had found only two who understood at all, and they had appeared either afraid or ashamed. It was apparent that they were relieved when he had abandoned his effort to communicate about their shared heritage. Well, he'd try to spend a little more time with his mother, now that the urgency of the crucial symbolic hunt was behind him.

His mother brought up the subject.

"Striker, your hunt is a wonderful success. It is good."

They had not talked for some time. He had not spent much time around the town, because his entire effort had been concentrating on the hunt.

"Yes, it is good."

"What will you do now?" she asked casually.

"What do you mean?"

"Well . . . Will you begin courting? Will you seek your vision-quest? And . . ." She glanced around to see that there was no one within earshot. "Will your quest be like that of *these* people or our own?"

Maybe it was only then that Striker realized that there was a choice. He had grown up listening to his mother's stories of the Prairie People, told openly and listened to by all. Then in quiet and privacy, he had been exposed to the secret part that was so important to her . . . The part that he must remember and cherish and pass on to his own children . . . The ways, the customs, the language. There had been a time when the secret had seemed deliciously important and a little wicked. He had enjoyed trying to locate others, though it had been frustrating, and in the end, fruitless.

Now, at this turning point in his life, he had been distracted by two completely divergent happenings that had required his full attention. There was the quest for manhood, part of which was the symbolic hunt, and the physical coming of age, which called for the establishing of a marriage and their own lodge. A thought now struck him in the aftermath of the experience with the deer and the brief conversation with Pretty Moccasin: Both of these distractions had been centered not around the ways of his mother's Prairie People, but the ways of those among whom they lived. These, the Shaved-head people, where he had been born, where he, Striker, lived in the lodge of Maple Flower and Green Turtle, his almost-father. He was sure that Turtle, who had been such an important part of his life, had no idea that White Moon had taught her son the ways and the speech of her own people. Still Striker resented Badger's taunting remarks that his mother was a "slave-wife." It may have started that way, but in his mind, the lodge with its family and the children of both wives was a solid and happy one. True, his mother was Second Wife, but to him that had only been by circumstance.

To further complicate his thoughts, he had no experience with the sort of terrain that his mother treasured and longed to see again, the prairie grassland. He had difficulty even visualizing a region where grasses stretched to the horizons in all directions, with nothing above but big sky. All his life, he had lived in the same town, amid forested hills. His mother's description of open prairie was hard to grasp, and he was not sure he'd like it.

He actually began to doubt the importance of her heritage to anyone but his mother. He was concerned about this. There was a sense of guilt, a feeling of disloyalty to her about his lack of conviction.

Now, her question hung in the air . . . *Which quest will you seek?* She must be feeling his indecision and he knew that his answer would be critical. He did not want to hurt her, but . . .

"I am not sure, Mother," he began slowly. "There is much to think on. I have been led aside by the importance of my hunt, but that is past now. I must be thinking of such things."

I'm not making much sense, he thought, *but how can I?*

It would help, maybe, if he could talk to someone outside the situation, someone he trusted. But . . . It would have to be someone to whom he could talk freely. Yet how could he, without their knowing the secrets of his mother . . . ? *Aiee,* it made his head hurt. He did not really trust any of the few whom he knew were aware of the heritage of the plains. He actually thought of confiding his dilemma to Turtle and asking his advice. He was certain that Turtle, his almost-father, would give good counsel. He always had. Yet, to relate the problem would be to betray his mother. Striker was uncertain how it would affect the relationships in the household. He supposed that in reality, his mother was as Badger had tauntingly said, a slave-wife. She had been, a long time ago, but to most of the town, it had probably been forgotten. White Moon was the wife of Green Turtle, and a member of the town. Striker wondered why

Badger had wanted to bring it up anyway. Probably merely to taunt Striker. Yes, that must be it, an effort to demean a rival for the affections of Pretty Moccasin.

This realization did very little toward a feeling of well-being. Still, Moccasin had apparently been unimpressed. He felt a thrill as he thought of her, and a joy filled his heart that she had rejected Badger for him. Now that their old relationship showed signs of rekindling . . . *Aiee*, maybe the world was a good place, after all. Anywhere would be good, he thought, with Moccasin by his side. They had always confided many things to each other until recently. Nearly everything, actually, except *the* secret, the private teachings of his mother.

Here, he met his doubts again, having come full circle. With the renewal of their friendship and its suggestion of more, he wondered whether it might not be appropriate to tell Moccasin his problem and ask her help. But then again . . . To do so would again betray his mother.

Maybe he could ask his *mother's* advice. No, that would be unfair. . . . Besides, *she* had asked *him*.

And he had not answered her question. He owed her that.

"Mother," he began. "I must think and pray on this now. I will tell you when I can."

White Moon smiled. She could not fail to notice that even in telling her of his indecision, he *had* used the language of her Prairie People.

15

Striker awoke the next morning with a remarkable thought. He could simply drop a few words of the prairie language of his heritage into a conversation with Moccasin and watch her reaction. She might not even notice, though he thought she would. If she inquired, he could say only that these were words of his mother's people, which would probably end the discussion. Moccasin knew, he supposed, the circumstances of Moon's marriage to Turtle. It was no secret, though seldom discussed now, as far as he knew.

Then, depending on her reaction, he could learn a little more about her attitude. That knowledge would be important to him. Although the two young people had been very close as children, and in growing up, there are some things that children do not discuss.

If they married, and Striker was to teach his children the ways and language of his mother's Prairie People . . . *Aiee*, how could this be done without the full cooperation of their own mother? To add to that, the primary instruction of the young would usually fall to an uncle. In this case, a brother of Moccasin. At the very least, their mother would have to know what was going on.

Mother, he thought to himself, *this is too great a task you have given me.*

Maybe he should not marry at all, and should simply leave, to go back to the Prairie People. That would remove the responsibility. Maybe, even, he could go, find the appropriate Prairie People and tell the story of the Lost Band, then return to marry. This idea had some appeal, but over all, he kept coming back to one thought . . . In any case, it would be much easier if he knew Moccasin's feelings about it. He must at least try to learn . . . Yes, he would test a few words, to begin a casual conversation about it. Meanwhile, he would continue to learn the use of the courting flute, before winter drove everyone inside, where he could not practice. He intended to be adept with the instrument when springtime and circumstances offered the opportunity to use it.

His opportunity to try the words of the Prairie People with Moccasin came in a completely unexpected way. Striker was some distance from the town, picking out melodies on the flute. It was an unusually warm winter day, sunny and still, a brief respite before the coming of the next onslaught of snow, ice, or freezing rain. He was taking advantage of such a day to leave the house behind. He carried a bow, but hunting was not his primary goal.

A movement caught his eye, and he turned as Pretty Moccasin approached, smiling.

"Good day to you, Striker!"

"You are not supposed to come to me yet," he joked. "I must learn to make better courting music."

"I know. But the day is good. I followed you."

She came and sat beside him on the silvery-gray trunk of the fallen tree.

"You could continue the flute," she suggested, "but I would rather talk."

Striker laughed. "I, too. I talk better than I play, no?"

"That is true," she giggled. "But, you improve."

"You have listened before, when I . . . ?"

"Of course!"

He wondered when and where. Then, an idea came to him. This was a wonderful opportunity to try the talk of the Prairie People. Neither had spoken for a little while, merely enjoying each other and the day. Striker took a deep breath and spoke, as casually as he could, in his mother's native tongue, taught to him so carefully and so secretly all his life.

"The warm sun feels good."

It was a thing to say, but what he said made no difference, really. It would open the conversation. At least, he hoped so. He had no idea what to expect, but he could never have anticipated the result. Moccasin stared at him wide-eyed.

"*What?*"

He repeated the phrase, adding his explanation as he had planned. ". . . in the tongue of my mother's people," he finished lamely. Maybe this had not been such a good idea.

She was quiet for a moment, and when she spoke it was in a purely conversational tone.

"Yes, quite warm."

It took a moment to realize that Moccasin had *understood* his trial remark. He had not translated it, only told her that it was his mother's language.

"I . . . *You?*" he stammered.

The girl seemed equally confused.

"I do not understand," she blurted. "I knew your mother was an outsider, but no one ever said much about it. You speak her tongue?"

"Some," he said cautiously. "But how do *you* know of it?"

"My grandmother," Moccasin explained. It was a game. . . . A secret between us. No one else knew."

"*She* was of the Prairie People?"

"I . . . I guess so. She used to tell me that I was special, and to teach me this secret way of speaking. She died when I was still small. . . . Several winters ago. Then, I had no one to speak it to. Are there others?"

"A few. Most are afraid or ashamed."

Moccasin sat staring ahead, fighting her way through the confusion.

"Striker . . . This . . . *Aiee!* I have always wondered why your mother's stories seemed familiar to me. My grandmother must have told some of them to me. She also always talked of going home."

"Your mother . . . ?"

"No. My father, I guess. My grandmother must have despaired of reaching him, and chose me, to carry on. My father was more interested in becoming a man of our . . . of *this* people."

"I remember your grandmother ," said Striker. "I could have . . . I wonder if my mother knew?"

"Probably not," the girl said seriously. "Grandmother was very shy and afraid."

"Surely, she would have known of my mother," said Striker.

"Probably. But she lived in fear. She did not dare to say anything." *How sad,* he thought.

"Did she ever suggest what you should do?" he asked.

"Not really. Just wanted me to know . . . *'Remember who you are, and be proud!'*" She chuckled. "Striker, this is *our* secret, now. . . . What shall we do with it?"

They agreed to maintain their secret. Neither would tell of their discovery to anyone. There was one exception, White Moon.

"My mother will be happy about this," Striker said. "She likes you anyway, and this will make her life good."

"Really?"

"Happy" was an understatement. Moon was ecstatic, and wanted to talk of nothing else.

"You can start home as soon as you marry," she suggested. "*Aiee,* I wish I could go with you!"

"But . . . Could you not do that?" Striker asked.

"No, no, my son. Look: It is not unusual for a newly married couple to go away together for a few days. It will not be thought unusual, and no one will suspect. But, a warrior's mother does not go on his wedding trip, no?"

"Mother . . . It may not be that Pretty Moccasin wants to return to the Prairie People. Her mother is of *this* town."

"But you said her grandmother taught her . . . *Aiee*, I *remember* that old woman. I had no idea . . . But, Striker, the grandmother must have told her. It is her *duty* to go back."

"Mother, I am made to think that this must go slowly. Moccasin has only just learned of her heritage. Until now, she had almost forgotten."

"*Aiee*, a pity! Yes, I understand. But will she talk to me of this?"

"Of course. She thinks it good that we three share this secret that was her grandmother's. . . . And, hers. But, Mother, please do not push her on this."

"No, no, my son. Would I do such a thing?"

He could see by the twinkle in her eye that she was teasing him.

"Probably," he chided.

Still, here could be a problem. He must make Moccasin aware of it.

"It is as I said," he told the girl. "White Moon can hardly wait to talk to you. You must remember, it has been her goal for a long time to return to her Prairie People. She would have *us* go *now*."

"Now?"

"Well, as soon as we are married. Go for our marriage quest, and keep going."

Moccasin chuckled, and he thought the sound was like the laughter of the stream over white stones. Then the girl became serious.

"Striker, I . . . This is all so new to me. . . ."

"I know. I only tell you this because my mother will want to talk to you about it. She is excited that . . . That we three will share this secret. But, she will surely suggest to you that we go to the prairie to her . . . to 'our' people."

Moccasin thought for a moment, then spoke. "It would be good, maybe. Not now, but sometime. Would you not be curious?"

"Of course. My mother always spoke of it. I think that for a long time she planned to run away when I was old enough to travel, just herself, with me. Then she bore Turtle's child, and it became more difficult. I think she depends on me, now, to make that journey. So, she will try to convince you."

Moccasin laughed. "Of course! I would expect her to do so. But then . . . Turtle is not your father?"

"No. I am named for my father, Striker. White Moon carried his child when she was captured. . . . Me."

"It is a sad story," Moccasin mused. "I can see why this is so important to her. Oh . . . Has she taught your sister . . . And your brother, Possum . . . Turtle's children . . . Has Moon taught them?"

"I think not. She must have decided that it was my quest to undertake."

"Striker," the girl said, with a trace of sadness in her voice, "my heart is heavy for your mother. I can see how she would feel. Like my grandmother, but worse. *Aiee*, to have had her son deny his heritage!"

"She had no one but you, then?"

"That must be true. It was my feeling that she was captured or stolen when she was still a child."

He nodded. "Like my sister, Fawn."

"Oh! I had forgotten. You have an older sister. But how . . . ?"

"Not really, Moccasin. Fawn was an orphan, it seems. My mother was looking after her. Turtle and Maple Flower were childless and wanted the girl. They took my mother, too, thinking Fawn was hers."

"Then Fawn, too, knows the prairie language, their ways?"

"I am made to think so. But, she has her own family now. She probably does not have time to think about it. I could ask her."

Moccasin nodded thoughtfully. Maybe . . . I am made to think this, Striker . . . If we decide to go and see, we should do so before we have a lodgefull of children!"

.16

During the moons of winter it was virtually impossible to do any courting. That would require a certain amount of privacy, and there could be very little. The cold winter winds forced everyone inside in close proximity to other family members. There was much socializing, of course. Games, smokes, gambling, stories for the young and for the old, carried out in the lodges of friends and neighbors. But, in such situations there is little romance.

Striker and Moccasin often exchanged smiles and glances, and occasionally a few words. Sometimes these words were in one language, sometimes the other, depending on others who might overhear. Striker was more adept at the Prairie People's language, because he had had more practice. Moccasin was able to understand somewhat more than she could speak, but her memory for the guttural and nasalized sounds of her grandmother's tongue was quickly returning.

Friends and neighbors saw what was going on. More accurately, they thought they saw. The shy, secret whispers in a shadowy corner, the quiet laughter over some private joke. It was obvious to all that a romance was brewing. Only White Moon knew completely the details of these secretive whispers. But she, along with everyone else, knew that when spring came, romance would, also.

Striker had learned that Moon had *not* given the knowledge of their heritage to her two younger children. She had not told Striker why. Striker preferred to think that it was out of respect for their father, Turtle. Possum and Yellow Bird were, after all, children of this town, not of the Prairie People. They knew, of course, that their mother was originally an outsider, but that was all.

The Moon of Long Nights was followed by the Moon of Snows, and then the Moon of Hunger. Hunting was poor, and supplies of dried meat and pemmican were running low. The lodge of Turtle and Flower was better supplied than most, because of Striker's big kill in the autumn. Still, it would be good to see the Moon of Awakening, when Sun Boy's torch began to glow with renewed fire and the world returned to life.

At last . . . Warming south winds were melting snow and ice. Long lines of migrating geese honked their way northward. The willows along the stream began to change, showing even at a distance a yellow-green tint that gave promise. The soft silver maples were laden with their dark red blossoms. These came so early that usually at least one ice storm struck at the same time. The fuzzy flowers, from which Turtle's First Wife took her name, would be coated with thick balls of ice. Sometimes it became heavy enough to break large branches, which would come crashing to the ground in a sparkling shower.

Striker and Moccasin, with their new-found closeness, found beauty everywhere. Melting snow revealed sprigs of green underfoot, as well as swelling buds on trees and shrubs. Streams were swollen, and babbled in happy conversation, after winter's frozen silence.

They watched the geese overhead, and talked of the songs they sang as they traveled. The big gray geese with black and white face paint gave a raucous honking cry. The other geese, the high-flying flocks of blue and snowy-white birds, had a different song, like the distant barking of a myriad of small dogs. The happy couple talked of these things and laughed together. They envied the birds their ability to travel, to see and experience faraway places. The age-old springtime urge to migrate stirred their souls, as the call of the geese may have done since man first stood upright and watched the long V-shaped lines overhead.

"Do you know," Striker asked philosophically, "why one side of their pattern is always longer than the other?"

"I never noticed that, but it is true!" she said, enchanted, watching.

"My mother told me. . . . A legend of her . . . of *our* People."

"Why is it, Striker, that one line is longer?"

"Oh," he said smugly, "there are more birds on that side."

Her curious expression changed to one of mock fury, as she struck him gently with an open palm on the muscle of his shoulder.

"You are *bad!*"

"*Aiee,* what did I do?" he laughed. "I only told you a tradition of our People. Is it not so?"

He pointed upward, and both collapsed into happy laughter in each other's arms. Then she pulled away and became serious.

"Striker," she said, "I am made to think that you play the flute well enough. You need no more practice."

"I have not played much since winter," he protested. "I did not even bring the flute today."

"Never mind," she said flippantly. "I am convinced to marry. Also, that we should go on our quest."

"Now?"

"After we marry. You have told me of the Sun Dance of the Prairie People, when all bands gather. Would it not be good to be there?"

"To *stay* with them?"

"I do not know, Striker. To see them, tell them . . . You said that your mother is afraid that there was no one left to tell of the massacre. We do not have to decide now. Let us find them first."

Now, Striker was surprised to find that he had not thought of exactly *how* this was to be accomplished.

"They move around," he said thoughtfully. "Their Sun Dance . . . I am made to think it is in a different place each year."

"In the Moon of Roses, you said?"

"Yes . . . Let us ask my mother about it. There may be some pattern in where they choose."

"Aiee, it has been so long, Striker," said White Moon. "I do not know. . . . They choose, each year, where the Sun Dance will be held next season."

"How would we find them?"

"Mmm . . . If you could find a trader . . . They usually know about the hunters who move around. They trade for skins, dried meat, pemmican. . . . A trader might know. Or, maybe you could find a town of growers, who live much as we do here. Our Prairie People trade with them sometimes. Kenza, maybe Pahni. . . . But they are farther north. Dangerous, too. Better to look for Kenzas."

"Pahni. . . . Dangerous, Mother?"

"So it is said. They are different."

"How so?"

"Aiee, I do not remember it all. They steal children."

"But many do!"

"True. But their gods are different. Our People look to Sun Boy, but to the Pahni, Morning Star is more important, it is said. Their priests chart the stars' movement, instead of Sun's."

"But why, Mother?"

"Aiee, you ask too many questions, Striker. I don't know. But there are tales . . . They give a virgin to Morning Star for a wife, it is said, so that he will let their corn grow."

"Each year?"

"No, no. Only sometimes, when their Morning Star tells the priests that he needs one. Then she is sacrificed in a ceremony."

"They kill their own girls?"

"No, no! A virgin they have stolen from another tribe. But never mind, just stay away from Pahni. Kenzas would be better, if you can find them."

"How would we recognize Pahni?"

"Oh . . . They are called Horn People. The men wear their hair shaved around all sides, and one big tuft on top. It is twisted and greased and shaped like a horn sticking up, so." She made a gesture with her index finger. "That is the hand sign for Pahni, too. . . . Horn People."

"Maybe we will stay farther south, then."

"That is good," Moon said approvingly. "I did not mean to alarm you. But, be careful."

"Of course, Mother," he laughed.

"When you come to a town, ask for their chief, to pay respects. It is only proper. It brings honor to him, and to the visitor." Her eyes twinkled. "Besides, you get more help that way. When will you go?"

"We had not decided. We want to marry first, and we will need supplies. We can also hunt as we travel."

"Yes . . . *Aiee,* I will miss you, my son. I wish I could go with you."

"You could . . ."

"No, my place is here, now. The other children . . . We would hold you back. No, my duty was to teach you. Yours is to go back, to tell *them.* And, so good, Striker, for you to have found one of our own to marry. It was meant to be!"

They went through the ritual of courting, though it hardly seemed worth the effort. There was a thrill, though, in the sensuous tones of the courting flute, and the knowledge that it would soon bring them together. People heard, and smiled, perhaps remembering the thrill and excitement of their own courtship.

The necessary time was spent, and the marriage ceremony took place. Striker and Moccasin were seated side by side before a symbolic fire, blessed with an offering to the spirits in the form of a pinch of tobacco. The two mothers of the new couple approached from behind them, and spread a soft-tanned robe around the shoulders of the pair, making them one.

They would spend the night in a specially prepared brush arbor outside the camp, and would depart the next day.

"How long will you be gone?" asked Turtle, who knew nothing of their real quest.

"We are not sure," Striker answered vaguely. He was saddened that he must be deceptive toward Turtle, the only father he had ever known.

"It is all right, my son," his mother assured him. "I may explain to Turtle later. I am made to think he will understand."

She now considered herself fortunate to have arrived in captivity in the lodge of a good man like this one. It could have been much worse. And she could have been dead long ago, even before the birth of her son, Striker. Life is never what one expects, but always interesting. She envied the young couple the life ahead of them, and hoped that they might avoid some of the tragedy of her own. As many good things, she wished for them, but fewer of the bad . . .

The young couple rose early the next morning, decided to return to robes for a little while, and then rose again to travel.

At the crest of the ridge to the west of the town, they paused to look back. The wisps of smoke from the morning cooking fires were wafting up through the treetops. They wondered when, if ever, they would see this place again. It was the only home that either had ever known.

The tall storyteller paused and seemed to sway a little as he stood.

"Are you all right?" asked Spotted Hawk, the Real-chief.

"I . . . Yes, a little dizzy," admitted the other. "Maybe I am more weary than I had thought. The excitement . . . To be here . . . All my life, I have waited for this, no?"

"Do you want some food? Rest? It is late."

"It might be best," admitted the newcomer. "But I do not want to interfere with the Sun Dance."

"As it should be," agreed the chief. This man certainly understood the customs and importance of the ways of the People. No doubt as to his credibility. . . . Hawk turned to the keeper of the sacred bundles. "Would this . . . ?"

"We have not started the three days of announcement," advised the holy man." I would have begun in the morning, but . . . I see no reason why we could not hear our brother's story. I can postpone for a day the beginning of the announcement." Spotted Hawk glanced around the circle, meeting the eyes of each band chieftain in turn and receiving nods of agreement.

"It is good," stated the Real-chief. "We will hold another Council tomorrow night to hear the rest of our brother's story. He will be a guest in my lodge."

"Wait!" called a woman. "What happened to Striker and Pretty Moccasin? They did not rejoin the People, or we would have no Lost Band!"

"True," agreed Story Keeper. "They could not find the Prairie People, so they returned . . ."

"Let him rest," called someone. "The story has kept for many lifetimes already."

"That is true," observed the Real-chief. "No one from the Lost Band has ever returned until now. But let our brother rest tonight. We will hear his story later. . . . Tomorrow at sunset!"

Shadows were hardly starting to lengthen when the crowd began to gather. There was much excitement in the encampment, even beyond that which was usual for the festival of the Sun Dance. It seemed a long time before Sun Boy painted the western sky with his most brilliant colors and slipped below earth's rim. When the fire was lighted and the darkness began to deepen, the storyteller rose to continue his tale. In the timber along the river, a hunting owl called his hollow cry.

Some stories must only be told after dark. . . . Creation stories of Old Man, for instance. And, since almost any story might deal with the influence of the Old Man of the Shadows, it was best to wait until complete darkness.

"It is as I said," Story Keeper began. "Striker and Pretty Moccasin could not find their . . . our People. They spent more than a moon crossing the prairie, stopping to ask growers, following a story about where someone thought the Sun Dance would be held. It must have been far to the west that season, because they never found it, and never knew for sure."

"They did not try again?" asked someone.

"Apparently not. It was told to me that when they returned from this failed search, Moccasin was already with child. This interfered with the next try, and by that time another child was on the way. I do not know whether they ever tried again to find the Sun Dance, but they did teach their children well, both the language and the ways of the People. As it was with White Moon, they were probably concerned with the tasks of staying alive. Each season, they must have talked about it, and once more decided 'maybe next year.'"

He paused, as if he had reached a turning point in the story. His audience waited . . . A section of cottonwood log burned in half and dropped into the fire, sending a column of red sparks high into the sky to join the innumerable of yellow points of light already there against the black dome. On the ground across the grassland, the corresponding yellow-green sparks of a myriad of fireflies danced and twinkled. There was no moon, and the night held a sense of things of the spirit. This was an important time in the experience of the People. Already, the keeper of the Story Skins was thinking of what he would paint to commemorate this event. . . . The year the Lost Band was found . . .

"Now," said the narrator, "there is a space in the story. I do not know why, but only as it was told to me. A part of the happenings was lost, because nothing much happened for a few lifetimes. Ah, I see you wondering . . . Then how do we know that the teaching was carried on? Think about it, my brothers . . . I am here . . . I know your ways, your tongue . . . *Ours.* Someone, several someones, did a very skillful task in the way they educated their children and grandchildren. Some of them, we do not even know their names. To them, the story, the tradition, the language and customs of the People was so much more important than themselves. I respect and honor their memories.

"There is another thing, too, that has occurred to me. Our custom, that of not speaking the name of the dead . . . What if the keeper of the secret, while he . . . or she . . . was teaching the young ones, met with accident or illness and died? Crossed over without giving away his name? No one could speak it, and it would be lost. I am made to think that something like that has caused the space in the story. . . . Maybe more than once."

There were nods of agreement. It could happen.

"Whatever the reason, there is a hole in the story, for several lifetimes, though we know that *someone* . . . Well, as I said. Now, the story begins again, lifetimes later, in the prairies to the north. This time, the band which the People called the Lost Band nearly was lost entirely. But again, there was one . . ."

Part Three
Stumbling Bear

.18

Stumbling Bear dove into the cold water, and surfaced, sputtering and shaking. In a few moments, he would be more comfortable, but that first plunge was always a shock. Near him, his friend Gray Fox emerged from his own dive, yelping from the chill.

"Come on in, Dog!" he called to another young man on the shore.

"I'm coming!" Lean Dog retorted. "Get out of the way!"

He, too, took a graceful dive and came up sputtering.

"*Aiee!* It is cold!" muttered Gray Fox.

"No, you are soft, Fox," laughed Lean Dog. "Bear and I find it quite comfortable."

"Then why do your teeth chatter and dance?" demanded Gray Fox.

All three laughed. They had been friends all their lives, and now were approaching manhood. There were strange urges demanding their attention. The girls who had been in their loose-knit group for childhood instruction had already begun to change. Their bodies were shaped differently than they had been before. More graceful curves, shapelier legs, fuller breasts. They were becoming women, and very quickly, too. The boys were stimulated and fascinated by the process, but the changes come a year or so later in the male of the species. They had been forced to watch the girls of their own age turn their attention to older boys and men.

One girl, who had matured quite early, had already been taken in marriage. A widower, Walks Like A Bull, old enough to be her father, had announced his intentions to her parents, who were quite willing. Their lodge was blessed with many children, of which Willow was the eldest. It was considered a good match, because the older man was a capable hunter and warrior, and could provide well for her. She, with experience in helping with the younger children in her mother's lodge, could serve the same function to her husband's motherless children.

This turn of events was a shock to the boys her own age, of course. Though they had not fully reached manhood, there was jealousy. Willow, with her precocious development, had been an object of attention and embarrassed whispers among the boys. The situation was made more tense by the fact that Willow was a natural-born flirt. Some women are born with a primeval under-standing of men. From an early age, they know and use the wiles and trickery that drive men to greatness or to destruction. . . . The sidelong glance, the hint of a smile, a slow moistening of the lips with a caressing tongue . . . A way of moving the hips and torso as she walks . . . All of these things promise pleasures beyond the imagination to the inexperienced male whose urges are beginning to awaken.

It had been a great disappointment, then, when their childhood companion graduated overnight to the status of wife and mother. The entire situation was the source of many ribald jokes among the young men, who felt that they had been cheated, somehow. They missed the flirting, and had forgotten that there had been a time when they had actually felt it objectionable.

But they survived, cajoled and teased each other and the girls. Before long, their maleness began to mature. They realized that there was an entire group of young girls a year or two younger than they who were beginning to blossom. Plain girls who had seemed unattractive suddenly came to full flower. It seemed odd to the young men that they had never noticed *that* one. . . . *Aiee,* she had been no more than a mouse last season, and now . . .

Today, the three friends were, for a brief time at least, not thinking of girls. They were enjoying the day, and male companionship. The warm autumn sun was a sensuous contrast to the chill of the stream's coolness. They swam, splashed, ducked, and wrestled playfully, and finally emerged to lie on the warm sandbar to rest. Life was good.

"We will be moving soon," said Gray Fox.

"It has been decided?" asked Lean Dog.

"I don't know. I am made to think so, though. It is time."

There was silence for a little while, each with his own thoughts. Probably, all of these thoughts were similar. . . .

"Maybe they will let us take part in the kill at the jump," said Dog finally.

"I hope so. We are nearly men, no?"

"Of course. Maybe we could ask."

"You could ask your uncle, Bear," suggested Fox. "He would speak for us, no?"

"Maybe. I will ask him."

"Well," said Lean Dog, "if we can't do that, we can still hunt on our own. I intend to kill a bear this year."

The others laughed.

"Of course," mocked Gray Fox, "and the sun will rise in the west tomorrow."

"No, I am serious," insisted Dog. "We will probably winter in the Black Hills, no? That is bear country."

"That is not the same as *killing* one!" leered Gray Fox.

"Of course. But I can do it."

"I would rather kill buffalo," said Stumbling Bear.

The others laughed.

"Bear . . . Bear is your brother, no?"

"I . . . Something like that, maybe."

"You are joking!" said Fox.

Stumbling Bear was very uncomfortable with this conversation. There were things he could not discuss. Yet, the others were waiting for his answer.

"Of course!" he said finally. "An old family joke. Something to do with my name. I've never understood it."

He jumped to his feet.

"Come on, the sun's getting low."

One more plunge, to wash the white sand from their skins. . . . They quickly emerged and donned breechclouts, tying the thong at the waist. Soon they would need shirts and leggings every day, but today had been warm. They were beginning to feel the evening chill, though. . . . They headed back to the camp.

As close as their friendship had been, there was one secret that Stumbling Bear had never shared with the other two. He would not, could not. As far as anyone knew, Bear and his family were Lakota, like the rest. They were proud of it. This was as it should be.

Of course, there were those who would remember that the grandmother of young Stumbling Bear had joined the People as a captive bride. But, she had assimilated well. She had been a good wife to Bent Arrow, and had borne him two children, a girl and a boy. They had grown to maturity as Lakotas, respected by their friends and neighbors. The girl, Dove Woman, had married, and was the mother of Stumbling Bear. The child had been named, in fact, by his grandmother, who had died shortly thereafter. There were those who also might have recalled that Bent Arrow's wife had some strange dietary taboos, carried with her from her own people. She would never eat bear meat, and sometimes went hungry because of this odd carryover. It probably occurred to only a few people that it might have any connection to the name she had given to her grandson, Stumbling Bear.

As he grew, probably none in his own generation were even aware that his grandmother had been an outsider. There was no reason for the subject to arise.

Bear had always been aware that his mother considered him special. Yet, does not every boy's mother think so? Dove Woman had managed to give her child a sense of importance without allowing him to develop the arrogance that might have accompanied it.

When young Stumbling Bear had experienced some ten winters, his mother's brother took him on a hunt. This was not unusual. Much of his instruction as he grew through the early years of childhood had been supplied by this uncle, Calling Elk. It was a custom, the instruction of a boy by a maternal uncle. A useful custom . . . There is a time in the life of most young people when the advice and counsel of a parent is largely scorned. It is good to have another grown-up with whom to consult, and this becomes the function of the uncle.

So, it happened that on this hunt at the tender age of ten winters, Stumbling Bear had learned the secret. At their campfire that night, Calling Elk had told the boy of their heritage.

"You mean we are *not* Lakota?" Bear asked in alarm.

"Yes, we are," Elk told him, "and of this we can be proud. But we have, also, a connection to this other nation, called 'the People' in their own tongue. This makes us special."

The heart of Stumbling Bear leaped with excitement. What youngster would not thrill at the thought of being a member of a secret society?

"How many of us are there?" he asked.

"Very few. You might remember your grandmother. . . . No, you were too small. She gave you your name."

"I have been told of her. . . . She was the outsider?"

"Yes. She had two children, me and your mother. She taught us to take pride."

"My mother knows of this?"

"Of course."

"Why did she not tell me?"

"Did she not always make you feel that you were special?"

"Yes, but . . . I . . . Well, she is my mother, no? It is so, with mothers."

"Of course," Calling Elk chuckled. "But we decided that I should be the one to teach you. I would be your teacher anyway, in the hunt and the ways of manhood."

"Then . . . You and my mother . . . No more know of this?"

"No more that we know of. You, now. I will start to teach you the language of our People tonight. You must never forget this, Bear. And, you must never tell anyone of it."

"Why?"

"It might be resented. We must pass it on to our children. I have none, yet, but will teach them. Someday, some of us must return to tell our People what happened, long ago."

"But was not my grandmother, your mother, the outsider?"

"Yes, but not the *first*. Many lifetimes ago, a whole band of the People was killed. There was a woman, White Moon, who was a slave-wife of the killers, and she taught *her* children."

"And nobody has gone back since?"

"We are made to think not."

"But why, Uncle?"

"It was never possible, maybe. The men are usually busy with hunting or war. Many have probably been killed. I am made to think that it has been the women who have preserved the secret and passed it down."

"I can speak of this to my mother?"

"Of course. But it is not wise to do so with others near."

"Of course . . . My sister?"

"Not yet. She is too small. Your mother will teach her when the time comes."

"*Aiee,* Uncle, this is . . . *Aiee,* I do not know what to say."

Calling Elk smiled. "When in doubt, say nothing. One learns more that way. But, let us begin with a few words. I will also tell you of customs and traditions. You have seen the Sun Dance, and the vision-quest."

"Of course, Uncle. You mean, Lakota?"

"Yes. There are some differences. . . . In the ways of our other, the Prairie People in the Southern Plains, these are separate. One goes on a vision-quest alone. The Sun Dance is not connected in any way. *Aiee,* Bear, there is so much to tell. . . ."

19

"**N**ow, your name . . . Stumbling Bear . . . Your grandmother chose it. I am not sure why. Maybe, to call attention . . . Our People, the secret ones, do not kill bears. It is a covenant since Creation."

"But, *why?*"

"It does not really matter. Only that it is so. An agreement: We will not kill you, Bears, and you do not kill us."

"My mother does not eat bear meat. This is why?"

"Yes. Sometimes it is hard to avoid or explain. Usually, just the mention of a family custom will handle it. A bear *hunt* is harder, to avoid the killing, sometimes. Once, I had to fall down and drop my bow. . . ." Elk laughed.

"But you are a respected hunter, Uncle."

"Yes . . . We must be *better* than most, to be able to appear clumsy or foolish at times. But look at the problems of our mother. She must *cook* bear meat, sometimes, when your father takes part in a killing. Yet she cannot eat of it."

"But *I* have eaten. . . ."

"Yes, but you did not *know.* Once you know of this . . . Now, you cannot. But you are old enough now, to decide 'I will not eat my namesake' . . . I am not certain, Bear, but maybe your grandmother named you Bear for just this reason, to make it easier for you."

"What happens, Uncle, if one of our People does kill or eat bear meat?"

"Ah! If he knows, and does it anyway, he dies."

"*Aiee!* It becomes poison?"

"No, no. He . . . or *she* . . . might die in an accident, be struck by lightning. . . . An enemy . . . *Anything.*"

The boy nodded thoughtfully, and finally spoke again.

"The vision-quest, uncle . . . Which one did you follow?"

"You thought of that. . . ." Elk mused. "Yes, it is a choice. . . . I did the Lakota search for my guide, because my friends were doing so. I am made to think that it does not matter much *how* one finds his guide, but that he *finds* it. And I did not want to appear too different."

"Could a person do *both*?"

"I never thought of that," admitted Calling Elk. "I wonder . . . Would one find *two* guides? Or maybe the spirits would be angry over it. . . . I don't know, Bear. Let us think on this. You have a few years to decide. One thing is sure. We cannot ask the holy men of our Lakota heritage about the other!"

Both laughed.

"Now," said Calling Elk, "let us start with Creation. In the beginning, the People lived inside the earth, and it was dark and cold. Then, somebody discovered some light, coming through a hole in the top of one of the caverns, where there were some roots hanging down. He climbed up the roots and looked through. . . . *Aiee,* he was looking through a hollow log, a cottonwood tree that had blown over and broken. And there was a sound, like a drum. He crawled through the log and looked around. There, straddling the log and holding a drumstick was an old man with long stringy hair, and he had a big nose. He was very ugly."

"The Trickster!" explained Bear. "The Grandfather . . . *Iktoemi!*"

"Yes," continued Elk, "I am made to think he is all one. The Crows call him Old Man Coyote, I am told. To Kiowas, he is *Saindi*. To everyone, all nations, he looks much the same, so possibly he is the same person, the Trickster. . . . Older than Creation, able to speak all tongues . . . The languages of people, all of the animals, birds, even fish. The whisper of the breeze through the pines, the rustle of grass, ripple of water . . . All are understood and spoken by the Trickster."

"And he created us . . . the secret Prairie People?"

"No, no! Only the Great Spirit could do that. I am made to think that he, too, is all one, by different names, but . . . No, we are talking of Trickster. He did not *create* us, but only brought us through the log. . . . Let me go on. Where was I, Bear? Oh, yes . . . First Man crawled into the sunlight and stood up, and looked at the beauty around him, and he was glad. Then the Old Man whacked on the log again with his drum beater, and a beautiful girl crawled out! *First Woman*. Another whack, and another . . . Each time the Trickster struck the log, another person crawled out and stood blinking at the sunlight."

Elk paused and a look of mischief flickered around his eyes and at the corners of his mouth.

"They would probably be still coming through," he mused.

"They are not?" Bear interrupted.

"No . . . Alas, a fat woman got stuck in the log, and no more could come out. For this reason, our People have always been a small nation."

Bear thought for a moment. . . . "That part is a joke, no?"

"Maybe so . . . What do you think, Bear?"

They both laughed.

"Maybe . . . Uncle, what do our Prairie People call the Trickster?"

"Oh, I did not say? He is the Old Man of the Shadows. He can turn himself into a tree or a rock, or any animal or person. He is the Old Man. Oh, yes, he decreed at that time that no one may tell his story except after dark."

The boy peered into the night. There was no moon, and the ghostly light of the stars was practically nothing to those who sat within the circle of the firelight. Bear scooted a little closer to their campfire.

"Why? What happens?"

Calling Elk leaned forward, a grimace of fear on his face. *"No one knows.* No one still alive, anyway!"

There was dead silence, except for the murmur of the stream and the sounds of small night-creatures. *Or maybe of the Old Man speaking in their tongues,* thought stumbling Bear. . . .

They stayed awake for a long time, and Calling Elk told more stories. Some, Stumbling Bear had heard.

"Uncle! Many of my mother's stories are those of the Prairie People!" Bear spoke in sudden understanding.

"Yes . . . You know, people remember and tell a good story sometimes. Anyone's story. Our People . . . the Prairie People, have done this to keep the memory alive of who we are."

Stumbling Bear had begun to take a certain pride in this unknown but just-discovered heritage.

"You told him?" Dove Woman asked her brother the next day.

"Yes," smiled Calling Elk. *"Aiee,* it was good, sister. He has great understanding. I told him of the Creation story, and started him on the language. He will mention it to you when opportunity offers."

She nodded, pleased. "Yes . . . Bear gave me a special smile when he returned. My heart is good for this, Elk. I thank you!"

Her brother shrugged. "It is something we must do. Oh, yes! Do you know . . . ? Bear asked me about the vision-quest, which to seek!"

"What did you tell him? You did the Lakota ceremony at the Sun Dance, no?"

"That is true. He asked if he could do *both.* Dove, I know he is a deep thinker. I think the idea of a quest, alone in the hills or the prairie, appeals to him."

She nodded thoughtfully. "I can see how it would, Elk. He is a special boy."

"Ah, because he is yours!" Elk teased her.

"Of course," she laughed. "But you have seen it. He watches and thinks. He can spend an afternoon watching a bird build her lodge in a bush."

"He sees, notices, and understands such things."

"Yes, I know. But he is also skilled with the bow, and in the games and contests. You have taught him well, Elk."

"I cannot claim all the credit, Dove. His mother started him in the right path. *We* have a fine boy here. It is good."

He turned and started back to his own lodge, and the heart of Dove Woman soared, more nearly like the eagle than like her demure namesake.

"How was your hunt?" asked Gray Fox.

"It was good, Fox," said Stumbling Bear.

"I see no great amount of meat from your kills," his friend teased.

"It is not that kind of a hunt, Fox. We talked. . . . A long time. My uncle told me many tales of Creation, and of the time when all men and animals spoke the same tongues."

"New stories?" the other asked eagerly.

"Not really. I don't know, Fox. We spoke of *Iktoemi*, stories like that. I am made to think that it is a custom in my family."

Bear was uncomfortable, not being completely open with his good friend. He hoped that Fox would not be offended. Instead, the other boy paused in open admiration.

"Ah, what a great custom! I wish that *my* family had such a thing."

Fox was making this very difficult, unknowingly, of course. Bear longed to tell him more, but he had been entrusted with a very important body of information. He could not break so serious a vow.

"Probably," he said carefully, "there are customs in your family, too, no? Is not your uncle your teacher?"

"That is true," agreed Gray Fox. "Maybe we will go on a hunt soon. My uncle Snake is a worthy hunter and warrior, too."

"Of course! Is it not as I said? Your instruction will come."

Which, of course, it did. That of Lean Dog also. The balance in the relationship of the three friends was restored. Only Stumbling Bear, of the three, was aware that he had received different instruction from the usual. More properly, *additional* information.

He briefly made his mother aware of his understanding.

"It is good, my son," she said, smiling. "Yours is a heavy responsibility, to teach *your* children."

"You will tell Kitten, too, when she is older?"

"Yes, your sister, and any other children I may have, too. When she is grown enough to understand. Your uncle will also teach his, when he has children. I am made to think that is soon, too!"

"His wife . . . ?"

She nodded, smiling. "Say nothing, Bear. It is hers to tell such news."

"Of course, Mother . . . But, soon, there will be several who know of our People. . . . The Prairie People."

Dove Woman laughed. "It will take some time."

"But . . . It is like a band *within* a band! A secret society, like the warrior societies!"

"Maybe so. I had not thought of it in that way," she mused. "No matter . . . Just so our story is preserved . . . And, honored."

The three friends had grown nearly to manhood since then. There were two boys in the lodge of Calling Elk, and another in the lodge of Stumbling Bear's parents. None of these had yet been taught of the family secret except Bear's sister Kitten. Kitten was already interested in boys, and did not seem to understand the importance of their responsibility, which bothered Bear immensely.

20

The three young men sat on the crest of a slight rise, watching the distant prairie. It was the Moon of Awakening and the buffalo might be moving. Not in great numbers, yet, but there could be small bands at this time. More likely, they might see elk. Smaller herds, more unpredictable, but a possible source of meat for the first spring hunts.

Somewhat later, the great herds of buffalo would follow the return of the sun and the grass northward, from this winter range. Then, the Lakotas would attempt a major hunt, a buffalo jump.

Today, it was mostly a chance to get away, after the confinement of winter camp. It was good to feel the sunlight on one's back. Winter had its own pleasures. . . . The long visits and smokes in the lodges of friends and neighbors . . . Games, stories, gambling. But by spring, food was always in short supply. Usually not dangerously so, but sometimes. The Moon of Hunger in late winter often found its name quite appropriate. That frustration, though, was more centered on the quality of the stored food. Dried meat grows old, and pemmican becomes rancid after a few moons, because of the necessary tallow mixed with the dried and pounded meat and berries. People have a craving for fresh meat, just as the grazing animals crave green grass after wintering on last year's standing hay and the rough browse of leafless cottonwood and willow along the streams. Sun's return stimulates the new growth, the renewal and rebirth of all living things. It is truly the Moon of Awakening.

There is a restlessness among humans, a frustrated migration urge, maybe, that makes us watch with envy the first flights of the wild geese as they return northward. If the three friends had been asked that day the reason for their presence there, the answer would have been simple: hunting. A more accurate answer might have been a simple urge to escape the confines of winter camp and the enforced closeness to others. Still, they probably did not even think of that. It was simply the Moon of Awakening. It was good to be alive and out on open prairie, and no further excuse was needed.

"Look," pointed Fox. "There, to the west. Something moving . . . Elk, maybe?"

The others studied a moment. Lean Dog placed his partly closed fists in front of his eyes. He peered through the tunnels formed by his cupped palms and fingers, shutting out excess light to see the distant objects more clearly.

"Mmm . . . Maybe. What do you think, Bear?"

"Are you suggesting they may be bears, or are you talking to our friend here?" asked Gray Fox.

They laughed together. Many things are amusing to friends who have long been together, which would not be apparent to outsiders.

"Both, maybe," chuckled Lean Dog. "Are they bear, Bear?"

"Stop it!" demanded Stumbling Bear in mock anger. He paused a moment, studying the figures through his own cupped hands. "Are they moving?"

"I'm not sure. . . ."

Bear scooted to his belly and took two short pieces of last year's grass stems. He cleared an open space and placed the stems in alignment, sighting across the two at the dark figures in the distance.

"Can you tell color?" asked Dog.

"Too far," both the others said at once.

At a distance on the prairie, form is more distinguishable than color. Beyond a few hundred paces, objects are sometimes distinguished by shape, but color assumes a sameness. A grazing animal might be reddish or gray or black or spotted, and only be a dark object against the lighter grass. A little farther, it might be perceived as a stationary object. A tree, rock . . .

"They *are* moving," Bear reported, squinting across his grass stems. "Three . . .Elk, maybe . . ." He sat up and looked through his cupped palms again. "But . . . *Aiee,* something is strange. . . . They seem to have humps like buffalo. Something on their backs?"

"Panthers, maybe?" suggested Fox. "Remember when we saw that elk with a big cat riding on it?" He giggled.

"Don't be stupid, Fox!" said Stumbling Bear irritably.

"It does look like that, though," said Lean Dog. "Something is wrong, here. And they are not grazing, but walking, steadily. Not running, that eliminates panthers, Fox."

This time they all chuckled, but this was nothing to take lightly, and they soon sobered.

"Should we tell the men?" asked Gray Fox.

"Maybe," suggested Bear. "One could go, the others watch."

They looked at each other.

"Who goes?" asked Gray Fox.

There was a dilemma. . . . All wanted to stay and watch, though there was a temptation to experience the honor of carrying such an important message.

"Let us draw sticks," suggested Bear.

"Good!" exclaimed Lean Dog, turning to find suitable stems.

He turned his back, broke and shortened the stems to length, and turned again. Three stems protruded from between his thumb and fingers, all approximately even.

"Shortest carries the message," said Lean Dog.

Gray Fox chose first, grasping the straw that appeared the shortest. That, of course, would be one of the longest. Fox knew the trickery of his friend from long association. He drew it out. . . . Medium in length . . . But the clever Dog might have made all the stems medium, short, or long, with only a little difference.

Stumbling Bear, like Fox, knew the wiles of Lean Dog. They had played this game all their lives. The shortest . . . Or would Dog do the opposite? He grasped the longest of the two remaining stems and drew it out of Dog's hand. . . . *Aiee!* He had guessed wrong. His friend's devious mind had deceived him again.

"Watch well!" Bear told the others. "I will be back!"

He turned and loped back toward the camp.

It took a little while to locate his uncle. Why he chose to seek out Calling Elk instead of merely the first adult he saw, he could not have explained. Maybe it was only because the news that he had to report was so bizarre. . . . He could depend on Calling Elk to understand *anything,* because of their secret shared heritage.

Bear spotted his uncle with some other young husbands, lounging and smoking in the warm spring sun. He managed to attract Elk's glance and motioned to him. Elk casually rose and sauntered over.

"Uncle!" Bear began eagerly, though quietly. "There is something strange to the west."

"A storm?"

"No, no, not weather. Some strange creatures. Come and see! Bring your bow!"

Calling Elk, at first amused, quickly realized that the young man was dead serious, and quite concerned. Still, there was no point in alarming everyone until more was known. He paused to pick up his bow and a quiver of arrows, and rejoined his nephew.

"Now, where are these creatures, Bear?"

"The others . . . Lean Dog and Gray Fox are watching them. I drew the short stick. . . . Never mind. Come! You will see."

Bear loped away at an easy jog, his uncle close behind. There could be no conversation for now.

They arrived at the rise and found the two lying flat, watching with fascination as the three distant figures approached. They could be seen much more clearly now, but still at some distance.

"One is clearly a big dog," Fox explained. "It carries a pack tied to its back."

"It is not a dog," argued Lean Dog. "No one has ever seen a dog that big. It must be as big as an elk."

"It *is* a dog!" Fox exclaimed positively. "No other animal carries a burden for men."

"Let us not argue," Elk suggested. "Now, what about the other two?"

"That is even more strange," said Lean Dog. "We thought at first that they were animals like the other, but with the upper body of a man. Now, we think that . . ."

"They *are* like the other, the elk-dog!" Gray Fox interrupted. "And people ride upon them."

"Yes," agreed Dog. "It appears so. But would not such a creature be dangerous? It would be like the biggest wolf ever seen. Or like a bear."

Calling Elk was studying the distant figures carefully.

"The one is surely a pack animal," he agreed.

"It walks not quite like a dog. Some new creatures . . . But is it not like the others, except for the burden?"

"It seems so," agreed Gray Fox.

"The colors are different," observed Bear.

"Yes, all three," said Lean Dog. "The one carrying the pack is gray, and one black and one almost yellow."

"Dogs come in all colors," insisted Gray Fox.

"They *ride* upon them!" Calling Elk mused. "I never saw anyone ride an animal, except for the time Badger fell on a buffalo calf and it carried him a little way. But this . . . Wait! Is that not the trader who visits us . . . ? And his wife!"

Calling Elk now rose and waved to the approaching figures, who altered their course as they neared the waiting young men.

"Welcome, Trader!" he called. "What is *this?*"

The Lakotas drew back cautiously, trying not to show the uneasy dread of the big animals.

"Greetings! Calling Elk, is it not? Do not fear our 'god-dogs' here. They are harmless."

"Wh . . . What *are* they?" gasped Gray Fox.

"What you see," laughed the trader. "A dog as big as an elk, and wearing a turtle on each foot."

Now one of the creatures tossed its head and shook itself, and the young men jumped back in alarm. Then it lowered its head and began to crop the new grass along the ground.

"*Aiee!*" said Stumbling Bear. "It eats grass, not meat?"

"Of course," answered the trader. "Is this not a wonderful creature? Look . . . Three of them carry me, my wife, and all of our trade goods. We travel faster, we can do more trading. Where is your camp?"

"Over there," Elk pointed. "But . . . Where did these animals come from?"

The trader shrugged. "We bought these from the Shoshone. Others in the west have them. They reproduce well."

"But . . . The *first* ones?"

"I do not know. There are stories of strangers who came, riding them. People with shiny metal garments, from far away. Some said they had knives made of the shiny metal, too, but they are probably lying."

"And what are these called?"

"Different names by different people, Elk . . . 'god-dog,' 'wonderful dog,' 'elk-dog.' There is a word, said to be used by the metal people for this creature: *cab-eye-yo*. Some call it that."

"Can it run?" asked Lean Dog.

"Oh, yes!" said the trader. "Like a deer, almost!"

"Would not the rider fall off?"

"Sometimes. But I will show you, later. How it runs, everything."

The next few days were spent in trading, exchanging stories, and watching the wonderful elk-dogs. It was not long until even the children were touching and petting the animals. Trader put his black through its paces. . . . Walk, trot, canter, and a wide-open run, while the people gasped in amazement at his control.

"Could this not be used in the hunt, or in war?" asked one of the band's leaders.

"Of course!" answered the trader. "There have been such fights, already."

"I was thinking more of the hunt," said the chieftain. "It seems to run as fast as a buffalo."

The trader nodded. "So it does."

"Then . . . Could one not ride up alongside a running buffalo and kill it with a spear or an arrow?"

"Of course. Some have done it."

"It is good. Where can we get some?"

.21

In a few days, the trader and his wife were gone, and the excitement of the new elk-dog creatures subsided to a degree. Yet they had made a great impression. It was apparent immediately how much easier it was to travel with elk-dogs to ride. And, the burdens that had been carried before on the backs of Trader and his wife were now carried easily on the gray elk-dog, while they rode the other animals.

There had been considerable discussion along the lines of procurement. . . . *Where can we get some of these?* Trader was encouraging, but not very specific. Many people possessed some, among those to the far west, he said.

"Some are experts at hunting with them," he explained in more detail.

He demonstrated how one might use a long spear in the right hand and under the arm, approaching a fleeing buffalo from the left rear.

"I have seen it done," he said, "but I doubt that I could do it. All the young men are learning, among those who have these animals."

"Could they be used to hunt elk?" someone asked. "Other animals?"

The trader was thoughtful for a moment.

"I am made to think not. I have seen them used only on buffalo. Let us think on this. Antelope run too fast, maybe. Elk . . . I don't know. . . . They have an inclination to run into rough country. . . . Rocks and trees. Buffalo run into open prairie, no? In a straight line . . ."

"That is true," agreed one of the older men. "But tell us, Trader. . . . If we were to try to get some of these elk-dogs. Could we trade for them? What would be something the people there need?"

The visitor glanced up sharply, a look of resentment and suspicion on his face.

"No, no, we would not want to *become* traders," the other man protested.

Trader smiled. "I understand. . . . You want one trade, for some elk-dogs. I do not want to become a dealer in elk-dogs, only to use three or four to carry our packs and ourselves. It is no problem."

"But, what would they want in trade?"

"Let me think," mused the trader. "You could steal a few of their elk-dogs," he suggested. "Some tribes have so many that they would hardly be missed. They steal from each other, like a game. Like war, but with fewer injuries."

Everyone laughed.

"But, Trader, then we would be in strange country, with animals we do not know how to handle, and maybe pursued!"

"That is true," the trader agreed. "Maybe it would be better to trade."

"So . . . What would they want?"

"Well . . . Let me . . . *Aiee,* I have never traded for elk-dogs, except these!"

More general laughter . . .

"I gave some furs, a bow case with quillwork, a few robes. . . ."

"Buffalo robes, maybe?"

"Of course . . . Wait, though! They kill buffalo now, more easily than before. More easily than you do, without elk-dogs. *Aiee,* we come around again! You need elk-dogs to catch buffalo to tan robes to trade for elk-dogs!"

There was laughter, but not much.

"We cannot trade for elk-dogs until we already have some? But then we would not need them!"

"Yes . . ." The trader seemed lost in thought. "Something you have . . ."

Suddenly he brightened. "Bear!"

"They use elk-dogs to hunt bear?" someone asked.

"No, no! The elk-dogs greatly fear bears. You hunt bear. *You* have many bears, and you hunt them with more skill. Trade bearskins for the elk-dogs!"

Stumbling Bear felt his stomach tighten. It appeared that the hunters of this band would now set out on a bear hunt. Usually, unless someone felt a need to prove his bravery, a bear kill was mostly a matter of opportunity. It had been fairly easy for Bear's uncle, Calling Elk, to avoid the confrontation of the Prairie People's sacred taboo. Also for Stumbling Bear himself, at least so far. But now, with the men eager to harvest bearskins to trade for elk-dogs, there might be pressure to participate. This was leading to a great deal of uneasiness on his part.

After the departure of the trader with his wife and his elk-dogs, an argument arose. One faction among the hunters and warriors wanted to initiate a great bear hunt immediately. They would obtain bearskins, trade for elk-dogs, and hunt buffalo from the backs of running animals this very season. Fortunately, cooler heads of older men, backed by the women of the band, raised some questions.

"We need meat, now!" one old woman complained.

"You can eat bear meat, Grandmother," laughed a young man.

"It is not enough! We need a spring hunt for buffalo, to start the season."

"That is true," agreed an elderly warrior. "We must first hunt buffalo for the season's food. Then, think about this new animal. It may be, too, that it takes a little time to learn to ride and hunt from the backs of these wonderful dogs."

So after much discussion, it was decided. The band would move toward the area of the buffalo jump, hunting as able en route, and would try for a large kill at the jump. Meanwhile, as opportunity offered, they would gather a few bearskins if they were able.

Stumbling Bear was able to relax, at least for now. . . .

It was a summer of many changes, one he would long remember. All in one season, Stumbling Bear was to face the rituals of manhood, both public and private. He had learned of the elk-dog, which would create many new ways among the hunters of the plains. It would also mark his first participation in the great kill at a buffalo jump.

For many generations, the "jump" had been used to hunt the buffalo. Each year the great herds came through on their annual migration, following the northward progression of the greening of the grass.

No one knew how the first jump had taken place, maybe by accident, many lifetimes ago. It was possible to go up or down the steep face of the hill on either side of the jump. Difficult, but possible. There were several paths, and a person or an animal in no particular hurry could easily ascend or descend. The same person or animal, trying to hurry, might easily stumble and fall, rolling helplessly downhill through jagged rocks and boulders. Some ancestor of long ago may have seen this, and contrived to hurry the descent of a small herd of buffalo. Those behind would push ahead, knocking others off balance and starting the destruction.

Between the two shoulders of the bluff was the cliff itself, a sheer drop of ten times the height of a man and some fifty paces wide. A natural outcropping of rimrock slanted away from the edge on one side. On the other, generations of hunters had carried and placed stones to form another wing to the deceptive trap. People on foot, flapping robes and yelling, would move a few dozen or a few hundred animals toward the long V, designed to crowd a running herd into a compact mass. The animals behind would push the hapless leaders on over the edge to crash to their deaths below.

At the bottom of the jump would be the most athletic and the most skilled of the hunters. Some animals would survive the jump. The hunters must finish off the crippled survivors, many of which would be dangerously aggressive, though severely wounded. Bows, spears, even war clubs might be employed in the melee of dust and noise and danger. There was also a constant risk from animals that had managed to descend by the twisted paths to each side. It was a time of danger but of great excitement and celebration, for there would be food in plenty.

This carefully orchestrated hunt had been effective for many lifetimes. . . . As long as anyone could remember, and before that. It worked, because of the herd instinct, the tradition of strength in numbers. There was another factor, too. *Pte,* the buffalo, sees poorly at a distance, but his senses of smell and hearing are acute. He would not see the jump ahead until too late, but would smell and hear the danger and would follow the herd.

The three friends were to be permitted, this year, to be drivers, those who pushed the herd toward the jump. They had participated before, hiding behind the rocks of the wings, to jump out and urge the stragglers on as they passed. That was exciting and dangerous, but this time, even more so. They would be out in the open, learning to move the herd without excitement until the time came to excite. They would be supervised and instructed by Thinks Like A Buffalo, or Buffalo Thinker, who had organized many jumps.

"It is important," Thinker explained to this year's drivers, "*not* to alarm them. Get them to move, without bothering them enough to think about it. We want *Pte* to think only that something is annoy-ing. . . . *Maybe I will move over there.* . . . Now, the wind is good. We have only a little breeze, and it will carry our smell to *Pte,* who will think: *Aiee! Those are a nuisance, but they cannot run very fast*

on only two legs. I will walk downwind, to keep track of their smell.
We must get inside his head, you see, think as he does.

"Now, some of you have done this before. New ones . . . Fox,
Lean Dog, Stumbling Bear . . . Watch the others. Watch *me*. Do not
let a robe flap until I give the signal. And do not yell until I do.
Then, yell as loud as you can. Keep yelling, keep flapping your robe.
Are we ready?"

They nodded, and the party moved out. They sky was graying,
just beginning to turn yellow in the east to herald the day. The camp
was some distance from the prairie where the buffalo grazed. The
scouts had reported great numbers to the south of the jump. The
drivers' task would be to split off a few hundred and maneuver them
in the proper direction. The hunters and those in the rocky wings of
the trap would also be moving into position. They must be
completely hidden before the drive approached.

Buffalo were scattered as far as the eye could see as dawn broke.
A few were lying down, some stood calmly chewing their cuds, and
hundreds more grazed eagerly on the bright new grass.

Buffalo Thinker studied the setting.

"Now," he said quietly, "you see, along a line from here to that
little rise to the west . . . Not many buffalo . . . We will walk
between, divide them there. Make that line *our* line . . . Then turn
and all start toward the jump . . . *Slowly*. We wait until the ones we
cut out are all moving in the same direction toward the rocks. *Then* I
will signal."

The others nodded, and Buffalo Thinker moved toward the herd,
walking slowly. The others followed a few paces apart, and single
file. Thinker threaded his way, avoiding a resting animal here and
there. Sometimes one would stand to stare inquisitively or snort and
run a few paces. *Do not break stride. . . . Keep moving,* the leader
had admonished. To *change* pace would be a cause for alarm.

A calf, hidden in a low spot, leaped to its feet with a bleat of alarm
as Stumbling Bear passed. It stood for a moment, then ran to and
fro, searching frantically for its mother, calling out again. Bear

glanced around, aware that . . . *Aiee!* A low warning grunt from behind him, and the thump of hooves at a trot. He remembered the admonition of Buffalo Thinker: *Do not put yourself between a calf and its mother. Keep the calf between you.* A quick glance . . . If he continued without breaking stride, another few steps would take him from between the two. The cow could approach her calf, or vice versa. The cow would surely see this, too, unless he confused her by changing pace. He dared not run. . . .

One step, another . . . How slowly he seemed to move. . . . His palms were wet with cold sweat as he gripped his robe and his short spear. He must not try to defend himself, for fear of destroying the entire hunt. The cow took another threatening step. . . . He had decided that if she came for him, he would fall as flat as he could, lie still, and try not to cry out. But now the calf suddenly ran past him, approached its mother, and began to nurse eagerly. The cow quieted.

Bear breathed a sigh of relief and continued his slow walk. Buffalo Thinker had now reached the little hillock and turned to survey his drivers. With a slow arm signal, he motioned for the line to turn and begin to move the divided herd toward the jump.

22

Buffalo began to lumber to their feet and move away from the approaching line. The scent of humans on the light breeze behind the line was of help now. Standing animals ceased grazing to stare upwind. Then they would turn, not yet alarmed, to amble downwind, away from the unfamiliar smell. Those that had not yet caught the scent moved also, driven by instinct. . . . *The herd is moving. . . . This direction . . . I must move, too. . . .*

Now Buffalo Thinker began to wave his robe gently. The animals near him moved faster. This was also a signal to the other hunters, who started to flap their robes too. In the space of a few heartbeats, hundreds of shiny black hooves were pounding the earth in a mad dash away from the strange two-legged creatures. Thinker now began to yell, a full-throated deep cry, and the other hunters joined in. Panic raced through the stampeding herd.

The leaders were now inside the rocky wings of the trap, and a few animals attempted to break out between the boulders. But here, they encountered more of the noisy, smelly, two-legged creatures, who flapped robes and screamed. . . .

The first of the leaders, a wily old cow, saw the danger and whirled back from the edge. But she was only to meet the crush of the oncoming horde, a solid wall of heads, horns, and shaggy bodies. Others tried to turn, only to be forced relentlessly back toward the drop. Animals stumbled and, sometimes injured, rose again to escape the threatening crush of the new danger: their own kind, crazy with fear. But now they were falling from the cliff, pushed to death by ones and twos and then tens and twenties. Dust rose from below as hunters rushed in to finish the kill on any survivors. There was a great danger in this, even, because shaggy bodies were still falling from above.

The drivers approached the trap, and Buffalo Thinker called them back.

"It is enough! Let the rest go!"

Most of the entrapped animals had either escaped or had fallen from the jump. Those remaining now made a successful break for open prairie. Stumbling Bear trotted to the rimrock outcropping, where people were beginning to move toward the cliff to see how successful the hunt had been.

"*Aiee*, did you see, Bear?" called Gray Fox. "I am made to think that we did well."

"Yes," agreed Buffalo Thinker, who happened to pass. "Some of you took too many risks!"

But his scolding was not too severe. Lean Dog joined the other two, and they hurried toward the jump's rim.

"Did you see that bull that turned back?" Dog asked the others. "I thought I was dead! He charged the robe I was carrying, instead of my body. *Aiee,* he brushed so close. . . . Nearly stepped on my toes!"

A cloud of gray-yellow dust was boiling up the face of the cliff from the melee below. There were shouts and bellowing and the sound of what must have been the blows of stone axes on the skulls of animals still alive. They could see nothing through the solid cloud of mushrooming dust. It appeared almost solid. . . . So solid, in fact, that for a moment in this time of fantastic achievement, Bear felt that he could step out onto the surface of the dust cloud and walk upon it.

No sooner had that thought occurred, than he heard a drumming of hooves behind him, and someone called a warning. From the corner of his eye, he saw a yearling bull, separated from the herd. It was lost and confused, frantically bellowing for its companions in a frenzy of fear. Bear stepped aside, and the young bull, seeming not even to see him, ran toward the cliff. There, it paused for only a moment, staring at the roiling dirt ahead with inefficient eyesight for the current situation. A long leap . . . The bull's front legs were extended as if it expected to find solid footing on the dust cloud's surface. It disappeared more quickly and completely than if it had plunged into water. More smoothly, too. The surface remained undisturbed. From below came the sound of a massive impact, accompanied by yells of surprise. Some at the top of the jump laughed at the unusual happening.

It was only later that they learned of the death of Little Snake. He was one of the older hunters and a man highly respected for his courage and his skill. He had been among the fallen carcasses, making sure that there were no injured buffalo that might recover enough to be dangerous. Snake had been crushed by one last animal, dropping out of the sky through the dust cloud. This would be recorded in the band's winter count pictographs, painted on skins. . . . It was the year that Little Snake was killed at the jump by a falling buffalo.

Now, with a great kill of buffalo came the chores of skinning, butchering, and processing the meat. Everyone worked at the tasks, down to the smallest child, who could shoo flies and birds away from the racks of drying meat.

There was ample cause to hurry. The odor and stench of rotting carcasses would soon offend not only the senses but the quality of the food supply. The goal would be to salvage and move, as quickly as possible, every usable part of the buffalo. . . . Meat, skins, sinew, even bones, horns, and hooves. With such a successful kill, of course, it was possible to be more selective, using the best of the bounty first. Mainly, though, the job consisted of butchering and transporting meat and hides to the distant camp for drying and curing.

The first night they worked late, building fires to furnish light. The next day the skinning and butchering continued, while overhead, buzzards drew slow circles in the clean blue of the sky, and waited. . . . They and other scavengers would salvage what was left.

The People, tired but with full bellies, would recount the tales of olden times, when Man and other animals all spoke the same tongue. It was then that Coyote had agreed not to compete with Man in the hunt, but to take as his share that which was left. It has been so ever since. Coyote pauses in his own hunt for mice to watch Man's hunt and share the bounty if he can. Man sees his fellow hunter, and may wave a greeting at a distance to wish him *"Good hunting, Grandfather!"*

By the second evening the jump was abandoned to Coyote and others of his profession. The night was filled with the distant song of the gathering scavengers. . . . Yelps, barks, chuckling yodels . . . Once, the howl of the great gray wolf who circles the herds to pull down the weak and crippled. He, too, would share this kill.

The work continued. . . . Drying and smoking meat, dressing and tanning skins, and later, pounding dry strips of meat to mix with berries, nuts, and melted tallow to make pemmican. This nutritious staple food was stored in casings made of the small intestines of the buffalo.

In a few days, the work was accomplished. Never finished, of course . . . Only the urgent part, which must be done immediately while meat and skins are fresh. The women would be making garments and lodge-skins for many moons from this glorious kill.

They moved the camp, half a moon later. It was good to avoid the area of a jump except when the hunt was expected or imminent. The jump was over for the season. . . . Well, maybe a fall hunt, but it was not yet time to decide. When the time comes . . .

A more urgent concern was that of the proposed hunt for bear. There was an area known for its bear population, usually avoided except for individuals fulfilling a vow or attempting to prove manhood. Now the goal was different. *Seek* bears, kill bears for skins with which to trade for horses.

Stumbling Bear was troubled. His secret heritage forbade the killing of bears, yet how could he avoid the responsibility of the coming hunt? He sought out Calling Elk.

"Could one ever choose to kill Bear for a greater good?" he asked his uncle.

"Surely!" Elk answered quickly, much to the surprise of Stumbling Bear. "It is your choice. Of course, you die."

"By the bear?"

"Maybe . . . Maybe some other way. An accident . . . Lightning . . . Sickness. But one way or another, you die."

"Then it is not a choice," protested his nephew.

"Oh, yes," insisted Elk. "It is simple. Some things are important enough to die for. All we have to do is to decide which ones are that important."

"But . . . If we are dead, we cannot carry out the purpose. . . . *Aiee*, Uncle, it makes my head hurt!"

"Mine, too," chuckled Calling Elk. "No one said that the responsibility of this secret would be easy."

The friends of Stumbling Bear, unburdened with such secret agendas, lost no time in boasting about how many bears they hoped to kill.

"Do you suppose," asked Lean Dog mischievously, "that the skin of the big bear-that-walks-like-a-man is more valuable than that of the black bear?"

"I never thought about it," mused Gray Fox. "I suppose so. It would be harder to get, and should be worth more in horses, maybe."

Stumbling Bear was quiet, uncomfortable with this conversation.

"Did you hear," asked Dog, "there was a man who killed a bear over at the jump, before we left?"

"Really?" asked Stumbling Bear.

"I heard of that," said Gray Fox. "Little Hawk, his name. He went back to see if he could find a knife he had lost, and there were bears there."

Fox went on with more details, but the mind of Stumbling Bear was far away, lost in his own thoughts. How could he fulfill his duty to his mother's heritage, and still take part in the coming effort to acquire horses? Other questions rose in his mind. . . . If he assisted in a group hunt, but did not take part in the actual kill, what penalty would accrue? Even Calling Elk was unsure.

"I am made to think," he pondered, "that it is how you feel in your heart. But, I don't know, Bear. Maybe . . . If we are really a *help* to someone who is to do the kill, we would have a problem."

"Then, if what we do gets in the way, helps prevent a kill . . ."

"Ah, that is another problem," said Elk. "If we *interfere* with the hunt, and cause it to fail, we are disloyal to that side of ourselves. If someone was killed because of our actions . . . *Aiee!*"

"And," Stumbling Bear answered thoughtfully, "if we do not help with this bear hunt, it slows the trading for the horses."

"It seems so."

"Uncle," said Bear suddenly, "we had spoken once of a vision-quest, like that of your people. . . . My mother's . . . *Ours.*"

"Yes . . . To go out alone, to fast and pray. But what . . . ?"

"If I were on such a quest, when a bear hunt took place . . ."

"Ah! I see. You could not go on the hunt because you are not in the camp. Yes!"

"Would it be proper to take such a quest?"

"Oh, yes. You have been made to think that you should go on a private quest, to fast and pray. You do not need a reason, only that you have been called to do so. *Aiee,* why did I not think of this?"

"I had not asked, Uncle. . . . What will *you* do when they hunt bears?"

"Nothing . . . I will stay behind. I have proven myself already, so my bravery is not in question. Oh, there will be my friends who will tease me about it, but they will only be joking. But you . . . You have yet to prove yourself, to gain respect and become a man. And this may do it. . . . A private hunt, alone, which is really a vision-quest . . . Yes!"

23

Before Stumbling Bear could complete his plans for a private vision-quest, there was a distraction. The band, some thirty lodges, had moved into an area noted for its bears. In a day or two they had settled in, and the scouts were gathering information.

Yes, there were bears. Elk, too, which was good. Fresh meat is always welcome, and dried meat and pemmican can be stored against future need. But the primary quarry of the hunters would be bear, both for meat and for the fur. There was a discussion in the council as to the quality of the fur. Winter furs, such as otter and mink, were far more desirable than those of the same creatures in summer. It was supposed that this, too, would be true of bear. But the bear sleeps through the winter. They would be not only hard to find but very dangerous when aroused.

"We should not wait a whole winter to try to trade for some horses," insisted Owl Dung, one of the more aggressive of the younger hunters.

Owl's opinions were respected in spite of his youth. His actions and accomplishments had made it apparent that he was a rising leader.

After lengthy discussion, a general agreement was formed by the council as to how the bear hunts would be carried out. Three or four hunters, for mutual protection . . . There seemed no need for more. It was generally agreed that to hunt alone in bear country would be foolish, and that there should be at least two for safety. This was not a ruling by the council, but a strong suggestion.

If a few bearskins could be collected, a party would head to the west to see if trading would be practical. . . . A trial run . . . The party would take some other items, too, a few furs and some examples of the fine quillwork done by the women of the band. It would be a small party, chosen by the most successful of the bear hunters. Two or three men, who might take their wives along. But first, of course, was to kill the bears.

"Let us go out on a bear hunt, we three," suggested Lean Dog. "We have as good a chance as anyone. It is a fitting way to prove our manhood. Maybe, even, we will be permitted to go to trade."

Gray Fox laughed. "Do you know how to tan a bearskin, Dog?"

"What do you mean?"

"Someone was talking about it today. The first step . . . Catch your bear."

"That is what I said," replied Lean Dog irritably, as the others chuckled.

"But it might not be easy."

"Of course. I never said . . ."

"I don't know," Stumbling Bear put in. "I am made to think that we should go with more experienced hunters at first."

"You are afraid!" accused Dog.

Stumbling Bear flushed in anger.

"I . . ."

"You know that's not true," said Gray Fox. "Our friend Bear has as much courage as anybody we know."

"Then why . . . ?" Dog began, but Stumbling Bear interrupted.

"It is only good sense to go with men of experience first. Besides, I may have something else to do."

"What do you mean 'something else,' Bear?" asked Gray Fox.

"I don't know yet. I must talk to Calling Elk, my mother's brother."

"Oh . . . You will hunt with Elk?" asked Gray Fox.

"Maybe. It has not been decided yet. That is all."

"See, Dog? There *is* a reason. Now, let him alone."

Stumbling Bear sought out his uncle, and the two made their way out of the camp a little distance. Bear related his tale as they walked.

"What did you tell them?" Elk asked.

"That I must talk with you."

"*Aiee!*"

"What will *you* do?" asked Bear.

"I don't know. . . . But I am not under as much pressure as you. Let us think about this. We could go on a hunt together, maybe," mused Elk.

"Just two of us?"

"Well . . . The council suggests three or four, for safety. And, we would have to report failure. . . ."

"Elk . . . What if I chose to take a vision-quest instead? The fast, the lone vigil of our grandmother's people?"

"Maybe . . ."

"You have told me that you took the Lakota ceremony, no?"

"True. You *could* do both. The private quest now."

"Would it be wrong, to use it to avoid the bear hunt?"

"I do not see how."

"What must I do?"

"Go out alone. . . . Pray and fast. . . . No food, only a little water. You have fasted before?"

"Not intentionally," Bear grinned. "I have been hungry."

Elk nodded, chuckling. "It is the same, for better purpose. There are pangs of hunger for a day or two. Then, at about the third day, the senses clear. . . . You will see and hear like never before. Then, come visions."

"As dreams?"

"Maybe. It is like being in a dream, yet knowing it is a dream, watching it at the same time."

"But . . . Is it asleep or awake?"

Elk shrugged. "Who knows? Either . . . Or both, or in between. Bear, it cannot be described, because it is like *nothing* else.

"You felt this when you took your vision-quest at the Sun Dance?"

"Yes . . . But I am made to think it is all the same. Fasting and prayer, to bring the spirit closer to the spirit-world. *How* is not so important to the spirits, or to the Great Father, who is known by different names to different peoples."

"And the quest will help me find my spirit-guide?"

"Maybe . . . Maybe not. That is its purpose. One purpose, anyway. It is not always successful. Maybe you are not ready yet. Maybe you do not *recognize* your guide. But why think of these things? Maybe you *will* be successful. *Probably.* At worst, you can try again."

"Try again?"

"Of course. A person never learns *all* about the spirit-world. Until he crosses over, of course. We would hope for *that* to be later."

"Then . . . How about this, Uncle? My friends are urging me to go on a bear hunt. . . ."

"Ah! Lean Dog, no?"

"Yes, that one."

"I thought so. A good man, that Lean Dog, but his judgment . . . Not grown up yet, maybe. Be careful. . . . Make sure his ideas are what *you* think is good."

"But I would not go, Uncle. I can say *no, I am led to seek a private vision.*"

"Good!" exclaimed Elk. "No one can even question such a decision. When will you go?"

Bear thought for a moment.

"Soon, I think. I should tell my mother the whole story?"

"Yes . . . She will be proud, Bear. . . ."

His mother was pleased, of course, that her son would undertake a tradition from the family of her people.

"My heart is good for this, Bear," she told him.

He could see the excitement in her eyes.

"You have spoken with Calling Elk?" she asked.

"Yes, Mother. Elk, too, feels that this is good. But . . . What of my father?"

"Do not worry. I will tell him. It is not unusual. . . . A young man plans a quest with the help of his teacher. . . . A private search for his spirit-guide . . . Your father will understand. He, too, will be proud of his son."

There was very little preparation to be made, and few belongings to carry. . . . His bow and arrows, fire-making sticks, a knife, a water-skin, a warm robe to sleep in, against the chill of night. Even in summer, nights are cool on the high prairie.

Bear told his friends about his adventure. Not much, of course. They were puzzled.

"But why, Bear? We are nearly ready to take part in the bear hunts."

"I . . . I cannot explain it, Fox. I am made to think that this is something I must do."

"You have had a vision? A dream that tells you?" asked Lean Dog.

"Yes, something like that. I have talked with my teacher, Calling Elk, and decided that this is something I must do."

"Your uncle should know," agreed Gray Fox. "He is greatly respected."

"Yes. I cannot tell you more. It is something I am called to do."

"How long will you be gone?" asked Lean Dog.

Stumbling Bear had not thought of that. It was not appropriate anyway. When will an event occur? *When it is time.*

"I don't know. When my quest is answered. I will see you then."

"And you will tell us of your experiences?" Lean Dog asked.

"Of course not!" snorted Gray Fox indignantly. "One does not share such things about his medicine quest."

"Maybe part of it," Stumbling Bear agreed. "I don't know, now. Maybe I will when I come back."

Bear and Calling Elk had devised a sketchy plan, so that Elk would have a general idea of his whereabouts. A day's journey to the northwest . . . That was mostly because it was not hunted frequently by this band. There is something exciting and inspiring about new territory, which might enhance his experience.

He started in the morning, well fed for the journey by his mother. He carried no food. His fast would begin as he traveled.

Twice he stopped for a short rest, on the advice of his uncle. Once he sipped a little water from the waterskin. On the second stop, he found a clear cold spring, drank deeply, and refilled the skin.

In the afternoon, he began to look ahead for an area in which to camp. He could see a blue range of hills in the distance, but he realized that they were more than a day's travel ahead. Nearer, however, he could see that there were scattered pines and rocky slopes. He wanted a place for a camp, one that would afford a high hill or promontory of some sort from which to see into the distance.

He located a tawny-pink intercropping that formed a bluff perhaps ten times the height of a man. Its face looked toward the south. From its height, he could see both east and west to perform the ceremonies that would attend the rising and setting of the sun.

As he made his way up the shoulder of the bluff, he began to gather fuel for his fire. There was plenty of dead wood from the scattered pines. This was reassuring. If the area was well-traveled, people would have used such fuel before now. The narrow game trail topped out on a flat area a bowshot across, and Bear paused to catch his breath. The view was magnificent, from the sparsely wooded hills below and to the west, to the rolling plain south and east. Here, he would camp.

A few steps away, in a little hollow, he selected the place for his fire. A little caution, maybe . . . A fire on this rim could be seen from a day's travel away. It would be only prudent to shelter it from casual view. He readied his tinder and kindling, and took out the yucca sticks. The whirling spindle created smoke and brown powder, and before long, a glowing spark. He tossed the fire bow and sticks aside, and gently lifted the shredded cedar bark containing the precious spark. He breathed on it from beneath, watching it grow and finally burst into flame. This torch he shoved beneath the kindling sticks and watched the hungry flames grow. He added a few more, and began to sing. Not in the language of his Lakota heritage, but in the other, that of his mother's people. The Song for Fire . . .

From the pouch at his waist he took a pinch of sage and another of tobacco. Each, he tossed into the fire to honor the spirits of this place. *Here I intend to camp,* such a ritual announces. *I honor whatever spirits might live here, and ask your help in whatever lies before me.*

He rose and walked to the edge of the bluff to watch and appreciate the changing colors in the west as Sun Boy painted himself to cross beyond Earth's rim to the other side for the night.

24

The evening grew chilly, and Bear walked back to the fire to bring his robe. With its furry warmth around his shoulders, he sat again on the rim, watching the stars appear, one by one. From the corner of his eye, he sensed a change in something to his left. Nothing for alarm . . . A quiet change. He turned to find the blood-red rim of the rising moon emerging from the distant horizon. He had never seen it so beautiful. *Aiee,* a good omen!

Bear felt that he could see it move, creeping upward, brighter and more radiant as more of the moon's disk was revealed. Stars in that part of the sky began to dim under its glow. It was a time of magic. He had watched the moon rise before, but this was a special night, one in which something wondrous might happen. No, that was not quite it. . . . Not that it *might* happen, but that one could *expect* miracles. His heart raced with the excitement of it all.

Soon the entire glowing circle, perfect in its roundness, could be seen. The color was lighter now, a golden yellow instead of red. It was possible to see in its light, distant features of the landscape that had been hidden in purple darkness before. Timbered slopes, rocky hills, rough breaks and gullies . . .

The air was still, and he became aware of a change in the sounds of the night. A myriad of creatures raised their separate songs to greet the rising moon. Tiny insects chirped and twittered. An owl sounded its hollow cry from a tree below the bluff. A coyote called, another answered. As he had before, Bear wondered how one or two coyotes are able to pretend they are at least six or eight.

Another sound, from the far distance . . . A scream, like that of a woman in agony. It startled him for a moment, until he realized what it was, the hunting cry of the big long-tailed cat. It made the hairs stand at the back of his neck. He was aware that he was not a likely quarry for the great cat. The hunter was some distance away, and besides, his campfire and his human scent would discourage the approach of such predators. Still, there was no ancient covenant with the cougar, as there was with Coyote, and with Bear among his mother's people. Man *could* be fair game for the cat, and her eerie scream did little for his peace of mind.

He thought of seeking rest, curled in his robe by the fire, but rejected the idea. This was his great adventure, and sheer excitement would not allow sleep. He might miss something. . . .

His empty stomach rumbled a little in complaint, but that was expected. A small sip of water . . . Soon that part of the fast would be behind him, and then what wonders he would learn! Either way, there would be no sleep tonight. He replenished his fire and returned to his lookout on the bluff.

He settled back to watch the silvery moonlight on the distant landscape. The night-creatures continued their plaintive songs. He did not hear the great hunting cat again.

He knew that he would not, could not sleep, so it was with great surprise and not a little alarm that he awoke with the rising sun in his eyes. There was a moment of total confusion. What . . . ? How . . . ? Was this how a vision takes place? He looked around him, expecting to see some wondrous revelation. Instead there were only the familiar rocks and trees and plants, and the songs of small creatures.

Day-creatures, he noticed. Of course . . . A vision of daytime would include day-creatures and sounds. He was wakening slowly, though. Was this sunrise a part of his vision, or merely the dawn of the second day of his quest? Or was he totally within his own dream?

Bear shook his head to clear it, rose, and stepped back to his fire, now reduced to white ash. He stirred the fluffy ash to reveal a few tiny coals and raked them·together with a stick. To this he added dry pine leaves and grass, kneeling to breathe life back into the fire. A wisp of smoke . . . A little heavier, now a dense white plume . . . The little pile burst into flame, and he was quick to add small twigs. Then, larger sticks. It was a little while before he rose, satisfied, and went the few steps back to the lookout. There, he faced the east and lifted his voice in the Song for Morning. It seemed odd to him now that he had even questioned whether this might be his vision. A ridiculous assumption, far too presumptuous. No, he still had a hunger pang or two, a connection with reality, not with things of the spirit. He was disappointed, and a little bit embarrassed.

Bear spent that day watching, waiting. He gathered a little more fuel for his fire, and offered another pinch of tobacco and a little sage. It seemed only prudent to do so, since he sought the company and advice of spirits.

But, nothing happened. In contrast to the previous evening, when miracles seemed imminent, there was nothing unusual. He was disappointed, and spent some time in racking his brain for some error in his preparations or his ritual ceremonies or his songs.

Finally toward evening, it came to him. He must be trying too hard. He had been practically demanding that a vision appear. Elk had told him not to be impatient, *That is not how it happens.* One must *allow* it to take place. Bear felt foolish as he thought about it. He should have known. At least, he had not figured it out, the nature of his mistake. Humbled, he did the simple evening chores of the camp, and sang for the setting of the sun.

It was longer this evening, between the time that darkness fell and the rising of the moon. Hardly less spectacular, though. The perfect roundness of the glowing orb was only slightly flattened on one edge. He could still see plainly the figures in shadowy relief on its surface. A face ... A rabbit ... There were several stories he had heard. It could be anything one wished, maybe. Or, anything the spirits wished. Maybe it was like staring into the glowing heart of a campfire, where the shifting tones of light and shadow form pictures in the mind. ... Dreams, memories, hopes ...

He was practically hypnotized by such thoughts as he stared at the rising moon. An owl, the silent hunter of the night, soared softly across his field of vision, blotting out a patch of stars as it passed. Fascinated, he watched. Without changing course, the creature crossed directly across the face of the moon and out of sight into a cluster of pines below the bluff. *A good omen,* he thought. Was not Owl the messenger among his mother's people? Surely, *now* something would happen!

Yet, it was another night of disappointment. Despite Owl's ghostly appearance, and the lavish painting of the moonlight over the earth, there was little to satisfy his hunger for truth and knowledge. Certainly, no inspirational gift, no sudden understanding of the mysteries of life and of the Other Side. Again, he did not expect to sleep. This time it revolved more around discouragement than expectation. At last, he curled up in his robe by the fire and drifted off.

The coming of dawn on this, the third day of his quest, was as exciting as the two previous mornings had been dull. There was a feel of meaning, of understanding, a significance to the world and everything in it. His senses were sharp and clear, and now he recalled Calling Elk's description of the experience of fasting. After the initial hunger and protest of the belly in uncomfortable spasms, the experience is said to change.

This must be it. ... He could feel the difference, the acute sharpness of all his senses. He could see more clearly. He saw objects at a great distance, things not previously noticed. The air was clear, clean, and exhilarating. Colors were brilliant and varied, the sky a bluer blue than he had ever noticed. The ever-changing colors of light and shadow on the hills presented an entirely new concept, an understanding of how all of Creation must be. And, without limit . . . He wanted to soar with the eagle high overhead. . . . His spirit reached out. . . .

Then, in some strange way, he *was* soaring, in spirit, with the bird above him. He could *feel* it, the wind beneath his wings, the sensation of lofty flight. *I am inside Eagle's head,* he told himself with a mixture of triumph and awe. He detected a rabbit, crouching far beneath him, trembling in a clump of dry grass, terrified at the mere shadow of the bird above. But Rabbit did not know that Eagle was not seriously hunting. Eagle had already killed, had fed her young, and was now soaring mostly for the joy of doing so.

Stumbling Bear returned to the rim of his bluff, enchanted with this new experience. Not only sight and color, but the acuteness of all his senses was sharpened. The sights, sounds, colors, the scents of warm sun on pines, the sounds of the small creatures in the dry grass . . . Not just their voices, but the rustle of their movements as they went about their ways . . . The wash of fear that they felt as a potential predator passed.

He felt like shouting. . . . *This is it!* He felt that he was able to travel across space and across spirit, to enter the minds and souls of the creatures around him.

Even the whisper of the breeze in the pines spoke to him: *Good day to you, Uncle!* That was a surprise. As an adolescent, he had never been addressed by this term of respect, always reserved for an adult male. He looked around, but there was no mistake. *And to you,* he answered in a whisper. In the voice of his mind and spirit, maybe. He dared not destroy the magic of the moment by speaking aloud.

For some time he sat there, experimenting, conversing, trying to send his consciousness into the thoughts of other creatures. There was a small herd of buffalo in the distance, and he reached out to experience their thoughts. There, he encountered the calm but concerned spirits of the old cows, watchful, maternal, protective, a little anxious sometimes as their calves strayed too far. A low call would bring the youngsters back at a gallop. Theirs were scattered thoughts, of play and warm milk and sunshine on their backs and the wonder of a great new world. The mind of a massive herd bull on the far side of the group was largely concern for comfort; grass to fill the belly, the receptiveness of some heifers nearby, and jealous resentment of a couple of young bulls whose ambitions might rival his own status.

Around the perimeter of the herd there strolled or trotted three or four wolves. Their thoughts were those of the hunter. . . . Seek, select an easy victim. . . . Maybe a calf separated from its dam, though that could be risky. A clever old cow could be dangerous to one who only sought to fulfill the necessary functions of the hunt. A likelier meal might be a sick or crippled animal, left behind when the herd moved on. There . . . Was that a limp, or merely a misstep? Ah, one to watch . . .

It was a day that seemed to have no reference or relation to time. Not a sensation of *endless* time, Stumbling Bear realized, but of an existence untouched by even the concept. The passage of time held no meaning in this spirit-setting, a world without such limitations. A spirit could soar on forever. He grew tired and slept, wakened again. . . . Or did he only dream that he slept and wakened? At times he could imagine that he was high above, circling with eagles. He watched his own sleeping form below, and there seemed nothing unusual in the event, as if he had done this before.

Sometimes the world seemed dark, sometimes bright and sunny, and he was never sure afterward as to the meaning of that. Were days passing, or was he circling the world in spirit, seeing the dark and light sides from afar? It was hard to define, in this strange, exciting realm where time had no meaning anyway. . . .

25

The young man woke, blinking in the light of the rising sun. No matter what he had experienced, or for how long, there was a definite feeling that could not be denied. It was morning. A real morning on a real day. The rock shelf beneath him was hard and cool, and his body was stiff with the night's chill.

There was another sensation, though, which he met with mixed emotions. He knew instinctively that his quest was over. This thought met with some resistance, even denial. He did not want to accept it. *I have not even met my guide,* his thoughts protested. Close on the heels of that protest came the memory of Calling Elk's instruction. One might not find his spirit-guide, especially if he tried too hard.

Tired, hungry, disappointed, and frustrated, Stumbling Bear sat up. Was this all for nothing that he had spent the past few days in fasting and prayer? He did not even know how many days, now. Well, there *had* been that flight of the spirit, a wondrous experience. . . . He could recall the thrill of soaring in the person of the eagle, cowering with the frightened mouse in the dry grass, and conversing with the breeze as it whispered through the pines. All of those experiences must count for something, no?

He sipped a little water. . . . He had precious little left. He must refill his waterskin as he started back. It was time, too, to break his fast. He carried in the pouch at his waist a few strips of dried meat. Now, he took out a piece, broke off a small bite, and began to chew. His stomach, awakening from the absence of intake for the past few days, rumbled gently as the juices began to flow. There were a few moments of cramplike pain as the adjustment took place. The chew of meat in his mouth enlarged as it took on moisture and softened. He swallowed part of it, chewed the rest a bit longer, and swallowed again. Another small bite, as he gathered his few possessions for travel. Not too much . . . But he could eat as he walked.

He descended the shoulder of the bluff, and as he reached more level ground, he caught a glimpse of motion in a tree ahead. What . . . ? A magpie or a raven, maybe? Possibly just a squirrel, or even a porcupine. But, it would be only prudent to know. He stepped to the right to clear his line of vision, partially obscured by a small pine. Now, where had he seen the movement?

In a tree perhaps a stone's throw away, a dark furry face peered around the trunk of a tall pine. A bear cub . . . Fairly small, so one of this season's birth. He smiled at the serious yet comical stare. This cub had probably never seen a man. It was black, with lighter markings around the face. The thought crossed his mind that at this moment, other men of the band were engaged in a hunt for just such cubs, or for any other bear. *You have nothing to fear from me,* he launched the thought at the creature in the tree.

Just then, another movement, a little higher and on the other side of tree's bole. A second cub, apparently the litter mate of the black one . . . This, however, was of a different hue, a golden honey-colored fur of great beauty. *Aiee,* such a pelt would surely be much more valuable than the usual black. This idea flitted through his mind, even as a feeling of guilt assailed him for having even given birth to such a thought. *Forgive me, brother,* he whispered with a self-conscious smile.

These confusing thoughts and ideas were interrupted by a noise behind him, and he turned quickly. A huge black she-bear was lumbering down the boulder-strewn slope toward him in a very determined manner. It took him only a moment to realize the gravity of the situation. Without even realizing it, he had placed himself between the big sow and her cubs. It was a very dangerous place to be. He should, of course, run to one side or the other, to allow her access to the cubs, but it might be too late. *Any* motion, in any direction, might be interpreted as a need for attack. That event seemed likely, anyway. But, what of the covenant of his mother's people, binding them to Bear since Creation in an inescapable agreement? He had no idea how the covenant worked, or even how to invoke its power. He must do something, however, and quickly. The bear was only a few paces away now, and certainly seemed intent on her lumbering charge, directly at the spot where the young man stood. There was no time to nock an arrow, even if the taboo of the covenant had not prevented it.

Stumbling Bear stood, palms sweating and his heart beating wildly. No time to think, even . . . He raised a hand toward the charging animal, palm forward and upright, in the hand sign of greeting. *I hold no weapon! I mean no harm!*

The bear seemed confused, and paused in her rush. A low growl rumbled in her throat. Still terrified, the young man managed to stand fast. The animal was so near now that he could see the hair standing on end from her ears to her tail. She stopped, watching him closely, glancing past him for a moment at her cubs in the tree.

"Mother," he spoke softly, right hand still raised, "you do not know me, but your people and mine are bound by an agreement since Creation. I cannot harm you."

The great head swung back and forth, the nostrils dilated as the animal tried to catch a scent. There was an indecisiveness to her manner.

"I was called Stumbling Bear," he went on, "by my grandmother, whose people know you well."

A question came to him now, not in words but in thought: *But here? How?*

"Her people came from far away," he explained, "but some of us follow their ways. We are your brothers. We do not harm Bear people, you do not harm us."

Others of your people hunt us. . . .

"Of my father's people, yes. They do not know of the covenant."

He was still sweating profusely, still terrified, and somewhat puzzled at this dreamlike scene. Was he actually *talking* to an animal that a short while ago he had seemed about to kill him?

The stiffly erect back hair of the bear was flattening into place, and another thought-question was thrust toward him.

What do you seek here?

"I seek my vision-quest. It is different from that of my father's people."

It is good. . . .

A strange thing was happening now. Maybe it was the sweat of his brow, trickling into his eyes to blur his vision. For whatever reason, the outlines of the bear's figure seemed to waver, as heat waves distort the distance on a hot day. In a moment he felt that he could see the shimmering forms of trees and rocks beyond and *through* the image of the bear. Alarmed, he rubbed his eyes, but it did not help. Surely in a moment now he would awake and it would have been a dream. The bear was starting to turn away.

"Wait!" he called softly. "What . . . ?"

The animal looked back briefly. *You have been tested,* came the thought, as the animal turned away again.

"But . . . I . . . Do not leave me!" he pleaded. "You are my *guide?*"

Of course, came the almost whimsical thought-answer. *What did you expect?*

"What must I do?" he called frantically.

But the bear was gone. He turned to look at the cubs in the tree, but there was nothing. Merely the whispering breeze through the sparse branches of the tree where he had thought he saw bear cubs.

He turned to stare again at the place the bear had stood. Had he imagined it? There was no trace, no tracks. He walked among the trees, searching for something. He did not know what. It would help to have some reassurance, some solid evidence that yes, it *had* happened.

The bear had stood about here. . . . Next to a tree . . . A dark tuft caught his eye, a few coarse hairs snagged in the rough bark of a small pine. Maybe the bear had been rubbing there. He plucked the hairs loose and carefully placed theme in his pouch. At least he had not imagined the entire scene.

Stupid . . . Stupid! How could he have bungled it so badly? He asked himself. He sat on a boulder at the foot of the bluff, completely dejected. Three, maybe four days he had fasted and prayed and had tried his best to do as he must. Aside from the one thrilling time when he had experienced the ability to move freely in the spirit-world his entire vision-quest seemed a failure to him. Maybe, even, that one soaring feat had been only a dream. His biggest failure, though, was his mishandling of the meeting with the she-bear. His *guide!* And he had not even known it. Surely nothing good could happen in the life of one so stupid that he had failed to recognize the most important event of his vision-quest. *Aiee!*

How could he even rejoin the band at the summer camp? He could imagine the questions, the scorn that might be heaped on him. All his friends had known that he was on a special vision-quest, somewhat different than most. Now, on his return, they would be curious. It was a private subject, of course, but he would be expected to give some suggestion as to his success. Gray Fox and Lean Dog would probably be even more curious. And in spite of the fact that one need not reveal any of the details, it would be hard. Anyone with any perception could see by his attitude that his quest had failed. He might as well announce it to his friends and family, or even in the council: "I went on a vision-quest, and nothing happened. Then, I met my guide and did not recognize her. I am not worthy."

Finally he rose. For a little while he considered not returning to the camp but heading out alone. That seemed impractical. He had no food, no garments except those he wore. . . . His main reason for rejecting such a plan, though, was that it would hurt his family. It was better, he decided, that they know he was alive and a failure, than to have them wonder all their lives if he had lived or died. Yes, he owed it to them. He started back toward the summer camp, but his heart was very heavy.

"Tell me about it," requested Calling Elk. "It cannot be that bad."

Bear had sought out his uncle as he arrived in the camp just before dusk. A brief stop to tell his mother that he was back, and then on to find Elk. He had blurted out his disappointment, and Elk had suggested that they walk outside the scatter of lodges.

"Worse!" insisted the young man. "I had one vision, or maybe it was only a dream. I don't know. Nothing happened. My spirit only flew around and came back."

"Maybe this had meaning, though," suggested Elk. "I want to hear more of that dream, but go on, now. Your guide? You did not find him?"

"*Her*," corrected Stumbling Bear. "Oh, yes, I met and talked with her. Not in words . . . I mean, mine were words. The answers came back as thoughts. But I did not know . . . did not even recognize that this was my guide, Elk! *Aiee*, I am aptly named, the Bear-Who-Stumbles."

"Now wait!" insisted Calling Elk. "Let us consider, here. You had a dream or vision of the spirit, you met and talked to your guide. Still, you think this was not a good vision-quest?"

"I did not *know* it was my guide, Elk, until she was gone. I got no advice, no guidance. I do not even know what is expected of me."

"Tell me all that the guide said."

"Well, it was not in words."

"I understand. But when . . . ? How did you learn who it was?"

Stumbling Bear blurted out his whole disastrous meeting with the guide animal, and paused.

"But," said Elk, "she said you had been *tested?*"

"Something like that."

"Bear, if you had not *passed* the test, you would not have been *told* of it. You would never have known! And you asked if she was your guide?"

"Yes . . . I guess so. I said something like 'You are my guide?'"

"And then?" Elk pressed on. "The answer?"

"Well, something like 'What did you think?' But not in words, Elk. In a thought, somehow."

"Yes, I understand. *Aiee,* Bear, you *are* pretty stupid." He paused to chuckle. "But, maybe not. I am made to think that you have a very powerful guide."

26

Now a new dilemma arose. Should he make known his encounter with the spirit-bear, or let it remain a private thing, his personal medicine? Stumbling Bear and his uncle discussed it at great length.

"There is no need to tell anyone of your vision-quest and its outcome," Elk pointed out. "You cannot be criticized for saying nothing. Or even that you cannot tell of it."

"But my friends will wonder."

"Of course. But they have no right to ask."

"They will wonder why I do not hunt bears, Uncle."

"Ah, but that is a separate problem. You already . . . Wait! Let us think on this! Maybe . . . You could explain that you cannot kill bears because your guide is a bear, and you have taken a vow. . . . The closer to complete truth, the better. Ah, yes . . . This may be as it was meant to be. It lets you explain without revealing the more important, the secret part. I am made to think that this is good, nephew!"

"You think I would not be called a coward?"

"You are not a coward, Bear. You have taken a vision-quest, alone, in bear country. Your friends may tease you, and probably will. But they *are* your friends. They know your courage. You did well at the buffalo jump. And a man's connection with his spirit-guide is not to be questioned, anyway."

Bear was honored by these last comments from his uncle. A *man's* connection with his spirit-guide, Calling Elk had said. His teacher, confidant, sharer of the secret of their ancestry, had referred to him as a *man*. The heart of young Stumbling Bear soared. He considered changing his name. . . . Maybe *Singing* Bear . . . No, he decided against it. One such major change at a time . . . He did not even mention that thought to Calling Elk.

Together, they outlined the story to be told publicly.

"The simpler and the less detail the better," Elk advised. "How is this . . . ? You wished to honor the customs of your grandmother's people by a lone vision-quest. You had learned that it was their way. You can take another quest at the Sun Dance if you choose, but that is another matter. I think it would not be needed, unless you are called to do so."

"But when . . . ?"

"That can be set aside. Let me go on. . . . You fasted, prayed, and on the third day . . ."

"It may have been the fourth, Uncle."

"No matter. On that day, your guide came to you in the form of a she-bear. You talked, and you now know that for you, it is a taboo. . . . You must not hunt or eat bears. Ah, this is good, Bear. It is maybe for this purpose that your grandmother *named* you. Now, you need not explain, and no one can question! Tell them all about the fasting," Elk suggested. "What it felt like . . . But maybe, least is best: At any question, you can fall back on *I cannot tell you*. That must be respected. But there is good reason to tell that your guide came as a bear. That helps with the other problems. *Aiee*, it could not have been planned better. You do have a powerful guide, nephew."

It was not quite so easy with his friends. Gray Fox and Lean Dog wanted to hear every detail. They had always shared most of their inner thoughts, these three. The other two knew nothing of Bear's secret heritage, so that made it somewhat easier. He could evade specifics, though, by either of two methods: *I cannot remember,* or *Of that, I must not speak.* He suffered the expected good-natured teasing, and endured the account of the bear hunt in which the two had participated.

A group of men had surrounded a clump of trees where there was believed to be a bear or two. As they tightened the circle, it became apparent that at least two she-bears and some cubs were in the thicket. It was a dangerous situation, and one young man had been badly mauled by a yearling cub. His wife, who had accompanied the hunters, saw what was happening and ran to help him. She picked up the spear of her fallen spouse and rammed it from behind into the tender area under the tail of the beast. Squealing with pain, the bear retreated.

"You should have seen it, Bear," Lean Dog told his friend. "The girl saved her husband. He would surely have been killed. *Aiee,* I would not want to fight her!"

The young wife had quickly been described as the "One Who Speared the Bear's Rump." Within days, her previous name, Pretty Morning, was all but forgotten. She would proudly wear the new name, shortened to "Bear's Rump," for the rest of her life.

"Did you two make a kill?" Stumbling Bear asked his friends.

"Not a clean kill," Fox admitted. "You have to realize, Bear, there is a lot of confusion, much happening. It is like the buffalo jump. Who caused which kill? We both had arrows in one of the bears. It takes a lot to put down a bear!"

Bearskins were being accumulated, and a trading party was organizing. The successful hunters of bear, with their wives, had dressed and tanned the skins, with the fur intact. Buffalo skins, except for winter robes, were usually not tanned with the hair on. Smooth leather was much to be preferred for garments, moccasins, and lodge covers. In the case of bearskins, however, the fur was a matter of prestige.

By custom, the hunter who made the actual kill received the hide of any animal and first choice of meat. Those who also participated had a share of the meat. No food should be wasted, ever, so in this way the two friends of Stumbling Bear had obtained for their respective lodges a good supply of bear meat for drying.

"It is different from buffalo or elk, but good," Gray Fox explained. "You should try it."

"I cannot," admitted Bear. "A vow."

"Yes . . . I forgot. . . . Your family, no? Your name?"

"Partly," he agreed. This seemed to be going smoothly. . . . "Partly, my vision-quest. My guide came to me as a bear."

He had decided to be quite open about that. There would come a time, maybe, when he would want to ornament his shield with the image of a bear, perhaps carve a fetish. To establish this now might eliminate explanation later.

"Ah, yes," said Fox, nodding understanding. "It is good. You must have a powerful guide, Bear."

Fox sounded a little envious.

"Probably not," Bear responded, as he should. "There is nothing special about me. I do some songs, a little medicine. Nothing special."

This was as it should be, the denial of any special gifts. That, too, would help to establish his status as one who has specific restrictions involving his personal medicine.

As the days passed, preparations began for the trading expedition to the west to acquire horses. Those most eager and eligible to go were, of course, those with bear kills. Stumbling Bear naturally assumed that he would not be included, and gave it no more thought.

Those who would go, however, were becoming eager. It would be a great adventure, one that they could relate to their children's children around story fires for many winters to come. It was an important year, this one, the year in which they would acquire the new animal, the horse. There was little else to be talked of that summer. Who would go, how many, the selection of the leader of the party . . . There seemed little doubt about that. It would be Bull's Hump, a popular young hunter who had already established his reputation. He had been highly successful in killing bears, and represented an ideal figure of leadership. He was tall, handsome, and successful, and would make a good spokesman when they reached the country of the people with horses.

There would be a large party. Partly for safety, that of strength in numbers. It might be better, too, to bargain from a position of strength. There was also yet another fact. No one knew much about how many horses they would acquire. The trader and his wife had handled three animals easily, but little was known about them. One more large question pertained to the trading. No one had much of an idea how many horses they might expect to have when the trading was done. To some extent, they would be at the mercy of those with the horses, who would have a better idea of their value. But again, the horsemen would be less likely to try to cheat a large and powerful party.

A day had not yet been set for the departure of the trading party. Some were still tanning bearskins and making preparations for travel, when Stumbling Bear encountered his friend Lean Dog.

"Ah, Bear, how is it with you?"

"Good! I have not seen you lately."

"No, we have been busy with preparations for the trading party," said Dog smugly.

"You are going?" asked Bear in surprise.

"Yes. Both Gray Fox and I. You could probably go if you wish, Bear. Bull's Hump wants many men."

"No . . . I think not," chuckled Bear. "I have no bearskins except my own, that of Stumbling Bear. I do not want to trade that. Where is Fox today?"

"He is not feeling well. His stomach . . . The summer complaint, he said. Cramps . . . He will be better soon."

"When do you leave?" asked Bear.

"It has not been decided. You will hear. . . . Bear, my heart is heavy that you will not be with us on this trip. We three . . . *Aiee,* what good times we have had. . . ."

"And will have again, Dog. There will be other parties, for hunting or trading. Next time, maybe . . ."

A day or two later, Bear encountered Gray Fox, and they paused to talk a moment.

"Your stomach is better?" asked Bear.

He wished, a moment later, that he had not asked. A look of anguish came over the face of his friend. Now he noticed that Fox had lost weight. His eyes were sunken, and he walked partly bent at the waist, as if his stomach gave him constant pain. In addition, he moved with short and apparently painful steps, as an old person would.

Fox smiled, and even that seemed painful.

"The stomach, yes. I am eating better now."

He did not mention his crippled gait and apparently painful limbs. It was not the way of Gray Fox to complain. Bear did not want to embarrass him with further questions.

"When does the trading party leave?" he asked, to change the subject. "Lean Dog said you are both to go."

"I do not know," said Fox. "I do not know whether I can go. I would have to feel much better, Bear. This has been half a moon for me."

"That long, Fox? *Aiee!* This must be a different sickness."

"Maybe so . . . I am too tired to wonder. Some others have it too, you know."

"This summer stomach complaint?"

"Yes . . . But it is more than that, Bear. I don't know. . . . I have had the summer complaint. We all have. It has none of this pain in arms and legs. . . . Well . . . I must go and lie down. It is good to see you, my friend."

Fox turned and shuffled away, leaving Bear saddened and confused. What was going on?

In the next few days, he heard of several others who seemed to have this same illness. The entire family of Gray Fox . . . That of another lodge nearby. Here and there throughout the camp people fell ill. The day for the departure of the trading party had not yet been determined, because several of its principal members were sick.

"You are Stumbling Bear?"

"Yes . . ."

"I am called Bull's Hump. I would talk with you."

"Of course . . ."

Bear rose from the willow backrest where he had been sitting. He was surprised and a little confused. Was the leader of the trading party about to invite him to go with them?

"Let us walk," said Bull's Hump bluntly.

The two fell into step and made their way past the last of the scattered lodges, down to a big fallen cottonwood by the stream. Here, Bull's Hump motioned for them to sit. Bear settled on the silver-gray bole and waited anxiously. *What could the man want?*

"I am told," began the older man cautiously, "that yours is bear medicine."

"No, no, nothing special," protested Bear. "I sing some songs, give some tobacco, but . . ."

"Yes, yes," the other interrupted impatiently. "But you do not hunt or eat bears?"

"That is true. A family tradition."

"And your guide . . . ?"

"A bear," admitted the young man. "But that . . ."

Bull's Hump waved him down. "There are others who do not eat bear?"

"I . . . I suppose so."

Stumbling Bear was beginning to be irritated by all this. The man had no right to ask such personal questions. One's medicine is a private matter.

"What is this about?" he demanded.

Bull's Hump paused and his face fell. "Forgive me," he said. "I am trying to learn . . . You know that some of those who will go to trade for horses are sick?"

"Yes . . . One of my good friends, Gray Fox."

The other nodded. "It is strange. None but those who would go on the trading party are sick. They and their families. I am made to wonder. Is this trading trip bad medicine? What do you think?"

"*Aiee*, I am not a holy man, Uncle. I could not know."

"Then you know of no cause, no reason. . . . Do you know of anyone who would object to such trading?"

"Of course not. I have friends who will go. That is their concern, not mine."

The other nodded, still puzzled. "I do not know. . . . I wondered if there is bad medicine in the plan of trading for horses. You know of nothing, then?"

"Nothing. I would tell you, Uncle. My vow has nothing to do with horses."

Bull's Hump rose, with a dejected sigh. "Well . . . So be it!"

They made their way back toward the camp, each lost in his own thoughts. In the back of Stumbling Bear's mind, there was an uneasiness. There must be something not understood, here. Was it to do with bears or horses, or his own family's secret traditions? Maybe all of these, maybe none. He longed for better understanding, and his heart was heavy again.

27

Gray Fox died in agony, almost a moon later. There were three other deaths with what appeared to be the same sickness. In each case it had started with nausea, looseness of the bowels, and pain in the stomach.

But it did not pass quickly, like the usual summer complaint. The bowel and stomach symptoms improved with the usual treatments, but then the other ailment appeared quickly to replace it. The muscles of the body ached constantly, and with any motion the pain increased, gnawing, stabbing, and twisting with increased severity. The hapless victim hesitated to move, lest it worsen the agony. Even the muscle activity of breathing in and out brought further torture.

Some did survive, learning to live with the constant pain. There seemed to be no pattern to who would be affected, except that the malady appeared in some families and not in others. Oddly, babies and very small children, often the most vulnerable to illness, were completely spared.

The medicine men had no explanation. It was a new experience, maybe a curse or retribution for some action that had offended the spirits.

Someone suggested that possibly it was wrong to try to acquire the "elk-dogs."

"But we have not done so yet!" protested another. "Besides, the trader and his wife were not affected by having horses."

"As far as we know! They may be dead by now. And remember, *their* ways are not like ours. The horses may be right for them but not for us."

"Trader said that many tribes and nations are using these animals," insisted another man. "He would have known if anyone had trouble."

That was the general opinion, but the mystery remained.

"Have you felt any of the pains?" Lean Dog asked.

"No, none," answered Bear. "You?"

"No . . . I don't think so. There was a time, maybe half a moon ago. . . . A little stomach pain. I have a few aches, maybe."

"Did this start when Fox was sick?"

"Maybe . . . About that time."

"I wonder why Fox was sicker. . . ."

"That was while you were gone, Bear, wasn't it?"

"Yes. Fox told me about your bear kills, offered me dried bear meat. He seemed well then."

"You do not eat bear, do you?"

"No . . . A family custom, and my vow."

Dog nodded. "So you did not try Fox's dried meat." It was a statement, not a question.

"No. Did you?" asked Bear.

"Just a bite or two. Not very good, I thought. It seemed sandy. . . . I thought maybe the piece I tried had been dropped on the ground and not cleaned well."

"*Aiee!* That is not like Fox's family. Their lodge is clean. . . ."

"So I thought. Maybe Fox was doing his own bear meat, and was careless. *That* could be," Dog suggested.

"But again, not like Fox. And, what about the others who died?"

"What do you mean, Bear?"

"I don't know. . . . Was there something they all did, or did not do?"

"Oh . . ." Dog shook his head, and suddenly his eyes widened. "Bear . . . I . . . I am made to think that every one was a bear hunter. . . . Or, his family . . ."

One by one, they counted. Yes, in each case, death had struck the family of a bear hunter. The other cases, those who had sickened but survived, were also connected in some way to the bear hunts.

"Should we tell someone about this?" asked Lean Dog. "Maybe there is a curse. . . ."

"Let me talk to my uncle, Calling Elk," suggested Bear. "Elk is wise in such matters. Let us say nothing until then."

"Shall I come with you?"

"No, no. Elk might talk more freely to me. I will tell you what I learn."

Calling Elk was puzzled.

"Only the families of bear hunters?" he asked.

"It seems so, Uncle. Could it be that some of *our* family's vow . . . I mean, could my grandmother's taboo be transferred to others who do not have such a tradition?"

"*Aiee,* I think not, Bear. I am made to think that one must know about it for it to harm him. He must know that he breaks a taboo. But something else . . . Is there something about the flesh of bears that causes the sickness and also is the reason for the taboo among *our* people? And, not all bear eaters are sick, are they?"

"I guess not . . . No, there are some whose families are still healthy."

"So . . . ," Elk continued thoughtfully, "it must be that some, but not all bear meat is dangerous, no?"

"To *them* . . ."

"Yes, of course. Any bear meat would be wrong for our family."

"Elk, Bull's Hump questioned me. . . ."

"Yes, I knew. He is trying to find answers, too. A good man."

"Do you think the sickness is because of horses?" Bear asked. "Bull's Hump wondered, I think."

"I know. He talked to me, too. I do not see how the horses could be part of it. We have none. No, nephew, I am made to think that there is something about bear meat. Not *all* bear meat, but *some*. Some of it carries bad medicine and causes sickness. I do not know why."

The next time he saw Lean Dog, he was puzzled at his friend's attitude. Dog seemed to want to say something or to ask something, but hesitant to do so. Stumbling Bear had related his conversation with his uncle, but Lean Dog seemed to feel that the conversation was incomplete.

"What is it, Dog?" Bear finally blurted. "Something you want to say?"

"Well, I . . . Bear, I must ask: Is it possible that *your* medicine, that of the bear, is causing this sickness?"

Stumbling Bear was startled, hurt, and a little angry.

"Dog, I have no such medicine. . . . I told you . . ."

"Wait, wait!" interrupted Lean Dog. "I do not wish to offend you, my friend, but look. . . . You have found your guide, a *bear*. You have never eaten bear meat. . . ."

"Because of *family* tradition, Dog. It does not matter to me that *others* eat bear. That is nothing to me."

"But your medicine animal . . .'"

"That has nothing to do with it," Bear snapped. "Dog, I have no power, no medicine. If I did have, I could not use it to sicken others, even if I wanted to. That would probably be dangerous to me. And I would have no reason to want to hurt anyone, anyway. *Aiee*, how can you talk this way?"

Lean Dog was quiet for a moment, and then spoke softly.

"Stumbling Bear, you are my friend. What you have just said is true, all of it. I know this, because I know *you*, and know that your heart is good. But look. . . . If these questions have crossed my thoughts, they must have occurred to others, too."

Bear was startled. "Dog . . . Are you trying to tell me that there are some who think this sickness is *my* doing?"

"I am made to think so, Bear. No one has said so to me, but that may be because you are known as my friend."

"*Aiee!* You know better."

"Of course. But I thought you should know of this. What will you do?"

"I don't know. Talk to Calling Elk first, maybe. Sleep on it, try to decide. There may be nothing I *can* do."

Calling Elk was as surprised as Bear had been.

"Lean Dog fears that some will think our medicine vows about bears could accidentally affect others," Stumbling Bear explained.

"*He* thinks that?"

"No, no, Uncle. Dog understands. He is a good friend. And no, he does not know our whole story."

"Good. I am made to think it would not be wise for him to know more."

"I agree. But it was good of him to warn me, no?"

"Yes, very good! Now, let us consider. . . ."

Elk was lost in thought for a little while, and finally spoke again.

"You said that Bull's Hump questioned you."

"Yes, Uncle. But he did not seem to be accusing in his questions."

"Hmm . . . Bear, we must make sure that everyone knows we have no objection to *their* trading in bearskins or eating the flesh of bears."

"They should know that!"

"Of course. But do they? We must show that our hearts are right."

"How, Uncle?"

"By supporting the trading party. I will talk to Bull's Hump. We grew up together. He is only a little older than I. Yes . . . And you will go with me!"

Satisfied with his conclusion, Elk rose and started off in search of Bull's Hump. Stumbling Bear followed, still somewhat confused.

The pipe passed among the three for a few circuits, and finally Bull's Hump raised the question.

"You wished to talk?"

They were seated outside the camp for privacy, on the same fallen cottonwood where Bull's Hump had questioned Bear.

"Yes," replied Calling Elk. "It has been told to us, Uncle, that some may wonder about our vows not to hunt bears."

"But that is . . . ," began Hump.

Elk waved him down. "Let me go on. You had talked with my nephew, here, of these things."

"Yes, only to see if he knew any reason for the bear-meat vow, which I know that your family practices. A friend of your nephew had died. . . ."

"Forgive me, Uncle," Elk spoke respectfully. "It was not my purpose to question, but to offer our support for the trading party. Our vows about bears are private, but we accept the right of anyone else to hunt, kill, eat, or trade bears. We would not try to stop it. I am made to think that such trade is good. We *need* the elk-dog creatures, if others have them. I asked to talk with you to find how we can best be of help to you. It was not my purpose to question otherwise."

"Yes," Bull's Hump nodded thoughtfully. "That is good."

"How could we show that our hearts are right?" asked Elk.

"Well," mused Hump, "you could go with us."

"You would let us go?"

"Of course. You have said that you support such trade."

"But we have no bearskins, nothing to trade."

"You can find something. Other furs, well-sewn garments or moccasins . . . Whatever. We need your presence, not your trade goods."

"It is good!" exclaimed Elk. "My nephew, here, will have to have his parents' permission, but my sister, Stumbling Bear's mother, will cherish this opportunity for him."

"Ah! I thought so! It is good."

He started to rise.

"Wait!" said Calling Elk. "Is there any explanation yet for the sickness?"

Bull's Hump sat back down.

"Not a good one. It has something to do with the bear meat. If it is well cooked, there seems no problem. The dried strips are dangerous sometimes. And, maybe some bear meat is good, some bad. But no one has sickened who had not eaten dried bear meat, as far as I can learn."

"*Aiee,* that is strange!"

"Yes . . . One other thing. Several who had handled the drying meat said that it had an odd feeling. . . . Sandy or gritty."

"Dirt?"

"Maybe . . . But one woman whose husband died said that as she wrapped him for burial, *his* flesh felt sandy to her, through the skin."

"She could tell *that?*"

"I don't know, Elk. She was in mourning. . . . Maybe her observations are not reliable."

Bull's Hump rose again, and then turned back.

"You might be interested," he said, "that I have stopped eating bear meat until after this trading trip."

"A vow?"

"No. Just caution," Bull's Hump said, smiling.

.28

The storyteller paused, exhausted again.

"So that," he recounted, "is how the people of the northern prairies obtained the horse. We traded. Some just stole a few to begin with. Others . . . Well, one tribe first saw horses when they were attacked by people on horseback. After the fight, they sat down to council, and traded for a few horses. Now I know that you . . . *my* People, had horses early."

"Yes," acknowledged Spotted Hawk, "we got them from the southwest. The Spanish . . . 'Metal People' came into our country. They were riding an animal never seen before. It was described by our scouts as a dog as big as an elk, which eats grass and wears a turtle on each foot. We were for a time called 'Elk-dog People.'"

"Yes . . . That was one of the things which made it hard for me to find you. At the time the 'Lost Band' was killed or captured, we were not called that. If it had not been that we recognized a few words, and stories of Creation . . . But, I get ahead of my story. Maybe I could rest again."

"Of course," agreed the chief. "But we want to hear it all."

"Wait!" called an old woman from the crowd. "You have not said. . . . What was wrong with the bear meat? Was it because of our covenant with the bear?"

"Oh . . . No, it was thought not. It helped for Calling Elk and Stumbling Bear to go on the trade mission. They did trade for horses successfully. The problem was not horses, but bears, and only *some* bears. Whatever the problem, it can be avoided by cooking. But it was found *not* good to use bear meat in dried form, what we now call 'jerky.' That was the danger. It must be cooked. This makes no difference to you and me, of course. We do not use bear meat anyway."

"Let him rest, now," suggested Spotted Hawk. "We will hear more."

"Of course," agreed Story Keeper. "The rest, most of it, is my own story."

When the band reassembled, Story Keeper appeared relaxed and refreshed again. It must be very hard, thought the listeners, to tell such a story after many lifetimes of waiting. Story Teller rose, and the crowd quieted.

"You have treated me well," he began, smiling. "It is as I have always dreamed it would be, to come among my own people. But let me finish the story.

"Calling Elk, Stumbling Bear, and the others had traveled far, had met with strange tribes with strange customs. At least, it seemed so. Blackfeet, Cheyenne, Shoshone, Crow, even some whose main occupation was fishing in the cold streams of the Northwest. All of these people were already using the horse, or, like the Lakotas, were in the process of trying to get some. Here in the Southern Plains, you were already using them. You know, then, the great changes which came about. This has nothing to do with my story and that of the Lost Band, yet it does.

"As I said, the rest of the story is that of my generation, my immediate family. There are other stories in between, some known, some very sketchy. . . . Some can be told, later. But let us look at the whole matter of this change. . . ."

Part Four

Story Keeper ⌁〜→

29

The coming of the horse turned the world upside down for the people of the prairie. People who had progressed from hunters and gatherers over the centuries to become growers of corn, pumpkins, and beans now saw a reverse in the process. The Absarokee, or Crows, split into two nations. They were still associated by blood, tradition, and annual festivals, but one segment leaned toward farming, the other to the hunt.

Consider the young men of all nations. . . . Consider the thrill. . . . Chasing buffalo on horseback, flying like the prairie wind itself must have eclipsed the joys of hoeing corn. A hoe, made of the shoulder blade of the buffalo lashed to a stick, is not as exciting as a lance or a bow.

People who had been fishermen moved away from the big rivers and out onto the plains to become horsemen. Now they could compete successfully with the more aggressive Blackfeet and Lakotas. Many of these horsemen developed skills of selective breeding, management, and training of the animals.

The young couple drew in their horses at the crest of the hill, laughing as they paused to rest.

"I won!" she chortled.

"Only because you caught me off guard," he accused, laughing. "You cannot start a race before you tell the other that there is a race."

"But you knew!"

"That there would be a race, yes," he admitted. "But not *when. Aiee,* you are a difficult woman!"

"Which is why you like me," she accused. "At least, I am made to think so."

She smiled provocatively, and his heart melted. Lark Woman was named for her lilting laughter, which rippled like the song of the prairie bird that was her namesake. Someone had once referred to her as a "manly-hearted woman," a great compliment among their people. A clever woman with courage and athletic skill was greatly to be treasured. Still, these qualities detracted nothing from the fact that she was *woman,* through and through. There were times when Blue Horse did not know how he could wait until they could marry and establish their own lodge. It had been for years a foregone conclusion that they would do so. Since their childhood and their beginning instruction in the Children's Society, these two had been close friends. . . . Helping, defending, each ready to fight for the other in the childish disagreements of youngsters at play.

They dismounted and sat while the horses grazed, shoulder to shoulder. These two animals, also, had spent much time together. The steel-gray gelding was perhaps half a hand taller than Lark Woman's spotted mare, but both families were known for their fine horses. Both families were pleased and proud that marriage seemed a logical conclusion for these two young people.

From the vantage point where they now sat, they could see at least two days' travel in any direction. To the west, a purple rim of mountains was barely visible along the horizon. It stretched north and south in a darker line against the dim blue of the distant hills.

"I would like to see the mountains," mused Lark Woman. "Will you take me there?"

"You can see them from here," Blue Horse teased. "No need."
Lark chose to ignore the remark, except to poke his ribs with an elbow.

"Seriously," she said, "do you think you will become a trader, like your uncle?"

"I don't know. There are things about it. . . . His mother was Arapaho, you know. . . . 'Trader People'. . ."

Horse made the hand sign for "trader," which also indicates "Arapaho."

"Yes . . . You two are close. . . . I thought maybe . . ."

"He would never urge me in that direction, Lark. It is mine to choose."

"I know. . . ."

She wondered whether Blue Horse had been asked to accompany his uncle on this season's trading. Well, she would find out.

They sat in silence, enjoying the fresh green of the rolling prairie. It was the Moon of Greening, April of the white man's calendar. The world was thriving in the luxury of Sun's awakening, the return of the grasses and the buffalo. In the distance to the south were herds of buffalo, grazing their way northward. In some areas the hollows and the south slopes of the gently rolling landscape were black with the thousands of animals. It was nearly time for the summer hunt.

To the north, at only a short distance, a band of about thirty antelope browsed or lay in the sun, the tiny fawns under close watch by their mothers.

A herd of elk could be seen to the west. On the bulls, sprouting furry antlers were barely discernible in the distance. A large herd . . . Signs were all good for a season of plenty, though it was best to take only a day at a time. . . .

Behind them, in a well-chosen bend of the river, was the camp. It was a strong band, some thirty lodges. Downstream a short distance, the horse herd grazed, loosely supervised by a few of the young men. There were hundreds of animals, hinting at the affluence of this particular band.

Lark Woman was proud to be a member of this nation, this band, and of the family she represented. Her father, Walks With Horses, was a respected subchief. Probably no man in the band carried more prestige except the chieftain himself.

Lark was the oldest child in her father's lodge, born to his first wife, Finds Water. There was a second wife, now. Walks With Horses had taken in Mink Woman, sister of Finds Water, after her husband was killed in a hunting accident. There were three other children in the lodge now.

She felt herself under a certain amount of pressure just now, because of her impending marriage to Blue Horse. Not much had been said of it, but this season would be the logical time, probably after the Sun Dance. She would talk to her mother about it. There were decisions to make. And, if Blue Horse were to go on a trading expedition with his uncle, Trades a Lot, when would the marriage be possible? She was not really eager for Horse to become a trader. She liked her life as it was. Except, of course, that she longed for her own lodge and Blue Horse to share it.

Over all of this, there was another concern, which no one who knew her would have suspected. There was a secret in her mother's past. During Lark's tenth summer, Finds Water had taken the girl outside the camp and revealed an astonishing tale. For generations, the family of Finds Water had been handing down a hidden agenda, from one to the next, in secret. The girl had been astonished. . . . Many lifetimes ago, the survivors of a genocidal raid on her ancestors had pledged themselves to carry on the language, customs, and traditions of "the People."

At that point, it had become confusing. . . . Does not *every* nation refer to itself as "the People" in its own tongue?

"But what people, Mother?" the bewildered child had asked. Finds Water had seemed a bit embarrassed for a moment.

"Well . . . Child, I fear we are no longer certain. One of those in the Southern Plains, I was told. But many things have happened since. An ancestor of ours was brought north, to the land of the Lakotas. We have been among Crows, Blackfeet. . . . But if we keep and teach our own ways, our tongue, our Creation stories . . . Someday we will return to the land of our people."

"But, Mother . . . these are our people, no?"

"Yes, that is true. We are doubly fortunate, you see. We have the advantage of both ways. . . . The people of your father, and our own, the secret part."

"And no one knows? Not even Father?"

"Very few. It must be kept that way."

"Why, Mother?"

"Because it is secret. If everyone knew, it would destroy it. Someday, it is said, there will be a leader, who will take us back to the People . . . *our* People."

It had been a shock, one that Lark was not entirely sure was pleasing. But to a child, a secret, with a sense of belonging that few could share, was deliciously enticing. She threw herself whole-heartedly into the learning of the language and customs of her mother's "People."

Now, with her impending marriage to Blue Horse, she could see another problem. With this one exception, that of the secret past of her ancestors, Lark had always shared her innermost thoughts with Horse. If they were to marry, her heart told her that she would wish to confide even this to her husband, though her mother had not done so, with Lark's father.

But what would be Blue Horse's reaction? It was a worrisome thing. . . .

30

It was not long before Lark Woman's question was answered. At least, one of the questions that rose in her mind. Trades a Lot, the uncle of Blue Horse, asked Horse to accompany him on the summer's trading trip. To his credit, Horse did speak with her about it before agreeing.

"It is good," he told her. "This would let me see if the life of a trader is for me. One summer's trading would let me know."

Lark Woman was silent, as thoughts raced through her head. Four or five moons . . . They had never been apart for more than a day or two. She was hurt, and felt a little bit rejected by his eagerness to undertake this long separation. She tried to remain calm, as she blinked back tears. This was a critical moment, which might affect the rest of their lives. If she showed resistance to the proposed plan, Horse would probably overreact and stiffen in his resolve to do this thing. That would push them apart, causing a rift that might never heal. This in addition to the dangers he might face while she sat at home to wait and wonder.

Careful, now, she thought. She must not drive him away. . . .

"It is good," she agreed cautiously. She gave him her most provocative smile, leaning against him so that he could feel the warmth of her body. "It would let you know how you feel about the life of a trader, as you say."

He studied her face for a moment, his thoughts confused by her physical nearness. And, she was agreeing too easily.

"But . . . ?" he said finally.

"But what?" Lark asked innocently. She drew away from him a little way. . . . *Not too far* . . . "Something else?" She ran the tip of her tongue along the edge of her upper lip, while he watched her, fascinated.

"I . . ." Horse stammered through his confusion. "I was . . . I thought . . . You started to say something else?"

"What? No, I think not, Horse. Maybe I was thinking I would miss you. Four or five moons, he said?"

There was a look on the face of Blue Horse now that was little short of panic.

"Trades a Lot's wife will go with him?" Lark moved a little closer again.

"I suppose so."

"*Aiee,* a trader's wife must see interesting things," she mused.

"She works hard, I suppose," Horse observed.

"Of course. Women do, Horse."

"Yes, I know. But the work of the trader's wife is a little different, I suppose. Packing, traveling . . ."

"I wonder if I would like such a life," Lark mused thoughtfully.

She waited for what seemed an eternity before Blue Horse finally answered.

"Well," he suggested, "You could see . . ."

"What do you mean?" she asked innocently.

"We could marry now, and you could go with me on the trading trip."

"What . . . ? Why yes, of course," Lark said, as if surprised. "Sweet Grass could show me the work she does. . . ." She gave Blue Horse a quick little hug. "Horse, what a great idea!"

Such are the ways of a clever woman, to achieve her goals and make her man believe that it was his idea all along. . . .

The marriage took place early in the Moon of Roses. The young couple had only a few days alone in the temporary lodge, well away from the camp. It was an idyllic time, as the richness and trust of an already strong friendship ripened into love in all its fullness. They watched the world around them.

They laughed together at the antics of a trio of fox pups across the stream. The furry creatures rolled and tumbled in mock combat, pretending to bite fiercely. Then one pup would break away and run wildly, pursued by the others.

They watched a great blue heron. . . . It stood in a shallow pool, motionless, watching, waiting for the quiver of movement that would betray the location of any small creature near the water's edge. . . . The hunter's prey.

They swam in the stream, in a deeper pool, made love on a soft buffalo robe as they dried in the warm sunlight and gentle south breeze. Then they lay looking at the sky, watching a red-tailed hawk trace his circular pattern in a sky that had never seemed so blue.

They made love again. . . .

Is not love at its best when it begins in friendship, grows to romance, and matures in a completion of trust and confidence? They even laughed together at their own sometimes inept love-making, knowing that this, like their friendship, would grow stronger and better over time.

They watched the sunset, and the rising of the moon, counting stars with delight as they appeared one by one. It was a time of magic, as if they had never seen such wonders. In truth, they had not, for they were now different people, man and wife as well as lovers. . . . They were attuned to the spirit, each of the other.

The shared warmth of their bodies was pleasant as they snuggled in the soft robes against the chill of the high prairie night, and that, too, was good.

Lark Woman awoke at dawn, to the song of birds in the trees along the stream. At her side her friend, now her husband. . . . (*Aiee*, what a delicious thought . . .) Her husband still slept, breathing slowly, his face serene and childlike. Lark hesitated to move, not wanting to disturb him. She studied his features. . . . Strong, handsome, yet gentle . . . How wonderful that they were now one, she and Blue Horse. . . . Now together in every way.

Even as she shaped that thought, a wave of guilt swept over her. In one way, they remained separate. Lark had refrained from thinking about it, in the excitement of their coming marriage. Now, with the sense of completion, the total trust as the two had become one in body and in spirit, came the guilt. It was *not* complete. She had still kept from him the secret of her family, their customs and ways.

Now, she was ashamed, embarrassed, and just a little bit afraid. What would Blue Horse say if he knew? Would he feel betrayed? She studied his peaceful face as he breathed softly. His breath tickled her bare shoulder, and she hesitated to move, lest she disturb him. . . . She would feel betrayed, if Horse had kept such a thing hidden from her.

No, she could not continue this way. He had given her his complete trust, and she felt that she had not been honest with him. And, she *must* be. She blinked away a tear, and took a deep breath.

Blue Horse stirred at this slight motion, and opened his eyes, smiling as he looked at her. He reached, to pull her into his arms.

"Wait!" she protested. "I have not been honest with you, Horse!"

He looked puzzled for a moment, and then smiled.

"Is it not the privilege of a woman," he asked, "to have small secrets from her husband?"

"No, no," Lark scolded. "This is not a small secret, Horse." She pulled away.

"It must be serious," he mused, pretending concern. "Another man?"

He smiled tolerantly, which bothered her.

"Of course not!" she said irritably. "But listen to me, now!"

He half raised up, leaning on his elbow.

"It *is* serious!" he said in wonder. "What . . . ?"

She laid a finger on his lips.

"Sshh . . . I will tell you, Horse. You know that there are some customs in my family which are different?"

"Of course. Family customs. Do we not all have them?"

"Not like mine!"

"What, then . . . ? Lark, I do not understand. You have never told me. . . ."

"I have told *no* one. It has been a secret for many lifetimes. None of the family has, ever. Only the children born to them."

"But you . . ."

"Yes, I tell you, Horse, because now we are one. I can have no secrets from you, because you are a part of myself, now."

"It is a *terrible* secret?" he asked.

"No . . . Well, I guess not. But a very large one. We are not of this nation. We are outsiders."

Blue Horse laughed. "Outsiders? Lark, everyone has outside ancestors. My grandmother was Shoshone!"

"Yes, but she did not insist that her children continue Shoshone ways."

"Well, some!"

"But not like *this*. Horse, we have our own language, Creation story, customs. We know of our Sun Dance, our vision-quests, all the customs."

"Like the family bear taboo . . . ," he mused. "Yes, I see some of this. . . . Lark, who do you mean by 'we'?"

"My mother, mostly. My brother will be told, when he is old enough."

"But there must have been others!"

"I suppose so. In other bands, in other nations, maybe."

"But how? When? And haven't husbands told their wives, women their husbands?"

"Maybe, sometimes. I don't know. But some have been captive wives; some of the men probably chose to adopt the ways of their wives' people. Some may have forgotten. . . ."

"Why do you now tell me, Lark?"

"Because," she said helplessly. "There has never been a marriage like ours. You are a part of me."

A tear crept into her eye.

"I understand, Lark, I am made to think the same." He held out his arms. "Come, tell me from the beginning."

"Yes," she said, tears now flowing freely. "But first, make love to me?"

31

In the next few days, little by little, Lark told him the story. Of the attack on the village, of White Moon's determination and her teaching of her son.

"That was before the horse?" asked her husband in amazement. "A long time ago!"

"Yes . . . There are some pieces missing, some others are known in great detail. A man called Stumbling Bear was one. His people were trading bearskins for their first horses. . . ."

"Ah! And he could not kill bears!"

"Yes. I will tell you more of that."

"But that is why your family has the custom . . . ," Horse pondered.

"Of course."

"Lark . . . This has been very important to you. To your ancestors. *Aiee!* How could they keep it going for so many lifetimes, yet tell no one . . . ? But *you* told *me.* Does that break a taboo?"

"I am made to think not. You are a part of me now, Horse."

"How can you be sure that I will not tell everyone we know?" he teased.

"Because you are who you are," she said seriously. "Otherwise, I would not have told you."

Now Horse became serious. "I am honored, Lark." He thought for a moment. "Do you suppose anyone has ever had enough trust before, to share such a secret with her husband?"

"Or his wife?" she asked. "I have wondered this. I hope so, but we cannot know."

"And did anyone ever go back?"

"I am made to think not, because they would have let it be known."

"But Lark, they would not know that *you* are here. Or others, in other nations . . . There may be some, like yourself."

"That is true. But around story fires, you know, people share Creation stories, and stories of olden times, when animals and Man spoke all one tongue."

"What has that to do with it?"

"Well, when we listen to stories, as traveling traders, will we not hear some that are our own?"

"Maybe . . ."

"And then, I would try a few words of the tongue. . . . I will have to teach you that. . . ."

"And if someone understands . . . Yes! I see."

"You will not object, then? If I search for my People?" she asked.

"*Aiee,* I will help you, Lark."

"But we must tell no one. Not even your uncle."

"Agreed. Lark, a trading trip is a good way to tell some of your stories, to hear others. . . . Who knows *what* we may learn?"

They returned to the camp, living temporarily in the lodge of Blue Horse's mother. There was much to be done in preparation for the trading expedition. Goods to pack, horses to select, both for riding and for packing. By common consent, Blue Horse and Lark Woman were primarily responsible for this selection. Trades a Lot and Sweet Grass, with more expertise in trading, would select and pack the trade goods.

The newly married couple were, of course, subjected to constant teasing and ribald jokes about their longer-than-expected stay at their private lodge. A "prolonged rutting season," one of Lark's young women friends called it.

Lark, blushing and laughing, treated it as a compliment. "May it be as good for *you*," she taunted.

"You would lend me your man?" retorted the woman.

"Of course!" Lark retorted. "But only what is left after I am finished with him."

"*Aiee!* I am made to think that is very little," observed another friend.

They assumed that meanwhile, Blue Horse was being subjected to similar treatment by the young men. It was an assumption that was quite correct, of course.

"You look tired, Horse!"

"Of course he does. . . . He has probably not slept for three days."

"Huh! Would *you* have?"

Through all of this teasing, Horse kept silent, blushing and smiling self-consciously.

"You will never know," he finally said quietly. "But now, I have work to do."

And he rose to go and sort out the horses they would need.

Lark Woman confided to her mother that she had told Blue Horse their family secret.

"Is this wise, Lark?" her mother worried.

"I am made to think so, Mother. I know my husband well. He will be of help."

"He *agrees* to this?"

"Oh, yes. He is excited about it. It brings us closer. Already, he is learning the tongue of our People."

"*Aiee!* He *is* serious!"

"Yes. Someday Horse will speak to *you* in that language."

A frightened look came over the mother's face for an instant, and then she smiled.

"Maybe . . . I am not quite ready for this, Lark."

"It is good, Mother. During this training journey we will be able to search for where our People might be."

"But Horse's uncle and *his* wife must not know. . . ." The concern came over her face again.

"No, no, Mother. We will only listen to stories. . . . Tell a few, maybe."

"Where will you go, Lark?"

"I don't know. Trades a Lot will plan. Is there any hint where our People might have been?"

"Ah, that is a long time ago, Lark. Many lifetimes. It has always been said that they lived to the south of here. South and east, maybe . . . In prairie with tall grasses. There was forest to the east of them, where the enemy lived."

"That could be many places," said Lark. "Well, no matter. We will listen to stories, tell a few. Traders are expected to be storytellers, no?"

"Yes . . . But do be careful, Lark."

There were seven horses, four to ride and three to carry packs. It was only a few days until the routine of travel was established. Travel, stay at any camp or village for a day or two, and depending on the trade, move on. The general plan, Trades a Lot explained, would be to head west toward the mountains, then southward along the front range.

"We will not cross mountains?" asked Lark, a little disappointed.

"You will see enough mountains, Lark," laughed Sweet Grass. "That is hard travel."

The general idea, Lark gathered, was to travel in a big circle, back eastward across the plains, and then back toward the band.

"Some traders," explained Trades a Lot, "have crossed the mountains to the west. We might do that, someday. But not this time."

"What is there?" asked Lark.

"More mountains," laughed Trades. "*Many* mountains. On westward, I have heard, a big salty water."

"Salt?"

"Yes. Another, far to the south. Farther than we will go."

Lark felt a prickling sensation along the back of her neck. She was just beginning to feel the thrill of the unknown, of exploration.

"You have talked to people who have seen these things? Tasted the salt?"

"Yes, Lark. Of course, they might have been only telling stories. But I am made to think there was much truth. Some traders I have met travel all year."

"But how do they winter?" Horse asked in amazement.

"They travel far to the south, where there is no winter. Then in summer, farther north. They migrate, like *Pte,* the buffalo."

"There are places with no winter?" asked Lark, amazed.

"Oh, yes. Places with no summer, too. Far to the north, I have heard."

Yes, thought Lark. . . . *Of course* . . .

In the stories of her mother's People, winter was the conflict between Sun Boy and Cold Maker. Cold Maker awakens in autumn, comes roaring down from his ice caves in some northern mountain, and attempts to extinguish Sun Boy's torch. Sometimes he does, almost. By the Moon of Long Nights it becomes depressing. Then the Moon of Snows and that of Hunger . . . Every year it seems that Cold Maker is about to win.

Then Sun Boy rallies, makes a new torch, and begins to drive Cold Maker back to his lair in the icy mountains to the north. At least, he always has. . . . This calls for the celebration of the Sun Dance, the return of Sun, the grass, and the buffalo.

Lark was fascinated. All her life, she had heard this story, with variations by the different narrators, depending on their own background. Now, for the first time, she began to realize that it is possible to go and see some of the places and things that storytellers describe.

Well . . . It might not be good to go too far north. What would happen if a person accidentally awakened Cold Maker from his icy lair? That might be like rousing a bear from its winter sleep. One should be careful. . . .

One evening, camped far from anyone with whom to trade, Trades a Lot opened a small pack they had not seen before.

"Lark," he said, "you seem to like to think of strange places and things. Let me show you . . ."

In the firelight, he spread out a collection of small stone objects. Arrow points, knives, awls, scrapers . . . These were of similar shapes and purposes, but varied widely in color. There were points of flint that ranged from white to brownish tan, blue-gray, pink, reddish, even shiny black.

"Some of these come from far away," Trades a Lot explained.

"Where did you get them?" asked Horse.

"From other traders, mostly. Some of these flints are fairly common. You have seen most of these colors."

"Yes, but . . ."

"This shiny black . . . That comes from far west of here. Many days' travel. The pink . . . Some of the stone-makers heat the gray stone under a fire after it is finished to make it harder, and it changes its color. This red pipestone, you have seen. Many pipes in many nations are made of this."

"Yes, my father has one," Horse said.

"Yes . . . Do you know that *all* of the red pipestone comes from one place?"

"Really?"

"Yes, it is true. This only goes to show how wide is the travel of traders."

"*Aiee!*"

"Yes, but here . . ." He unwrapped an object the size of a fingertip from a soft piece of buckskin. It was an oval thing, the size of an elk's tooth, but adorned with several colors and very highly polished.

"What is it?" asked Lark.

"A shell," said Trades a Lot proudly, turning it over to reveal a ragged opening along the underside. "It belongs to one of the creatures who live in the salty water I spoke of, to the west."

"Where did you get it?"

"A trader . . . He had several."

"*Aiee,* it is beautiful," said Lark. "Has it a purpose?"

"Only its beauty, I think," Trades a Lot answered.

Carefully, he rewrapped the cowry shell and retied the pack.

Lark lay awake a long time, staring into the night sky, after the others were asleep.

What wonders lay ahead?

32

They traveled far that summer, trading, telling tales around story fires from the mountains across the prairie to the forested areas. They followed old trails, worn by centuries of moccasined feet, and by clawed, padded, and hooved feet centuries before that. The Moon of Thunder passed, and the Red Moon. They visited and traded with many different peoples, some familiar, some whose customs were entirely new. In each place they would spend a day or two, and before they left they would have a better knowledge of each new people they encountered.

Lark Woman became their principal storyteller. She had a flair for it, and became better at it with more experience. Very early, she realized that many of the nations they visited would not be able to understand the tongues she knew. Their own, or that of Blue Horse's Arapaho uncle . . . She had even learned a little Shoshone from a captive youth. And then there was her own, the secret language of the people from the southern prairie. That one she would hold in reserve, until the proper time.

They found themselves using hand signs constantly, and Lark found it practical to do that in her stories, too. The running storyline in a mix of languages was soon accompanied by hand signs, which were familiar to virtually everyone. Lark could hold an audience entranced with her own excitement as she told stories of olden times, those of several nations. Not all at once, of course. It was best, she had found, to begin with a story that had many different variations. A simple one, such as how Bobcat lost his tail . . . There were at least six versions of that one, some more imaginative than others. Usually someone in the crowd would respond with another version, and another. . . . With the audience becoming involved, it was a simple matter to lead the stories to those of Creation. Many of these were similar, but Lark hoped someday to find someone telling *her* Creation story. Stories of Bobcat and Rabbit and Coyote are all very well, but anyone may tell them. Stories of Creation are, somehow, more personal, more important. A storyteller telling of Creation will naturally tell his own story, that of his own, *the* People.

It was in a town of growers, on one of the streams where the prairie meets woodland on the east, when it happened. It was late in the Moon of Ripening, almost to that of Falling Leaves. The weather was good, with warm autumn days and cool crisp nights. The trading party had completed the southern swing of their tour, and were working their way back toward their own country before the onslaught of winter. Lark had been trading story for story with the local storyteller. He was an interesting old man with a quick sense of humor and bright, sharp eyes, which seemed to miss nothing. The crowd was actively involved. The local audience is always a good one, she had noticed, in a town where there is a skilled storyteller.

The two storytellers had been tossing Bobcat stories back and forth, much to the delight of this responsive crowd. Lark had noticed that among people to the north, Bobcat usually lost his tail by freezing. . . . He sat too long gazing at his own reflection in a still pool, maybe, while the weather changed suddenly. Bobcat's long and beautiful tail, hanging down in the shallow water, was frozen there. He had found it necessary to chew it off to escape, and Bobcat has had a short stub of a tail ever since. *Is it not so?*

The old man had told such a tale, and she decided to counter with that of her secret heritage. In their version, Bobcat, hiding from a hunter, had taken refuge in a hollow tree. But unfortunately, his tail, long, soft, and beautiful, hung out through a knothole, and was seen by the hunter. The man gave a tug or two, and Bobcat did his best to keep quiet.

Ah! said the Man. *I will use this fur to decorate my bow case!*

He chopped off the tail at the knothole, and since that day, Bobcat's tail has been short, no? *And to this day, we decorate bow cases with fur. Is it not so?*

The listeners loved the story, and the old storyteller nodded approvingly. It was his turn now, and he thought a little while. Finally he made a suggestion.

"Let us talk of Creation," he suggested. "How did we get here? Each of the different nations has its own story, does it not?"

"That is true," agreed Lark Woman. "Usually, from inside the earth."

The old man nodded. "Yet there is one I heard of, where the people were at the top of the sky dome, and had to wait until mud hardened to slide down onto firm ground."

"Where did the mud come from?" asked Blue Horse.

With experience, he was learning how to assist a storyteller with timely questions. He prompted Lark's stories sometimes.

"From beneath the water," said the old man. "The whole world was water, until the Water Beetle dove down deep enough to bring up mud. Beaver had tried it and failed. Loon, also. But Beetle did it. Then Buzzard flew back and forth over the mud, drying it with his wings. Where his wingtips brushed the mud are valleys and mountains. But it is as our visitor says. Most nations came from inside the earth. Sometimes through a hole, sometimes by climbing. The Mandans, they tell us, climbed up the roots of a giant grapevine and out into the sunlight. Our own story is similar. But I have heard of another, a little bit different. . . ."

"Tell us, Uncle!" pleaded some children in the space near the fire.

"Yes . . . Let me see. . . . How was it . . . ? From the Southern Plains, I think. These people lived underground, in darkness mostly. Then one day, they saw light overhead, and climbed a rocky slope to try to reach it. As they did so, there was heard from time to time a noise. . . . It was a booming *thump*. . . . *thump*, which seemed to shake the ground. It was a little bit frightening, but they were drawn to it, like butterflies to a flower.

"The first man crawled through a round tunnel, which proved to be a hollow cottonwood log, an ancient tree which had blown over and broken open. There, sitting astride its bole, was an old man, ugly and tall, with a big nose and long stringy hair. . . ."

"The Trickster!" cried someone.

"Yes," the storyteller chuckled. "Is it not strange that the Trickster, by whatever name, turns up in everyone's Creation story? Now in this case, he held a stick, and as he whacked the log again, a woman came out. She was First Woman, wife of First Man. They stood up in the sunlight, and it was good. Another whack of the Trickster's stick, and another man crawled through the log. Each time he struck, another man or woman. Soon they were dancing, singing, and praying, rejoicing in the sunlight."

Lark Woman's heart was racing. This was the Creation story of *her* people. . . . The first time she had heard it, except in secret. The eyes of Blue Horse were wide, also. Could it be? There was one thing they could ask as a test, an inside joke.

"Are they still coming through?" Lark asked the storyteller.

"Ah, no!" the old man said sadly. "Alas! A fat woman got stuck in the log, and no more could come through. Thus, that nation has never become big."

So . . . He knows about Fat Woman, Lark Woman realized. *It IS our story!*

Her head whirled. All her life, she had waited for this, and now she did not know what to do. She must speak to the old man, verify, learn whether he knew the whole story of the band that had been exterminated. And how much else did he know?

"Well, it is late," the storyteller was saying. "It is time for me to seek my rest. Thank you, daughter, for your stories. Maybe we can talk further."

It was an open invitation.

The listeners dispersed, chuckling happily over a pleasant evening of stories. Lark Woman waited until the crowd had thinned, and then spoke to Horse.

"Are you coming with me?" she asked.

"Of course!"

They approached the lodge of the old storyteller, and gently shook the deer-hoof rattle over the door to announce their presence.

"Is it too late, Uncle?" Lark called, as the flap swung open.

"No, no! Come in. We were expecting you."

He spoke in his own tongue, and now seemed to wait. Maybe *he* was not sure. . . .

Lark thought a moment, and finally resolved to try. . . .

"We were not sure," she said, using the secret tongue of her mother's people. The face of the old woman at the fire broke into a broad smile.

"My wife knows, too," the old man explained, unnecessarily. "Your husband, also?"

"Yes."

"There are others among your present people?"

"My mother, a younger brother . . . That is all we know of. You?"

"*Aiee,* we are the only ones here, except for our son and his wife. They have shown little interest. Our hearts have been heavy for this. We thought we were the last! Your partners in trading? They know?"

"No, no. The uncle of Blue Horse, here, is Arapaho. The trading looked like a good way to search."

The old man nodded. "You have found no others?"

"Not yet. You think there are some?" Lark asked.

"We do not know. I had thought not, but maybe . . . *Aiee,* my heart is good for this!" He hugged himself with pleasure.

"Uncle," began Lark, "we know nothing of where our people might be, or how they are called. Can you help us with that? We know only that they were once in the Southern Plains. Tallgrass country."

"Yes, so it is said. That was before the horse, but our tradition says they had horses early, from the Spanish, the Metal People to the south. Before we had them here. For a while, I was told, our people were called Elk-dog People. . . . Horse People, because of this."

We knew only of 'Prairie People,' of which there are many."

"True. *Aiee,* I still cannot believe it! This is a wonderful thing! I wish we could go with you as you search. I am made to think you will find success."

"Thank you, Uncle."

"Where will you go now?"

"We are headed home," Blue Horse said. "The season grows late. We will trade again next year."

"It is good!"

"Where should we go, Uncle?" asked Lark. "South?"

The old man nodded. "I would think so. Both your traditions and mine say so. Oh, yes . . . You know of a man called Stumbling Bear?"

"Yes . . . Part of our story, no?"

"Yes. Some pieces are missing."

"A woman . . . White Moon?"

"Ah, yes! We are made to think that we have what we have because of her. Ah, I envy you your search, Lark Woman."

They said good night, and departed for their own camp.

"Come back and tell us what you find!" called the storyteller.

"It is a promise!" said Lark.

33

Trades a Lot and Sweet Grass might have suspected that there was something odd about the behavior of their traveling companions. But, probably they did not notice. Blue Horse and Lark were newlyweds that summer. As such, they were expected to behave in strange ways. They could slip away for privacy, and draw no special attention except for a smirk or a knowing smile.

They did consider revealing their discovery to Trades a Lot and Grass, but rejected such an idea. To do so would reveal also the secret that had been kept inviolate for many generations. Lark had no idea whether they would honor the tradition. Horse, too, had his doubts. Much as they liked, admired, and trusted their companions, it would simply not be appropriate. Besides, it would place an unfair responsibility for silence on people who had no real reason for knowing.

They reached the camp of their own band late in the Moon of Falling Leaves. It was time to prepare for winter, and the site had been selected in advance. The prairie grasses were taking on their wide range of colors for the season. . . . Golden yellow for the plume grass, deeper reds for the tall turkeyfoot, and a variety of pinks to yellows for some of the lesser species.

It was a good time of year, with a blue haze over distant prairie that was unique to the season. Waterfowl honked their way south for the winter in long lines high above, sounding like the barking of a myriad of small dogs in the distance.

Lark was eager to talk with her mother, to tell her of their discovery. But that was not to be, yet. All their friends came to welcome them back, and small talk went on until far into the night. Everyone wanted to visit, to ask questions and inquire about the adventures of the season.

"*Aiee,*" said Lark Woman finally, "we are tired. "Let us rest, and we will have a story fire, tomorrow evening, no?"

The crowd of well-meaning visitors began to thin out, and finally Lark had an opportunity to take her mother aside.

"I have something to tell you," she confided, her face beaming.

"*Ah!* You are with child! Wonderful!" exclaimed the older woman. "When are you due?"

"What? No, no, Mother. I am not pregnant!"

"You are *not?* Why not?"

"Mother . . . No, that is not it!"

"Then *what?*" A look of concern crept over the still handsome face.

"We have found some of our People."

"Of course! There are many bands. . . . Wait! You mean *ours? The People?*"

"Yes, yes, Mother." The tears were streaming down Lark Woman's face. "*Ours!*"

"Lark . . . Look, we must talk. Now. It is late, but *aiee!* Let us go outside a little way. . . ." She raised her voice. "Lark and I are going outside!" she called to the rest of the family.

It was a logical move, an opportunity to empty the bladder and attend to any other personal preparations necessary for the night's rest. No one would think otherwise.

They stopped, a bow shot's distance from the nearest of the lodges.

"Now! Tell me. What is going on?"

Quickly, Lark Woman told of the old storyteller, how he had related the creation story. . . .

"*Ours?*"

"Yes, Mother. He knew of the Man of the Shadows, thumping on the log, even the joke about Fat Woman! He speaks our tongue, too."

"*Aiee!* Does he know of others?"

"Only their son, who seems not to care. He believes, though, that there may be some. He urged us to search."

"How is he called?"

"I . . . I'm not sure, Mother. We only heard him called the storyteller."

"What else did he tell you?"

"Well . . . He knew of White Moon, and of Stumbling Bear."

"He *did?*"

"Yes . . . He also said that we came from the Southern Plains, as we have been taught. For a while, they were called Elk-dog People, because they had the horse very early."

"But how . . . ?"

"From the Spanish . . . Metal People. They came from the south, long ago."

"Ah, yes, I had heard that. They did not stay. . . ."

"That is true. But some of their horses did."

"Ah, Lark! This is so exciting! What will you do?"

Lark shrugged. "Nothing, for now. It is good to be with you again. Horse and I have talked of trading to the south, and searching, next season. The trading went well."

"Trades a Lot and Grass know, then?" There was a trace of alarm in the woman's voice.

"No, no, Mother. Well . . . We have not talked of it, but . . . We will see, come the proper time. Maybe Horse and I will go, alone. We promised to go back and talk to the storyteller. Maybe he will have more information."

"*Aiee!* And he knows about Fat Woman!" she mused softly.

It was time to prepare for winter, and none too soon. There was frost on the grasses nearly every morning now. When they went to the stream just after daylight, a thin crust of ice was noticed at the water's edge.

Lark spent much time with her mother, who longed for more information about their meeting with another of their own people. . . . *The People.* There was not much to tell, of course. They had spent only a little while with the old storyteller, but it was enough to send the blood racing, the imagination on flights of fancy. Now, after many generations, would come the reunion, the return to their own people. And they, Lark and Blue Horse, would be a part of it. They must begin to plan.

Now there arose a complication. How could they accomplish what they wished and needed to do without their partners' cooperation? The trading venture had been good, and the two couples were compatible. But now, it seemed unlikely that they would be able to undertake the search that they intended, without the knowledge and cooperation of Trades a Lot and Sweet Grass. In fact, would it not be dishonest to try to conceal their true motives?

"Maybe we should tell them," Lark suggested to Blue Horse. "It would be very hard without their cooperation."

"No . . . Not yet," said Horse thoughtfully. "I am made to think that this secret has only been successful because *no one* has known, ever."

"But, I told *you*," she reminded.

He smiled, and slipped an arm around her waist.

"That is different," he said. "A special situation . . . There may have been others, like the wife of the old storyteller. But to have others, not really concerned, not bound by marriage . . . *Aiee,* Lark, I think not. It would be too risky."

"You are more sincere about my People and our secret than I!" she accused laughing.

"So be it," said Horse seriously. "I am a very fortunate man, to be the one to share your secrets."

She smiled, pleased. "Then how could we do this?" she asked.

"We cannot say to Trades a Lot, 'Look, we must go this way, or that way,' and not be able to give a reason *why* we must."

"That is true," she agreed. "Then what . . . ?"

"We must separate, go in different directions," Horse said. "This year or next. I know you are eager to start this search, Lark. But maybe another year of partnership . . . Then go separate ways."

"Well . . . ," she hesitated. It was a big step. "If they happen to go in a direction we want for *our* purposes . . . South, it should be. Has Trades said what he intends next season?"

"We have not talked of it, Lark. That would be the best approach, maybe. I will ask him. Yes, this is where we must start. You know, we have never sat down, we four, to talk over the season just past. That is a thing we should do, anyway, no?"

"Yes, of course. That will lead into what we should plan for another season."

It was easy to suggest that they discuss the successful trading venture. The natural course of the conversation led to mention of the coming season.

"I had thought we might go farther south next year," said Trades a Lot.

There was now no need to bring up the matter of next season's plans. Trades was already thinking along these lines. Horse and Lark exchanged glances. Now might be the time to question whether they should undertake a joint venture again. Lark was thinking quickly. If Trades a Lot was planning to go in the direction that they should take anyway, why bring up the question at all?

"It is good," she said quickly, before Horse could inject any question. There would be plenty of time to modify their plans later, if need be. Meanwhile, they could begin to prepare for travel to the south, with no one suspecting its real importance.

"We can stop and ask the old storyteller if he knows any more information," Lark told Horse later. "Yes, this will surely work out well."

Lark told her mother of these developments, and the older woman was pleased.

"I wondered how you would deal with the partnership. Horse's uncle knows nothing of this?"

"Nothing, Mother. I would not have objected, I think, if we had need to tell them. Trades and Sweet Grass are good to travel with. But Blue Horse thinks it better to tell no one."

"Yes, that is true. The fewer who know, the safer the secret. Horse is right. Is he a good husband, Lark?"

Lark blushed. "Mother! What a question!"

"Well, a mother wonders, child."

"I . . . Mother, how would I compare? He is all I know. Now *stop!* You are teasing me. . . ."

"Of course. I am sorry!"

The two women giggled together. Lark felt closer to her mother, after the long absence. And it was good to make woman-talk.

"Lark, I am serious now. When is your moon time?"

"I don't know. Soon, I think," Lark answered. "I feel that I am ready. Why do you ask?"

"Well, it has not happened since you returned. I have started and finished. We used to start about the same time. Of course, you have been traveling. That affects it, sometimes. I just wondered. And of course, you have a husband now, too. That can make quite a difference."

"It does!" laughed Lark Woman. "But . . . Oh! You meant . . ."

"Some women with a husband may go for many moons without a flow," observed her mother, teasing. "At least, so I am told."

Lark's head whirled. Such a thought had not even occurred to her. When *was* her last moon time? They had been still traveling. . . . They had been back with the band for nearly a moon, now. The jokes of her friends about a "prolonged rutting season" came to mind. But no, surely not . . .

"But, Mother, I feel ready. . . . A little bloaty and fat. Surely I am about to start."

Her mother smiled. "Maybe so . . . Of course, the feelings are much the same, you know, when one is with child or needs to start. . . ."

"That is not it!"

Lark's temper flared, and there were tears of frustration in her eyes.

"Maybe not. I only mentioned it," agreed her mother. "Time will tell."

It was half a moon later that Lark finally conceded that her mother had been right. She had become moody, irritable, and even downright unpleasant to be around, much to the bewilderment of Blue Horse. It was good, of course, that their union had been productive. But, it was terribly frustrating that her pregnancy would be completed during the height of the trading season, in the heat of the summer. The trading venture would be in strange country, among unknown nations.

For a while, Lark tried to tell herself that she could be pregnant just as easily anywhere, and resolved to follow their plans. Yet, with the coming of the winter moons and the great changes in her body, she gradually had to admit . . . There would be no trip south for her this coming season.

34

Lark insisted that Blue Horse go on the trading venture without her.

"You will be able to learn more, maybe," she told him. . . . "And, I promised to let the old storyteller know. You can tell him. . . . Maybe he can give you more suggestions for our search, and the year will not be wasted."

"*Aiee!*" Horse laughed. "How could a year be wasted, in which we have a child, you and I? But, I think I should be with you."

"Look, Horse . . . If you were here when the time comes for birthing, the women would only chase you out. Go on, see what you can discover."

After considerable discussion, they arrived at a compromise. Horse would go on a trading venture with Trades a Lot and Sweet Grass, but it would be a shorter season. They could see his need to return before the coming of the child. At least, he could be near. That event, the women had estimated, would be near the end of the Moon of Thunder, in midsummer. Possibly, even, in the early part of the Red Moon.

"A hot time to be birthing," Lark's mother observed. "But, better than the Long Nights Moon, or the Moon of Snows, I think. It is too cold, then."

The trading party would start a little earlier this season, so as to return before the time came for the child.

In all of the planning, the secondary mission of Blue Horse was kept quiet. He would seek more information for a later expedition that would also involve Lark Woman, and the quest for her people.

"Where is your wife?" asked the old storyteller. . . . "I had hoped to talk with her again. . . . A fine woman, and a great storyteller."

"That is true, Uncle. Lark had wished to speak with you, too. But she is heavy with child now."

"Ah! Good!"

"We will return early, so that I can be near when her time comes."

The old man smiled. "That, too, is good."

"My wife wanted you to know that we are eager to find more about her people. She has made a vow to find them. Only the pregnancy keeps her from it now."

The old man nodded. "It is sometimes so. Let me remember. . . . *Hers* are the lost people, our secret? You follow *her* quest?"

"That is true. And, my uncle and his wife know nothing of any of it."

"Yes . . . That is as I remembered it, when we spoke last season."

"Can you tell me any more, Uncle?" asked Horse.

"I have thought long on this," the storyteller said. "There is very little to go on. South, as we have said, but not too far south. You have said that your uncle, the trader, is Arapaho?"

"Yes."

"That is good. Have you been to Arapaho country, where prairie meets mountains?"

"Not that far south. Should we try there?"

"Maybe . . . I was only thinking that Arapaho are 'trader people.' Some of them travel widely. You could encourage your uncle to visit *his* people, and you could talk to them, ask who has traveled in the Southern Plains, where *our* 'People' may be."

"Yes . . . A good plan, Uncle, for next season, maybe."

"So I thought . . . Oh! Another thing! Last season, I mentioned that our son did not seem interested in his heritage."

"Yes. I remember, Uncle. That made the heart of my wife very heavy."

The old man laughed. "Yes, I remember that! I thought maybe she would go and find him, to scold him for not caring!"

"It is her way!" admitted Horse. "I, too, thought she might do that."

"But wait! " the old man went on. "Another thing . . . When we told Snake . . . our son . . . of your quest, he began to show much more interest. He has asked many questions. I am made to think that he would like to talk with you, Horse. He has spoken of trying to *find* our People! He had never been interested before."

"May I talk to him?"

"Of course. Come, I will take you to their lodge."

Spotted Snake rose to greet the visitors. A woman, seated by the fire, held a small baby, and a toddler played nearby.

"Snake, this is the trader of whom we spoke . . . Blue Horse. . . . He was here last season, you remember."

There was a moment of confusion on the face of the young man, and then a sudden understanding.

"Yes, of course!" He smiled. "Let us walk and talk, no?"

The three men strolled through the camp and beyond the last of the lodges.

"Your family is with you?" asked Spotted Snake.

"My uncle and his wife. My wife is not with us. . . . She is heavy with child."

"Ah . . . But it is she . . . ? My father said . . ."

"Yes. Hers is the secret of her People. I am trying to learn all I can for a search next season."

Snake nodded, but seemed puzzled. "But your uncle and his wife . . ."

"No, they do not know. He is Arapaho, on his father's side."

"Uncle!" he called at the door of the lodge. "It is Blue Horse. May I speak with you before we leave?"

The old man stooped to come through the door flaps, and stood to full height outside.

"Yes? What is it, Horse? A problem?"

"No, no. Only a question. It came to me that I do not know your name, except 'the storyteller.' How is this? How are you called?"

The old man laughed.

"I have been called many things, Horse. Some, better than others. Now, I am mostly the storyteller, because my name is too long and confusing. 'Bear Digs for Badger on a Foggy Morning.'"

It was easy to see that it could be a problem. Horse was sure that such a name had been a way to recall a scene on the morning of the child's birth, or in his infancy. A pleasant scene, watching a digging bear . . . But it would be a hard name to shorten in conversation. . . . *Bear*, or *Badger*, neither told the story. Surely, some of his childhood companions must have teased their friend by calling him "Foggy Morning."

Horse smiled. Yes, it must have been a problem.

"So," the old man continued, "I answer to 'the storyteller.' Not a name, yet it is. It tells who I am, in a better way than bears and badgers."

The twinkle in his eye told that the old man's sense of humor had created some jokes about this at the expense of others.

"It is good, Uncle. I wanted to know, that I might tell my wife of you when I return home."

The storyteller nodded, pleased. "A fine woman," he noted. "My best wishes to you both with the child. May our trails cross again next season!"

"May it be so, Uncle! Thank you!"

As Horse turned away, another thought struck him, and he paused.

"Uncle," he said, "may I ask . . . ? How is it that you have never made the search, yourself, for your People?"

The old man smiled sadly.

"Ah, that story is too long, Blue Horse. Each time I was ready to start, something would happen. We lost a child, my wife and I. . . . Even before, the *birth* of that one, as in your own family. Another season, I broke a leg. . . . My buffalo runner stepped in a hole and fell with me. You may notice that I limp. Even after that, I vowed to go *someday.* But then the smallpox came, and many people died in this band. Finally, I decided: *It is not meant for me to make this search.* I thought maybe Snake, my son . . . It was a great disappointment to have him lose interest. But *now* . . ." His face brightened.

"Uncle," said Horse, "would you consider going with us next season?"

The old man was startled, but recovered quickly.

"I think not," he said with a smile. "The cold of many winters settles in my bones on chilly mornings. But, I thank you. I will think on it. You will be back."

The last was a statement, not a question, and the storyteller continued.

"I am made to think that it is you and my son, Spotted Snake, who will make the search together."

He started back toward the camp, where Trades a Lot and Sweet Grass were nearly ready to go.

"How is it?" asked Trades. "A name?"

It took a moment to collect his thoughts. The conversation with the old man had taken unexpected directions. . . . Yes, the *name* . . .

"Might as well be," said Horse. "His real name is a whole story in itself . . . 'Bear who Digs For Badger on a Foggy Morning' or something like that."

"*Aiee!* Could he not choose one for himself?"

"Probably. But I am made to think he *enjoys* stirring up the question. He says most people would call him the storyteller, anyway."

"It is good!" agreed the other, swinging into the saddle. "It is bad enough, to be called 'Trades a Lot.'"

35

The trip back to rejoin the band in summer camp seemed long to Blue Horse. In the earlier part of the venture, there had been curiosity and the possibility of new information and adventure. Then there was the old storyteller, a fascinating man and a pleasant distraction. . . . Spotted Snake, who now seemed a powerful ally in their search.

But, as the days passed and midsummer neared, Horse began to worry. He missed Lark tremendously, but was also concerned about her pregnancy. Was it going well with her? He began to feel guilt. *I should not have left her,* he thought a hundred times. What if something went wrong, and she needed him? What if she bore the child early for some reason? And, there was always some question about exactly where the birthing would happen, anyway. *When it is time,* the old women said.

Horse became restless and irritable, and when the last of the trading stops was completed, and they headed on the last leg of the journey, it was none too soon for Blue Horse. He thought about leaving the others and riding ahead, but there was no practical value in it. He could not travel much faster alone, unless he abandoned the pack horses for Trades and Sweet Grass to manage. That thought was appealing, but was quickly overcome by his sense of responsibility to them. They traveled on.

Back in the summer camp, Lark Woman was becoming restless. She had quickly progressed through the early part of her pregnancy, the emotional mood swings from tears to laughter and back. Part of that had been before she had realized its cause. Once she had a reason for this irrational sensitivity, she felt much better. Her nausea subsided, and the mood swings seemed to smooth out. It was a happy time, despite the absence of her friend and lover, Blue Horse. She tired easily, but she was happy in the expectation of the child who would be hers. Hers, and that of Horse. She spent much time in dreamy contemplation of what such a child might look like. She dreamed about it, sometimes, and was careful to remember all she could about the dreams, because dreams are important. They are the doorway between sleep and awake, and as well, between the everyday world and that of the spirit.

Unfortunately, there was nothing of great importance revealed in these dreams. She dreamed of the child as if it were born already walking and talking like an adult. She found that amusing, and looked forward to sharing such a thing with Blue Horse. She could virtually see the expression on his handsome face as he smiled about it. The same face, actually, as that worn by the remarkable infant in her dreams.

It took her a little longer to realize that the talk of the little one was not just small talk. She could never remember after she woke what the infant had said, but it always seemed to make sense at the time. The whole thing was frustrating, but rather amusing.

Then came the night. . . . She had dreamed, and came awake suddenly in the darkness of her mother's lodge with a new realization. . . . The language spoken by the infant with its father's face was the secret tongue of its mother, that of the Prairie People. . . . *Aiee!*

She was never able to tell, in her dream-state, the sex of the child. It was a person, one with a powerful spirit, but one who was first an individual. Sometimes it seemed to her that it was a girl-child, one who could be a warrior woman, perhaps. At other times she saw this as a strong young man-child, much like his father as she remembered *his* childhood. Lark did not care, particularly, and in the dreams it did not matter.

At about the beginning of the Moon of Roses in early summer, the dreams seemed to stop abruptly. It was at this time that she was becoming almost painfully aware of her swollen belly. Each day, it seemed, the child within her grew larger and kicked harder. This part of the pregnancy was obviously that in which the infant, already complete, was simply gaining size. Its motions disturbed her rest. Probably this in turn inhibited the dreams. At least, she could tell herself that it was a reason why the dreams had ceased. Discomfort of the body makes it more difficult to feel the things of the spirit.

There came a morning when she rose and was surprised to find that her belly has assumed a new shape. She could not describe the difference, but it was there. It *felt* different, and she spoke of it to her mother, as soon as they were alone.

"Mother, something is happening. My shape has changed. I can breathe better."

"Let me see. . . . Ah! Yes. Your baby has dropped. It is good. No more than another moon, now."

"Another *moon?*"

"Yes, probably no longer than that. Maybe much sooner. Sometimes, after it drops, birthing happens quickly. Do you feel your belly harden sometimes?"

"Well, yes, Mother . . . But that has been happening for some time now."

"Yes, I know. But . . . Well, I am made to think that you will know when the time comes. Sometimes the water breaks first. If that happens, your time is near. A day . . . no more!"

As it happened, the mother was becoming concerned. Lark Woman was big, the child carried low, and everything seemed ready. But nothing happened. . . . A few practice contractions from time to time, sometimes enough to rouse a little attention, and then nothing.

"Maybe it is a boy," guessed an old neighbor and friend, skilled in the ways of such things. "A man-child takes longer to do *anything*, no? They are more stubborn."

The other women laughed at the joke, but this was a generally accepted theory. . . . If it is later than expected, there is more likelihood of a male child.

"It takes longer to grow the extra parts," said the old woman solemnly in much explanation. "But that is good that they do, is it not?"

The other women giggled.

"Some, even longer than others," one observed.

"And some men take longer to do anything, all their lives," another contributed.

"Well, I wish mine would return," said Lark peevishly. "We will both worry if he is not here when our child arrives."

"Maybe it is that the child is waiting for him to return," said the old woman with much experience.

"But I am not *trying* to keep this active child inside," retorted Lark. "*Aiee*, look at him kick! He wants out. If it is 'he.' And I want him out! I am not keeping him in!"

"Of course not, child. Not on purpose. But you have more control than you know. And, maybe the child does, too. Who knows? Maybe he waits for his father's return."

It was the beginning of the Red Moon, hottest of the year, when Blue Horse, Trades a Lot, and Sweet Grass returned. One of the scouts, the "wolves" who constantly circled the area of the camp, rode in to tell Lark Woman.

"They will be here by midday, maybe," he said, reining away to return to his duty.

"Thank you!" called Lark after him.

Now, she must hurry to look her best, no small job when she felt her most unattractive. She combed her hair, washed her face, and tried to smooth her buckskin dress, the only garment she could still wear. She paused a few moments as one of the now familiar practice contractions tightened her belly.

The skin covers of the lodges had been rolled up to allow the summer breeze to flow through during this, the moon of most heat. This provided shade, yet ventilation. In case of the infrequent summer rainstorm, the lodge covers could be quickly rolled down, to be raised again after the storm had passed.

Lark had thought as a child that these, the lifted lodge covers of summer, were an amusing thing.

"It is like a herd of big spiders, holding up their skirts," she had once told her mother. Lark had experienced only three or four summers, at that time, and it had become a family joke.

It was this appearance, though, that greeted Blue Horse on his return.

"Spiders with skirts held high," he greeted. "It must be the Red Moon!"

He swung down from the saddle to meet his wife as he said this, and Lark flew into his arms.

"Ah!" said Horse. "Who is this person between us?"

He touched her belly, almost reverently, and took her in his arms again. "*Aiee*, it is good to see you, Lark. My heart has been heavy!"

"And mine!" she answered, laughing and crying all at once. "I am happier now. You are well?"

"Oh, yes . . . Lark, there is much to tell."

"You have found our People?"

"No, no. But I know more."

There were friends crowding around, welcoming the travelers. Lark glanced around nervously.

"Better wait . . . You can tell me later."

"It is good. The storyteller sends his greeting."

"Ah! You saw him?"

"Yes . . . Met his son, talked to him. He is now interested, Lark. Well . . . Later . . ."

He turned to unsaddle and visit with friends and family. Lark hated to share him, only for a little while, but she knew that it must be. And now, he was home.

They had still not managed to get away and talk when the contractions started. The first few were much like those she had experienced in "practice," but they were different, somehow. It took a few of them to realize that. Now, although shorter, they became predictable. Soon, Lark could tell when to expect the next. That was both good and bad.

The old neighbor, an expert at birthing, held a hand on Lark's belly for only two cycles of tightening and softening.

"*Aiee*, this is it!" she said, as proudly as if she had accomplished it herself. "The child is ready to come out."

The lodge cover was rolled down for privacy, and men were banished from the area. During this hurry and scurry Lark's water broke, splashing down her legs and into her moccasins.

"Good!" exclaimed the old neighbor. "It will not be long now. See, child, as I told you! You needed only for that man of yours to return. You waited for him!"

36

At last they were together, alone, and could talk freely.

"It is so good to see you, Horse. I was afraid our child would not wait."

He smiled and touched her cheek.

"I thought that, too. *Aiee,* I have missed you, Lark!"

He stared at the round face of the infant in her arms. "And this little one . . . Yours and mine, Lark. Is he not beautiful?"

"Yes . . . I am made to think 'handsome.'. . . He looks much like his father. Look! He is wide-eyed with wonder at this new world he has found."

"Maybe," Horse agreed. "About the wonder, anyway. "But see . . . There is understanding in his eyes!"

"Yes, I thought so, too. Wisdom, almost. This is a special child, Horse."

"Of course! Yours and mine!"

They laughed together, and it was good.

"Lark, there is so much to tell you," he went on.

"I have been eager to hear. You found more of our People?"

"Not exactly . . . You remember the old storyteller?"

"Of course. You saw him again, you said."

"Yes. We talked long. He wished you well, Lark. You made a great impression on him. But, you remember, he spoke of a son? One who had no interest in his heritage?"

"I remember. My heart was heavy for the old man. He deserves better from that son, Horse."

"This is what I am trying to tell you! After we were there last season, that son began to take more interest. I talked to him. His name is Spotted Snake. Lark, he is excited, and would go with us to search next season. His father is very pleased at this. It has brought *them* back together."

"It is good! Horse, would it not be a great thing if we could join this People of ours as two or three families. . . ? A band of our own. At the time of the Sun Dance, maybe, in the Moon of Roses . . ."

He laughed at her. "*Aiee,* Lark, you are dreaming. We have not even found them yet!"

"That is true," she agreed. "But each day brings us a day closer to it."

He was a bit unsure of that logic, but only chuckled at her sincerity. "You are serious about this."

"Of course! Now, tell me more. You talked much to the old man, you said. What is his name? We never knew, did we?"

Horse laughed. "No . . . One of those odd things. A long name about bears and badgers. No one uses it."

"We thought of him as the storyteller," she recalled.

"Yes, that is true. And apparently, so does everyone else."

"Then that is his name?"

"It might as well be, I guess," said Horse. "But, he still wants to keep his bear-digging name. I am made to think, Lark, that he enjoys having a long and confusing name."

She laughed. "Yes, I remember his sense of humor. It is good, Horse, all of it."

"Yes, so I thought. I wished for you to be there, Lark."

She smiled, touching his face gently. "And I wished for *you* to be *here.* We have never been apart very much. It was lonely. But now, you *are* here. It is good, Horse. And now, another thing . . . We have been dressing skins for a lodge cover. We will have our own lodge this winter. You and I and this little one. *Our* little one . . ."

They quickly fell into the new life pattern. It was easy and such a thrill to be a family of their own that all other thoughts were put aside. There was the confusion and extra work involved with a small baby, of course. . . . The awakening at night to a hungry cry; the concern when the infant did not seem *quite* happy and they could not determine a reason.

There was some concern for a name for this precocious child. None seemed to fit well. "Little Horse" was used by some, and was appropriate in a way But it was clear that this child was an old spirit, a person of his own, and not just a smaller version of *anyone* else.

"He does not need a name yet," said Lark Woman. "There is time for that later, before his First Dance and the naming ceremony."

So, the infant was called by a variety of names at first, by family and friends.

"When the time comes," Lark said confidentially, "we will know what his name is to be."

The moons of winter passed quickly with the pleasant distraction of a rapidly changing infant in the lodge. It was apparent that there were to be special qualities about this child. Aside from his understanding ways and the wisdom in his eyes, there were characteristics that delighted his parents. He was mischievous, one who seemed to understand and laugh with others at a joke or trick.

"I think he *understands* the joke!" Horse said on one occasion.

"No, he only laughs because we do," said Trades a Lot.

Lark smiled. "That may be true, partly," she conceded. "But, look at him. . . . The wisdom in his eyes . . . There is something more there."

It was a bit uncomfortable to discuss such things with Trades and Sweet Grass, because their lodge had never been blessed with children. They had achieved only one full-term pregnancy, a tiny infant who lived only a day, and then gave up, mewing pitifully, too weak to nurse. The couple had given up on the possibility of children, and had made for themselves a life of a different kind.

Now, the preoccupation of Blue Horse and Lark Woman with their undeniably special child caused the two couples to drift apart. They had less and less in common as "Little Horse" grew and developed. There was no disagreement or rancor between them. It must have been painful, especially for Sweet Grass, to see the joy of Lark Woman with her child. For a little while, Sweet Grass would hold and rock the infant, a sad smile on her face. *She would have made a wonderful mother,* Lark thought. But it had not come to be. And now, though the instinct was there, it must remain unfulfilled. The two couples had different interests and concerns now, different friends. They continued to drift apart.

During the first season in their own lodge, Horse and Lark considered long about a trading venture. The baby was small, but healthy, and would probably travel well. But Lark was protective, and in spite of her eagerness to search for their People, she hesitated to leave the security of their familiar surroundings.

"It is different, now," she confided to Horse.

Besides, there was the uncomfortable prospect of having to discuss plans with Trades a Lot and Grass. Lark and Horse talked of this at great length. Could there be a compromise?

"Maybe I could go with them as far as the people of the storyteller," suggested Blue Horse. "Then, return to you and Little One, here."

Lark's face fell. "Maybe we could go, too," she said suddenly, her face brightening. "Then, return when they move on. It would give us a chance to stay a little while to talk to Spotted Snake and his family."

Horse thought for a moment.

"It is good, Lark," he said finally, "but we must explain to Trades. Well, maybe that will make it *easier!* I will talk to him."

It could not have been easier, as it turned out.

"Trades, I would talk with you of the coming season," began Horse, as they lighted their pipes and settled down to talk.

"Yes, I too," responded Trades a Lot. "Horse, I am made to think that we should follow the season north this year."

"*North?*"

"Yes, we have never traded much to the north of here. It was my thought to go that way, swing east, and visit the pipestone quarry. I have never been there, and have only traded for the stone."

"But, I . . . ," began Horse.

Trades a Lot waved him down.

"Now I know that you and Lark may not want to take your Little Horse into unknown territory this season. But he can travel. He will do well."

"But Trades, we . . ."

"Let me go on, Horse. It might be well for you to take a shorter trip, to a trade area we already know. You are experienced, now. Go to the south, to the village of that old storyteller. . . . You have become good friends. What is his name? Digging Badger?"

Horse laughed. "I don't know. . . . 'Storyteller,' to me. But, Uncle, I am made to think that your plan is good. I will have to speak with Lark, of course."

"Oh, yes. But think about it, Horse. This may be the way to do it."

Horse was already convinced, and knew that Lark Woman would be, too. It was an ideal plan, to avoid any discomfort over the new family status of the younger couple.

"*He* brought this up? Trades a Lot suggested it?" Lark demanded.

"Yes . . . I think, Lark, that they may have been uncomfortable, too. This is a good plan. No one will be embarrassed."

"A wonderful plan! We can travel at our own pace. . . . Where else shall we go, Horse?"

"Wait, wait," he laughed. "Let us go and talk to the storyteller and Spotted Snake. Then, decide where or whether to trade somewhere else this season, too."

There was a sound from the cradle board where the infant was propped, and the two looked quickly. The Little One, as they had begun to call him, was beginning to smile and to focus his eyes. Before long, he would sit. But just now, he was smiling broadly, waving his arms, and to all appearances, trying to enter the conversation.

Both his parents laughed.

"See?" said Lark. "He approves. By that time, Horse, he will be nearly ready to walk!"

"*Aiee,* let us not make him grow up too fast," said his father. "Let us enjoy him a little while."

Lark smiled, with the expression on her face that only a mother is permitted.

"Horse," she mused, "does it seem to you sometimes that we have had this child always?"

He smiled and put an arm around her waist.

"I was thinking that, too. And Lark, I wonder how we ever got along *without* him. I know he is more work for you, but . . ."

"But he is *ours,* yours and mine," she finished. "And he is to be a special man."

They had arrived at the camp of the band they now regarded as Storyteller's people on the previous day. It had taken some time to greet old acquaintances, and to pay respects to the chieftain of the host group, as was only proper. Only now, a day later, had they had opportunity to talk in private with the old man and his family, and that of Spotted Snake. It was an exciting time, one that had been long awaited.

It had been four years, in fact, since Horse had first met Spotted Snake.

"I feared something had happened to you," said Storyteller, "but I should have known better. I am made to think that this is meant to be."

"Meant to be?"

"Yes . . . It cannot happen, our return to the People, until the time is right. It has been many lifetimes now, many generations, no? The acorn does not fall far from the tree, but it takes a long time to make an oak from it. The time was not yet. It still is not, maybe."

"But we had hoped . . ."

The old man shook his head. "We do not know enough yet, of our People."

"But we know their story, Uncle."

"Yes . . . Until the time our Forest Band was killed. What has happened since? There have been many changes. The horse . . . The coming of white men . . . The Metal People, Spanish, who brought the horse, but never came this far north . . . The Fran-cois, French, who came to trap and trade. Then the Yen-glees, whose tongue is different yet. They all fight each other, and are very strange, though they bring some good things. Knives, fire-strikers . . ."

"But what has this to do . . . ?"

"I am made to think, Horse," said the old man, "that this will take more knowledge, more planning, than we had thought. All my life, I had dreamed that someday, I would learn where the People are, and I would go there, to live happily ever after. Now, doubt that this is so. Seldom do things happen as we plan."

"You *doubt*?"

"Not that we must do it, but that it will be simple. I may not see it in my lifetime." He paused and pointed to Little Horse, who had not outgrown the child-name despite his four years. "It may happen in his time. We become impatient, all of us. When the time comes . . ."

The old man took another puff on his pipe and seemed to lapse into reverie. Horse was shocked. He had been counting on much help from the old storyteller, but this . . .

Well, it *had* been four seasons, and things *do* change. Each season, a different problem. That first year they had simply been unable to find the camp. They learned later that there had been a battle between Crows and Lakotas, and that this band had moved westward from their usual range to avoid the danger of being drawn in. Another season, a sickness struck, carried in by a party of white trappers. Everyone in the Northern Plains scattered, avoiding social contact for a season. Still another, bad weather and a poor hunt . . .

"We *have* learned, though," said Spotted Snake. "There are some others. At least, we think so."

"Yes, that is true," said Storyteller. "I had forgotten. . . . A trader, last season, heard our Creation story, and said that an old woman among the Assiniboines, the Stone-boilers, told the same story."

"But are they not far to the north?"

"Yes, but you know how active traders are now. It has always been so. People trade goods and slaves, they intermarry, move somewhere else. Maybe a slave or two, carried northward . . . Whole nations move. The Mandans and Hidatsa say that they came from far to the east, beyond the Big River, on a *salty* water."

"But that was *long* ago, Uncle."

"And so is our story, now."

"You . . . You think we should not *try?*"

"Oh, yes . . . We must try even *harder*. But we should know all we can, first. This will take much planning."

A little later, Snake drew Blue Horse aside.

"You see how my father is. . . ."

"He has changed," observed Horse.

"Yes . . . Some days are better than others. It must be hard. All his life, he has dreamed of this reunion, the chance to rejoin his People. Now, it is about to happen, and he is uneasy about the change."

"I can understand that. A big step."

"Especially for one his age. I have thought, these past few years, that he would lead us on this quest. But, I think now it must be you and I."

Horse was startled. "But I . . . Snake, I am not one of the People, except by marriage. My wife, Lark Woman . . ."

Spotted Snake laughed. "I had forgotten that. But no matter. You *are* one of the People now. Your loyalty has proven it. Now, let us talk of what we know, and what we suspect. I have heard of a family among the Shoshone who seem to have many stories of old times which resemble ours. Our People . . . *this* people, are usually at war with Shoshones, but maybe you, as a trader, could find them."

"Maybe . . . We have the same thoughts, then, a band of our own, several families? Lark and I had thought to join them at the time of the Sun Dance some year."

"It is good!" agreed Snake. "We are not ready, of course. My father is right about that. But let us begin some planning. Could you trade with Shoshones this season?"

"I think so. The uncle who taught me is Arapaho, and they trade with everybody. I can rely on that connection."

"Ah, yes . . . 'Trader People' in hand signs, no?"

"Yes . . . That goes a long way."

They talked for some time, trying to set up some long-range plans. It was foreign to the customs of both, to look beyond the needs of tomorrow, except for storing supplies for the coming winter. It helped, somewhat, that their secret had required some thought for the future.

It was a frustrating and unsatisfactory council for both men, however. Both had a general idea of what was needed or desirable, but the task seemed too great. To plan a venture such as this, involving families from two and probably more nations, and to do it all in secret. *Aiee,* where to start?

"I wish that my father was still in his prime," said Snake sadly. "*He* could have led us!"

"I have no doubt of that," agreed Blue Horse. "He can still be helpful, if he will."

"Odd," mused Snake. "I have the same feeling. He is pushing *us* to do it. Well, let us try!"

A vague and tentative plan evolved. For the coming season, they would plan not to meet, but to investigate separately some of the rumors of others who shared the secret of the Prairie People of the Southern Plains. Then, *next* season . . .

That night, Horse and Lark Woman spent a long time in conversation. Both realized that they had counted far too heavily on the leadership of the old man. Probably, Spotted Snake had done the same. Now, with the changes they could see, the lack of direction, the forgetfulness, it was apparent that the storyteller could not furnish the leadership necessary.

But, who *could?* Spotted Snake obviously did not feel adequate. Blue Horse, part of the great secret only by his marriage to Lark Woman, did not feel qualified in any way. Lark herself had carried the secret well and had drawn Horse into it. Yet, while it would not be unheard of for a warrior woman to lead such a quest, Lark was not a warrior. She was a wife and mother now.

They finally tired of talking and spent most of a restless night frustrated and unhappy, with little sleep.

The next morning was spent in trading and in visiting with people whom they had met previously. In the course of all this, various people remarked on the child of the trader Blue Horse and his wife, Lark Woman.

"A fine boy," they agreed approvingly.

Then came the old storyteller to the temporary camp of the visiting family.

"I would visit with your child again," he told Lark. "There was not a chance for us to become acquainted yesterday."

Lark noticed that the old man's eyes seemed bright and alert this morning, but thought little of it. One has days that are better than others at any age, no?

The boy seemed to take to the old man immediately, and in a short while they were chattering like old friends. Not as older and younger persons, but as two adults, friends of long standing, who enjoy each other's company. It was almost as if, somehow, they were continuing a conversation begun long ago.

What a strange feeling, thought Lark as she watched the two.

Finally the old man rose, smiling. "This is a special child, Lark Woman," he told her. "This is the one."

"What? I do not understand, Uncle. I know he is special, but every mother knows that of her child. Why do you say he is the one?"

"Ah," said the old man, "I had hoped to find him before I die. I thought maybe it would be my own son, Snake. Then I thought maybe your husband. . . . A leader, that one, but with us by marriage rather than blood. It could have been *you*. . . . It might have been a woman. But now you have a family. Still, it is appropriate that this child is yours."

"But why, Uncle? What do you mean?"

"You have not yet guessed?"

"No . . . What?"

"This is the one. . . . How is he called?"

"Several names, Uncle. Little One . . . Little Horse, for his father. None have seemed right. But . . ."

"Ah, yes. There is a reason. This child is the one who will lead us back to our People. This one is the keeper of our legend, the secret of our heritage. He will have preserved the story. He is the Story Keeper."

There was a flurry of talk among the listeners around the story fire at the Sun Dance.

"*You?*" said Spotted Hawk. "*You* are that child? You have told us that is *your* name."

"That is true," said the newcomer. "I did not seek such an honor. It was thrust upon me. The rest of the story is mine."

.38

"**A**iee!" said Story Keeper. "There have been times when I doubted that I would ever be here before you, my People . . . Our People, to tell the stories I have just told, much less my own. Yet, here I am. Here you are. The story is nearly finished. This part will not be long, because my story is insignificant compared to what I have told you. Those who came before were the great ones. Striker . . . White Moon . . . Stumbling Bear . . . Lark Woman, my own mother . . . And yes, others of my lifetime . . . Old Bear Who Digs in Badger's Den, the Storyteller. His son, Spotted Snake. My own father, Blue Horse, who has become one of us . . ."

Story Keeper took a deep breath, and it was clear that this was, for him, the climax of a lifetime of loyalty.

"But," he said, his voice stronger now, "let me go on. . . ."

From the time I was small, as long as I can remember, my mother impressed on me that I was special. Of course, most mothers think so, about their own sons. It is right to do so, no? This was a bit different. My special treatment as a child was less that of an *honor* than one of *responsibility*. I must do well, learn well, all the things we teach our children, for all the usual reasons, and *more*. I must do all this *because* I had a special mission. I have to admit, there were times when I wished that I had no more responsibility than the other children, my friends. Even worse, I could *tell* no one. Ah, for a child to have a great secret, yet one he cannot share? Yes, I see some chuckling. . . . It *was* funny, sometimes. But let me go on.

When I was old enough to understand, my parents began my instruction in the secret culture of my People. . . . *Our* People, yours and mine. *That* was good. There were a few with whom I could talk in this, our own language. My parents, my grandmother . . . But we traveled in the summers. My father was a trader. . . . Yes, I have told you that. Not every summer. Sometimes, because of weather or war or events in our own band, that where we lived. Twice, Lark Woman was with child again. I have a brother and a sister. The first time I stayed with my mother while my father traveled. That was before I knew all about the secrets. The next time, I had seen probably twelve winters, and went with Blue Horse. When we returned, I had a brother, as well as a sister.

But it was on these trading trips that I really began to sense the importance of my responsibility. I had not asked for it, and still resented the extra duty, I suppose, but *aiee!* People who were obviously important among their *own* People would seem eager to talk to me, and as an adult. This I can tell you, was a heady fragrance! Unfortunately, I could not share it with my friends when we returned to our home band in the fall. But, I did meet and talk with some interesting people who shared the great secret. The old storyteller, of whom I have spoken, as well as his son, Snake, and his family.

I was still quite small when we met the Shoshones, and found a family of our People there. I still remember the emotions, the tears of joy as we met and talked.

We heard of a Blackfeet family who might have traditional stories like ours but were never able to find them. At least, they never admitted it. It must be hard, after so many generations of secrecy, to openly talk of it. Or maybe they only knew a few stories similar to ours in the first place. Some of those leads came to nothing, but even they were interesting and exciting. I began to enjoy my responsibility, and learned to speak several languages as I went along. Maybe this special calling would not be all bad. I met a young woman, a Crow. . . . But more about that later.

The years passed, and each of the families was preparing for the season when we could all join and travel to our People at the Sun Dance. We were still not sure when, or even where, and everyone was hesitant to ask too many questions. So, we drew strength from each other as we traveled, and our band, though scattered, began to become a reality. The Lost Band, as you have called it, was found again. Yet, while *we* were found, the rest of the nation was still lost. We did not know for certain how to find you. Yes, you chuckle, but think on it. We could not ask too many questions, and did not want to spoil our coming effort by going too fast.

And, our leadership was uncertain. You will remember that old Storyteller had virtually anointed me the leader of this reunion, while I was just a child. Had I known all that, *aiee!* But I was not old enough or experienced enough to handle it, yet. Between my father and Spotted Snake, they kept searching, pushing a little, withdrawing a little, searching for news of others who might belong to us. Both were good leaders, and might have been able to bring the People back. Yet, this gave a few years to search and plan.

As I look back now, I am convinced of one thing: The whole plan was set in motion by old Storyteller. He saw that some time was needed, to learn more about what we were doing. He did not want any headstrong young people to cause problems, to stir up troubles we did not already have. So, he picked a young person. Myself, as it turned out. This allowed them to wait until the time was right, and to bring some order into our band.

Finally, after we found each other and those living among the Shoshones, it seemed time to elect a leader. No one wanted the responsibility, least of all, I. But I had been selected by Storyteller . . . . As I think now, because I was *not* ready yet, to give Snake and Blue Horse time to organize what they were doing. So, it was not much of an election when the time came. More nearly, it was a matter of discussing when to undertake the journey.

By this time some momentous things had taken place. I had married my Crow sweetheart, and our lodge was already blessed with a child.

More importantly my parents, still trading, had traveled the eastern slopes of the mountains and had contacted people who knew of the Mountain Band and the Red Rocks of our People. They did not try to make contact, because they were told by the Cheyennes that those bands had gone eastward toward Tallgrass country for the Sun Dance of the People. This, of course, verified the legends that we had been told.

By now, we had begun to think how effective it would be, to walk in at the time of the Sun Dance and announce our return. We could travel with the several families and arrive as the other bands do, to take our place in the circle, the following year. So, we began to plan *that*. Food, supplies for a long journey, learn where the Sun Dance would be held.

We did so. . . . We asked the Omahas, Missouries, and even Pawnees, and got vague directions as we traveled. Finally, some of the Kaws were able to tell us where our Sun Dance was to be.

Then, we began to be concerned. *What if we are not welcomed? Will we be believed?* It was decided that I would come on in, and see what sort of reception I received. And, my brothers and sisters, your welcome has been wonderful. I am made to feel at home.

Story Keeper paused, and his eyes brimmed with tears again.

"But . . . ," said spotted Hawk. "What happened to the others?"

Just then there came an interruption. One of the wolves loped into the encampment, rode almost into the circle of firelight, and slid from his horse, to make his way toward the Council circle. Night had fallen now, but the concern on the scout's face was apparent in the firelight as he approached the Real-chief.

"What is it?" asked Spotted Hawk.

"My chief, we see the fires of a party camped to the north, maybe half a day's travel."

"How many?"

"From the fires, maybe twenty or thirty."

There was a flurry of talk, quickly silenced by Spotted Hawk. It was apparent that a party that size was no threat. An encampment of the entire nation of the People would not be vulnerable to any approaching group.

But Spotted Hawk was a quick thinker. He turned to Story Keeper.

"Your party?" he asked.

"Yes . . . We decided that I would come on in to tell our story. The main party would stay three days back, and then approach. They will be here tomorrow."

"That was not necessary," said Hawk. "We saw who you were when you knew about the Eastern Band."

There was general laughter, even from the Eastern Band, the butt of the joke.

"How many have you?" asked Spotted Hawk.

"Four families . . . Mine, my parents', that of Spotted Snake, and that from the Shoshones. Maybe nineteen, twenty."

The chief nodded, and turned to the keeper of the sacred bundles. "Can we hold up the Sun Dance one more day?"

"For *this,* of course, my chief!"

"Let it be so, then. We will celebrate the return of our Lost Band."

And so it happened. A delegation of young warriors of all the other bands set out at daylight with Story Keeper to greet the newcomers and escort them in.

"It is too bad," said Spotted Hawk, "that your old man, the storyteller with the difficult name, cannot see this day."

Story Keeper looked down from his horse, a puzzled expression on his face. Then he laughed.

"Oh, but he can, Uncle. He is with us. I am made to think his confusion was only to force the rest of us to do something. No, he is ageless. You will meet him later today, with the rest!"

That night, there was much feasting, dancing, and rejoicing, and for the first time in many lifetimes, there was no empty seat in the Council circle.

Author's Comments

This is a fictional account, not based on actual events. Yet, there have been similar times and places in history where a loyal group of people have struggled to preserve their own culture and traditions, sometimes against great odds. Some succeeded, some failed.

Judeo-Christian history is full of such examples, from the Babylonian exile of the Jews to the persecution of early Christianity. There were secret meetings and coded communications, with the knowledge that discovery meant death in the arena with the lions.

In the last century, many American Indians were forbidden by the federal government to conduct their own traditional ceremonies, or even to speak their own languages. Much of their culture was lost, but some modified ceremonies to make them acceptable as patriotic or religious symbols. Others continued in the secrecy of remote locations, or in the privacy of homes. As late as the 1970s, a small group of these people was discovered in the heart of a major American city, secretly carrying on their carefully preserved traditions in their own language.

What is the significance of these efforts? Maybe, none. Certainly, more of ancient cultures has been lost than has been saved. The effort may fail, but *can* succeed, sustained by the dedication of a few who are convinced of the importance of the effort, and the justice of their cause. "Each one, teach one . . ."

And the salmon struggles upstream to the place of its birth so that it may reproduce before it dies.

DON COLDSMITH